PAINTING THE CORNERS

Carolina Waves Series Book Five

TINA GALLAGHER

Galsalla Press

Painting the Corners

Carolina Waves Series Book 5

By: Tina Gallagher

Published by Galsalla Press

Copyright © 2021

Cover Design: Qamber Designs

Editor: Jeannine Luby

Chapter One

TREY

A BLACK TOYOTA Camry pulled up and I grabbed my bags and walked toward it. The driver popped the trunk and stepped out of the car.

"Trey Youngman?"

"Yep."

He took my bags and dropped them in the trunk and smiled over at me as he slammed the lid shut.

"I'm Joe," he said, and I shook his extended hand. "Holy hell, Trey Youngman in my car."

He opened the back passenger-side door.

"It's nice to meet you," I said and settled into the back seat.

After slamming my door shut, he jogged around the front of the car and got behind the wheel. I looked out the window as we pulled away from the extended stay hotel that's been my home for the past few weeks, glad to be moving onward and upward.

"I don't normally take such a long fare, but when I saw the name and where this one was going, I couldn't pass it up," Joe said. I nodded in response when he glanced at me through the rearview mirror. "I've followed your career since you started playing for New York. I thought they sent you down too soon. Sure you had some control issues, but nothing you wouldn't have worked out in time." He shrugged and smiled back at me. "But now it looks like you're getting another shot. Good for you."

Again I nodded and as the car merged onto the highway, I shifted further into the seat and rested my head back. Staring at the ceiling, I prayed for patience. If this guy keeps chattering like this for the whole two-hour drive, I'm gonna need it. The Waves are all about being fan friendly. This is a perfect opportunity for me to practice.

I made sure to keep both my face and voice neutral as I answered his questions about my former teammates and baseball in general.

"Seriously though," Joe said. "They never gave you enough credit. Maybe it's because you were in New York. Things are always tougher there." He shrugged. "I don't know, but I've never seen anyone paint the corners like you. You are a true artist on the mound."

"Thanks, I appreciate that."

It's about time someone besides me realizes that. Yes, I grew up with every advantage and was lucky enough to play on elite teams and have lessons with the best instructors but when it came down to it, I had to do the work. I'm the one who has to deliver when I'm standing on that mound alone. But people always lead with the fact that I was born with a silver spoon in my mouth and overlook those things.

Joe was about to say something else when his phone beeped.

"Sorry, I need to check this." After easing over to the side of the road, he put the car in park. "What the hell are the chances?" he said more to himself than me. Then he turned and looked over the seat. "There's someone else going to Myrtle Beach. Would you mind sharing your ride?"

I opened my mouth to give a resounding *hell no* but reconsidered before the words came out. Maybe another person in the car will take Joe's attention off me. Because if I have to put up with two hours of polite conversation, I'm seriously going to lose my shit. And I know that won't go over well with my new team.

"Nope, I don't mind."

He tapped his screen, then shifted the car into drive and pulled back onto the highway. I listened with half an ear as he continued to talk. This ride, more than losing my license, is my punishment for the collection of speeding tickets I accumulated in New York last year.

Of course, my father could have taken care of those tickets with one phone call, but he decided to be a prick instead. So the judge took away my license for six months. Which pissed me off, but wasn't the worst thing in the world when I was living in Manhattan and could just step out of my apartment and hail a cab. But I'd been sent down to Triple-A in Scranton a few months before the sentencing then got traded to Fayetteville shortly after, and not being able to drive in those cities really sucked.

My first instinct was to hire a private car service, but the therapist I'd started seeing in an attempt to become a better person made me realize that wasn't the best move. It was just me using money to avoid the consequences of my actions. In both places, my hotel was only a few blocks away from the stadium and since I wasn't going out every night—or any night for that matter—it wasn't necessary to have a car at my beck and call.

Which is why, after last night's game when I got called up to the Waves, I had to figure out a way to make the hundred-mile trip. I hoped someone from Fayetteville's staff would be able to take me, but supposedly no one was available. So a ride share was my only option.

I'll be paying for Joe's round trip and of course, I'll give him a big tip as long as he gets me to First Allegiant Bank Park in time. Which might be throwing money at the problem, but it's definitely for a good cause.

The last thing I want to do is fuck up this opportunity because I was late getting to the stadium, or because I was rude to my driver. Both of those things seem like a stretch, but it's hard to shake a reputation like the one I cultivated in New York so I know I'm going to be on a short leash with my new team. It wouldn't take much for the Waves to send me back down.

As if he read my thoughts, he said, "Our other passenger is just off this exit, then we'll head right to the stadium so you get there safe and sound in time for tonight's game."

"Thanks."

"You two can split the fare on the app."

"That's fine. I got it."

He turned right then pulled over to the curb and put the car in park.

"That's something you and the lady can discuss," he said, before getting out of the car.

I leaned my elbow against the door and rubbed my eyes. It's been a long day and it's not even noon. Taking in a few deep breaths, I focused on happy thoughts like my therapist always suggests. This ride will be over in a couple hours and I'll be back in the major leagues where I belong.

The door opened and the scent of cinnamon filled the car as the other passenger settled in next to me.

"Thanks for letting me ride along. My car broke down and I need to get back for a three o'clock meeting."

Opening my eyes, I looked over at the woman on the other side of the seat and blinked. Twice.

Her husky voice didn't prepare me for its pixie-like owner.

"No problem," I said, taking in her petite form and bright pink hair before looking into her violet eyes.

"I'm Nori."

She held out her hand and surprised me with her firm grip as I shook it.

"Trey."

Joe got back behind the wheel, started the car, and pulled out into traffic.

"Sit back folks, I'll get you where you need to go in no time."

"You're a lifesaver, Joe," Nori said as she released my hand and wiggled into her seat.

Frowning, I rubbed my hand against my thigh, trying to stop the tingling her touch had caused. I studied the woman next to me, trying to figure out what that's all about. She's definitely not my usual type. Tiny women with pink hair and tattoos who smell like dessert are nowhere on my list.

NORI

I DON'T KNOW what the deal is with the guy sitting next to me but he's been staring for ten minutes straight. He's pretending to have his eyes closed, but I can feel him watching. At least I'm not sensing disapproval, which is what I'd expect from someone who looks like him.

I mentally shook that last thought away. I don't want people judging me at a glance, so I shouldn't do it either. Even if he is a clone of every prep school, upper-crust guy I grew up with, not to mention my ex-fiancé.

"So you gonna be pitching tonight?" Joe asked.

Trey's whiskey-colored eyes fully opened, sweeping over me before turning toward the front seat.

"They stressed that they wanted me there today so we'll see."

Apparently the guy is a baseball player. That wouldn't have been my first guess for his profession. I would have figured finance or some sort of fancy corporate job. Although, with his straight nose and symmetrical features, he could definitely be a model. Not to mention his eyes. Their color is amazing, but contrasted with his raven hair, it's truly spectacular and give him a unique look.

My fingers twitched and without thinking, I reached into my purse and pulled out my sketchbook and pencil. With a few quick strokes, I had the outline of his square jaw and perfectly-shaped head. After adding his nose and eyes I paused, my pencil poised over the paper, and shifted my eyes to look at his mouth. His lips are plump and nicely-shaped and I drew them as I imagined they'd look if they weren't set in such a grim line.

But I have to give the guy credit. If I didn't have such a good bullshit meter, I wouldn't even be able to tell he's annoyed by Joe's constant talking. He's being very polite, but I grew up surrounded by people who showed one thing on the surface while something very different was going on inside.

I'd just put the finishing touches on my sketch when

Trey shifted in his seat and leaned his head against the window. The light hit his profile perfectly and I flipped to a clean sheet to capture it. I worked quickly, the scratches of my pencil the only sound in the now-quiet car.

It didn't take long for a decent profile to take shape. With quick flicks, I added his hair and smiled to myself. The short messy style looks tousled and carefree but I'd bet my entire last commission it's the result of a $200 haircut and $50 worth of product.

I added some shading to his jaw and smoothed it out with my pinky then my thumb. After adding in a few more details, I looked over at him to check my work and found him watching me. Crossing my legs, I rested my sketchpad against my knee, hopefully blocking his view of the page.

As I felt his eyes on me I continued working, even though all I wanted to do was snap the book closed to ensure he couldn't see. While adding dimension to the black-and-white sketch, I kept picturing those eyes in my mind. The amazing color would be challenging to duplicate in graphite, but I think I could capture them in acrylic or oil. It would take just the right mix of reds, yellows, and blues and a lot of trial and error to get an exact match but it would be worth it.

I glanced over at Trey and was surprised to meet his gaze. His eyes widened just a bit, then shifted toward my purse before meeting mine again.

"Are you an artist?" he asked, I'm assuming in an attempt to distract me from the fact he'd been blatantly staring.

"I am."

"Portraits?"

"Sort of." I tilted my head from side to side. "Portraits are my first love, but I make my living painting murals."

"Like on the side of buildings?"

"No. I mean, I have done that, but now, I mostly do them in people's homes." His brows drew together and I turned my phone so he could see. It's much easier than trying to explain. "This is what I drew for my meeting today. The client wants a fairy garden painted in her daughter's playroom."

"Nice."

"Thanks."

He turned back toward the window and I figured the polite chit-chat was over, but I was wrong.

"How long does it take you to actually paint something like that?"

"This design will take about two weeks since it's pretty large and there's a lot of detail," I said. "Thankfully it's close to home so if I get the job I won't have to travel far."

"Is that how long most of your jobs take?"

"No. This last one in Fayetteville just took the weekend, but it was a pretty simple design."

"What was it?"

"My client's husband is a huge Penn State fan so I transformed his man cave into his own

little Happy Valley. It was her anniversary gift to him."

"Nice gift."

"He seemed to like it."

"Do you have a picture?"

I flipped through my gallery and pulled up the panoramic photo I'd taken then handed him my phone.

His fingertips brushed against the screen as he moved the picture left to right and back again before nodding and handing the phone back to me.

"That doesn't look simple to me."

"Compared to some things, it is."

"Do you have a card?"

"Like a business card?"

The corners of his mouth curled slightly as he nodded. That was such a stupid question. What other kind of card would he be asking for? My cheeks were probably as pink as my hair as I reached into the side pocket of my purse, pulled out a card, and handed it to him.

He studied it before tucking it into his shirt pocket, then shocked the hell out of me by asking about my process and then my favorite project. I'd just finished showing him pictures of the latter when Joe spoke, pulling my attention to the front seat.

"I'm gonna drop Trey off at the stadium first then circle back around to drop you off."

I glanced at my watch, surprised we've been on the road for just about two hours.

"That sounds good." I looked at Trey. "My email address is on my business card if you want to pop into the app so we can split the cost."

"No worries," he said. "I got it."

"I can't let you do that."

"Sure you can. I was going this way anyway."

"If you're using that logic, so was I."

He smiled at that. Not a slight curling of the lips, but a full-blown, dimple-popping smile that transformed his face from amazing into something truly spectacular. I took a mental picture so I could sketch it later. Like as soon as he stepped out of the car.

"That's true," he said. "But seriously, I got it."

"Well, thank you. I appreciate it."

I fought the urge to fidget or obsessively tuck my hair behind my ear, or bite my fingernails like I would have done years ago.

Joe turned off the interstate and we moved in stops and starts through traffic. Before long we pulled up in front of First Allegiant Bank Park.

"Is there another entrance where I should drop you?" Joe asked.

Trey glanced out the window and looked around.

"This is fine." He looked at me and patted his pocket. "I'll be in touch when I buy a house."

That said, both he and Joe stepped out of the car. I heard the trunk pop open and glanced out the back window. Trey was mostly hidden by the trunk lid, but his ass peeked out just enough for me to appreciate. Which I did.

I jumped in my seat when they slammed the trunk shut. Shifting to face forward, I watched through the rearview mirror as Trey shook Joe's hand, picked up his bags, and walked toward the stadium entrance.

Joe got back behind the wheel and smiled at me over his shoulder.

"We'll get you to your destination in no time," he said.

"Thanks Joe, you're a prince."

I reached into my purse for my pencil and sketchbook, but instead of flipping the book open, I placed it back in my purse and rested my head against the window.

The image of Trey's smiling face is burned into my mind and I'm sure it won't go away any time soon. And when I draw it, I want to take my time and savor every single pencil stroke.

Chapter Two

NORI

JOE HANDED me my duffel and I slung it over my shoulder. He closed the trunk and stepped back.

"I have another bag," I said.

"Oh, sorry about that." He popped open the trunk and looked inside, then over at me. "Are you sure you had another one?"

"Positive." I peered into the empty trunk. "Shit."

"What does the bag look like?"

"It's just a plain black computer bag."

"I handed Trey all the bags that were on this side. Yours must have gotten bumped over." His brow wrinkled. "I'm so sorry. I didn't realize."

"It's not your fault. How could you know?" I stepped back so he could slam the trunk shut. He looked so upset, I tried to lighten the mood even though I was crying inside. "On the bright side, at least I know where to find him."

Joe apologized at least a hundred more times and I

assured him it would be fine. I chuckled to myself as I made my way up the walkway. If my usual paint splotch bag hadn't ripped, there's no way it would have been mistaken for Trey's.

Thankfully my designs are saved to the cloud so I still have something to show the client, even if it is just on my phone. Hopefully I'll be able to screen share to a smart TV. The specifics of the design will be a lot easier to see on a larger screen. I usually go in with paper sketches as well, but those are in my bag so the digital copies will have to be sufficient this time. I reached out and rang the doorbell, hoping for the best.

Molly, my new client, was thrilled with my design and was both understanding and sympathetic about my missing laptop and sketches. After getting her verbal approval on the design, I borrowed a tape measure and double-checked the room dimensions she'd given me. They were close enough that I wouldn't need to adjust anything on my sketch.

We chatted over tea, discussing specifics of the design, and I showed her paint samples online and made note of her preferences. Then I went through my calendar and blocked off two weeks that would fit into both of our schedules. Before leaving, I promised Molly I'd email a contract for her to eSign later tonight.

I practically skipped back down the sidewalk and got into the waiting car with a triumphant smile on my face. Besides the fact the commission on this job will pay my expenses for a couple months, Molly is pretty well-connected and has already mentioned some friends who want to see the mural when it's done. Hopefully some of them will want one of their own.

The driver dropped me off at First Allegiant Bank Park. I thought about just having him wait to take me home but I have no idea how long I'll be here. I'm sure they don't just give random women access to the player of their choice.

I walked up to the front gate and approached the attendant who greeted me with a smile.

"Hi, this is going to sound strange but I need to get in contact with Trey Youngman." Her smile faded as her eyes drifted down toward my stomach before meeting mine again. "Oh no, it's nothing like that." I let out a nervous laugh. "We shared a car earlier and the driver handed him my computer bag. I really need to get it back."

She looked me over from head to toe before waving a security guard over.

"Tell him what you just told me," she said.

"Trey Youngman and I shared a car from Fayetteville earlier today and the driver handed him my computer bag when he got out. I just want to get it back." The security guard crossed his arms over his chest and stared at me. "Look, I get that he's probably playing or whatever and even if he isn't you won't just take me to him, but I really need that laptop. Could I at least leave a note for him?"

He moved his hands to his hips and nodded once.

"I guess that'd be okay."

"Great! Thank you so much."

I reached into my purse and pulled out a small notebook and a pen. After flipping to a blank page, I wrote Trey a note explaining the issue being sure to include my address and phone number before signing my name. I ripped out the paper and folded it in half then handed it to the guard.

"I appreciate this." I placed the pen and notebook back in my purse and hiked it and my duffel bag more securely on my shoulder. I smiled at him then the gate attendant. "Thank you both for your help." Might as well push for extra sympathy while I still have their attention. "My whole business relies on that laptop so I really need to get it back."

The guard held up my note.

"I'll give this to the locker room manager. After that, it's out of my hands."

I thanked them both again then walked over toward a large statue of a baseball player and sat on the bench just off to the side. Grabbing my phone out of my purse, I swiped it open, pulled up the ride share app, and requested a car.

I firmly believe that if you want something done right, you need to do it yourself.

Unfortunately, right now, I need to rely on not one, not two, but three people to do the right thing. As I settled in to wait for my ride, I said a quick prayer that they would.

TREY

I SAT SLUMPED in the corner of the bullpen watching the game. Rusty Russell looks nearly perfect on the mound. He's hitting all his spots and has struck out seven in three and a half innings. Scratch that. A perfect slider makes it eight strikeouts in four innings.

As the Waves headed to the dugout and Houston took the field, I stood and stretched my back then twisted side to side before touching my toes. With the way Rusty is pitching, I'm not sure I'll get a chance to throw, but need to stay loose just in case.

Throughout warm-ups and even sitting here in the pen, the rest of the relievers have given me a wide berth.

There aren't many secrets in the league and it's pretty obvious these guys have heard the rumors that I'm difficult at best and a total dick at worst. I'll admit there's some truth there but it's not like some of the guys in New York were easier to deal with. Any conflicts weren't entirely my fault.

But the Waves have a whole different vibe so I'm going to need to play nice to fit in. This team has given me a chance and I definitely don't want to blow it and get sent down to Triple A again. Or worse, be released altogether.

I settled back into my spot at the end of the bench as the Waves' catcher, Leo Marakis, stepped into the batter's box. Leo is my former college roommate and teammate, and is one of the few people I'd call a friend. He comes from a big, loud Greek family who didn't give a shit about my family or its money. Plus he saw past my arrogant asshole facade and helped me become not only a better pitcher, but a better person. Around him and his family anyway. And now he's supporting me while I try to change for the better so I'm decent to everyone else, too.

Leo took two balls outside before getting served a fastball down the middle that he sent sailing over the shortstop's head. Even though the ball nearly reached the warning track in left-center field, he only ended up with a single. As our college coach Benji Alvarez used to say, "Leo isn't blessed with speed." But that's okay because he's got a rocket launcher for an arm and frames pitches better than any catcher I've ever worked with.

Marquez and McMullen both walked, then Jack Reagan sent a hanging curveball sailing into the upper deck in centerfield adding three more runs to the Waves lead, putting them—I mean us—ahead 5-0.

I shifted my eyes as someone sat next to me. Closing pitcher Malik Walters settled against the back of the bench, stretched his legs in front of him, and crossed his ankles.

"Stay loose. If Rusty keeps throwing like he is, you're gonna be closing this game," he said.

I glanced around before turning to fully face him.

"Yes, I'm talking to you newbie."

That's exactly what has me so shocked, even more than his words.

"Oh." I cleared my throat. "Okay."

"You ready?"

"I'm keeping loose so once I go through my routine, I'll be golden."

"Good to hear." He jerked his head toward the other end of the bench and the rest of the pitchers. "Just do your job and don't be a douchebag and everything here will fall into place."

I nodded then turned my attention back to the field when the crowd cheered. The designated hitter, Phillip Riddle, stood at second base, but I have no idea how he got there.

Malik stayed next to me for the next two innings as Rusty continued to dominate on the mound and the Waves hitters kept putting numbers on the board. The bullpen coach, Miles Eaton, confirmed what Malik had said, I'd be closing the game. So at the end of the seventh, I stood and worked through my routine.

Despite the butterflies in my stomach, I felt great and every one of my bullpen pitches looked perfect. Eaton even commented on a few, giving me an extra boost of confidence.

After the Waves got out in the eighth, I jogged out to the mound where Leo was waiting.

"You didn't meet Rusty on the mound. I must be special."

"You're special all right," he said around a shit-eating grin. "We're gonna show these guys how well you paint the corners. Just like the old days." He handed me the ball. "Let's get this over fast. My hamstrings are tight and my lower back is killing me."

"Got it."

He jogged back behind the plate and I threw a few warm-up pitches, getting a feel for the mound and the rubber. After my last one, Leo threw the ball down to second base, and we were ready to start the inning.

The first batter stepped up to the plate and I stood on the mound waiting for Leo's sign. It's not the pitch I would have chosen, but I learned back in college to never shake him off. He definitely knows what I should throw better than I do.

I took in a deep breath and placed my foot on the rubber. Wrapping my fingers around the ball, I rotated it to find the perfect grip on the threads. I focused on Leo's glove as I went into my windup. My arm extended, reaching back, over the top, then forward, before I released the ball, and settled into a perfect follow-through. The fastball sailed right over the inside corner of the plate, thigh high, for a called strike one.

We followed that with a fastball on the outside corner that the hitter fanned at but couldn't catch up to. I'm happy to say, I'm throwing hard today. Not triple digits, but I'd say high-nineties for sure and my pitches are making a perfect popping sound in Leo's glove.

After that, we stayed in that same spot, but slowed things down with a curveball. The batter swung way ahead, catching a piece of the ball with the end of his bat, ticking it right into Leo's glove for the first out.

Leo called for a similar pattern for the next two batters, and while they each fouled a couple pitches off, one guy flew out to center and the other hit a line drive right at Jimmy Chavez for the third out. The crowd cheered and Leo slapped me on the back as the rest of the team met on the infield to celebrate the 12-0 win. Not a bad first game with my new team.

After giving an on-field interview, I walked toward the dugout then through the tunnel to the locker room. A couple more reporters approached as I entered and I answered their questions about my pitching and told them how happy I am to be with the team and everything else they wanted to hear.

I passed Leo's locker on the way to my own and he turned to look over his shoulder at me.

"We're still going out to grab something to eat, right?" he asked.

"Sure. You'll have to drive me though. I don't get my license back for another three weeks."

He pulled his shirt off.

"Do you need to go to the hotel first?"

"No, I'd rather eat first. Once I get to the hotel, I'm probably gonna crash. It's been a long couple days."

"Great, I'm starving. Take the fastest shower ever and we'll get out of here."

"Sounds like a plan."

I made my way over to my locker, toed off my cleats, and removed my pants, then sat to take off my socks. The locker room manager, Toby Wheeler approached.

"Excuse me, Trey?"

"Yeah?"

"One of the security guards asked me to give this to you."

He handed me a note.

"Thanks."

I was about to read it when another reporter

approached. Placing it on the top shelf of my locker, I turned to face her, reciting a different version of the same answers I'd given to the other reporters. When I was done, I headed to take a quick shower. Leo's not the only one who's hungry.

Chapter Three

NORI

I WRAPPED my hands around my ancient laptop, ready to throw it across the room. As good as that would make me feel, logically I know the joy will be fleeting and I'll be left without a computer. Even through my aggravation, I know this laptop is better than none.

Setting it back on the table, I sat back in my chair and waited for the image to load. I have no idea how I used to get anything done on this computer. Then again, the wait probably didn't seem as bad before I had my super-speedy Surface.

I heard the garage door open then close and looked at the clock as Crispin entered the kitchen.

"You're home early," I said.

He dramatically flopped into the chair across from me. Then again, Crispin does everything dramatically or "with flair" as he prefers to say.

"Yeah, I'm feeling a little bitchy today so after I finished my last client, I decided to come home."

"That's not like you."

"I know," he said around a dramatic sigh. "But I figure, I own the place, right? And I have a perfectly capable manager who can handle things when I'm not around. Why not let her once in a while?"

Crispin shares my "if you want something done right, you need to do it yourself" belief so to say I'm shocked is an understatement. That salon is his baby. He bought it with half the money his grandmother left him when she died. A chunk of the other half paid for this house.

"Is everything okay?"

"Yeah, I'm just..." He trailed off, then shrugged and shook his head. "But I'm sure it's nothing some wine won't cure."

Jumping up, he walked over to the wine fridge on the other side of the kitchen and pulled out a bottle.

"It's only four o'clock."

"Yeah, but according to Alan Jackson, it's five o'clock somewhere. And even if that weren't true, it's close enough." He uncorked it then reached for a glass. "Are you having some?"

"No thanks. At the rate this computer is going, I'll be working all night. Wine makes me sleepy."

He took a long drink standing at the counter then refilled his glass and came back to the table.

"I told you to use my computer. You'll never get anything done with that dinosaur."

"I know, but I'd hoped to hear from Trey by now so I wouldn't have to bother you."

"Do not even start." Crispin rolled his eyes. "You've been my best friend since junior high. When are you going to accept my help without a fuss?"

"Hello? I live here, don't I?"

"Yeah, and how long did it take me to convince you to move down here with me?"

"Not that long." He snorted then took a sip of wine. "I mean, initially you were living with—"

"Do *not* say his name."

"You already had a roommate so you didn't need me."

"Honey, I've needed you every day since we met in Mrs. Geiger's science class."

I stared at him, my mouth hanging open, then blinked to bring him back into focus. Crispin is always dramatic but he's rarely sentimental. When he is, it chokes me up.

"Same here." I chuckled. "You know, that first meeting could have ended up with us hating each other instead of becoming best friends."

"True." He finished his wine and got up to grab the bottle. Sitting back down, he refilled his glass. "But you were too cute to get angry at."

I ignored the cute comment because I know he just said it to get a rise out of me.

"Why would you have gotten angry at me?"

"You said my name sounds like a cereal."

"That's because you said Nori isn't a name, it's what you wrap sushi with."

"And I wasn't lying. It is what you wrap sushi with."

"I wasn't lying either. Your name does sound like a cereal."

We both burst out laughing, which is exactly what we did way back when. It had been my first day in a new school where I was as much an outsider as I was in my father's house, which I'd moved into the week before, right after my mother died. I was scared and lonely and probably depressed, but Crispin made me feel those things less.

And spending time with him made me feel better about myself and my life in general.

"So you haven't heard anything from Trey?" I shook my head. "Did you call the stadium to make sure he got the note?"

"Yeah, I spoke directly with the locker room manager Toby Wheeler. He said he gave the note to Trey after the game last night."

"He had a big day yesterday. Maybe he just crashed after the game. I have faith he'll contact you."

"Well just in case, today I worked on figuring a new laptop into my budget."

"Give it a few days before you totally panic," he said, then bobbed his eyebrows. "So how was it sitting next to him for two freaking hours? Is he as handsome as he looks on TV? What does he smell like?"

I raised my brows higher with each consecutive question. He finally stopped speaking so I could actually answer.

"It was like sharing a ride with any stranger. Yes, he is handsome, but I have no idea if it's more or less than he looks on TV. I haven't watched baseball since you stopped playing, remember? And he smelled like some expensive cologne that you could probably name with one sniff, but I have no clue about."

He stood and walked into the living room and returned with my small sketchbook, a knowing smirk on his face. After dropping it on the table in front of me, he sat back down with one elbow on the table and rested his chin in his palm.

I blew out a breath and shook my head.

With his free hand, he opened the book and flipped through page after page of the sketches I'd done of Trey, stopping at the one of his beautiful smile that I finished late last night.

"They're all amazing, but this one…" He trailed off and fanned his hand in front of his face. "Girl, this one is something special. I've never seen a smile like that on Trey Youngman's face, not even when New York won the play-offs a couple years ago." Pushing his wine glass out of the way, he leaned forward. "You're an amazing artist with a vivid imagination, but I doubt that even you'd envision that particular smile on that particular man unless you'd seen it."

I looked down at the sketch and felt my face heat as I thought back to Trey flashing that smile at me. It's been a long time since a man made me blush like that.

Crispin sat back in the chair, never breaking eye contact.

"That's what I thought." He reached for his wine and took a sip. "And if that man flashed that smile at you, trust me when I tell you that you'll be hearing from him."

"I hope you're right."

But as I said those words, I couldn't be sure if it's because I want my laptop back or if I'm hoping to see that smile again.

TREY

STANDING IN THE SHOWER, I bent my head, letting the hot spray pound against my shoulders. Even though I only threw twelve pitches last night, chances are I won't be pitching today. So after my workout, I decided to take a shower so I won't have to later.

I turned off the water and grabbed a towel. After dragging it through my hair, I ran it over my chest, arms, and legs before tying it around my waist. Heading back to my locker, I sat and rested my head against the back of the chair. The last few days really have been a whirlwind.

When I got home after dinner last night I thought I would have crashed, but ended up getting my second wind. I put *Schitt'$ Creek* on Netflix and binged through two and a half seasons before finally dozing off as the sun was coming up. It's a good thing I set my alarm or I'd probably still be sleeping.

My ass was dragging when I first got to the stadium a few hours ago, but thankfully my workout woke me up enough to be functional. Falling asleep in the bullpen would definitely make these guys think all the talk about me is true.

After fully drying off, I stepped into a pair of sliding shorts. Grabbing a T-shirt off my shelf, I sent a small piece of paper whirling to the floor. I slipped the shirt over my head then picked up the paper.

I opened it and read the note quickly then a second time, a little slower. Dragging my fingers through my hair, I tried to picture the pile of bags in my hotel room. I like to think I'd notice an extra one but I never really looked at the number of bags, I just shuffled them from Joe's car to the locker room then into and out of Leo's car before tossing them in a heap and climbing into bed.

I'm not being arrogant thinking this might be Nori's way of getting to talk to me again. Women have done all kinds of strange things to get my attention. Granted, despite her appearance she seemed relatively normal, but you never know. I placed the note on top of my cell and finished getting dressed.

The old me would have ignored the note, but I'm

trying to get rid of that guy. He was cocky, arrogant, and entitled and people really didn't like him. When I get back to the hotel later, I'll check and if I do have the bag, I'll give her a call.

As I headed out to the bullpen, I thought about my conversation with Leo last night. He confirmed my suspicions on why my new teammates were giving me a wide berth. But he also echoed Malik's words and believes that if I do my job and don't act like a prick, I'll fit in just fine.

Leo is the only person who knows all my issues and why I act the way I do sometimes. Hell, he's the one who made me realize it. In college, he witnessed enough interactions between my family and me to get a pretty good picture. With some added details from me, he fully understood my whole poor-little-rich-boy existence.

Playing for New York was always my dream but after a few months of therapy, I know now that being that close to my family wasn't the healthiest thing for me. Even though I was on the road half the year, they still managed to make me feel like shit. And when that happens, I do stupid things and make other people feel just as bad.

I reached the bullpen with plenty of time to spare before the first pitch is thrown. Figuring I'd be sitting for nine innings, I stood by the wall and took in the whole stadium. Nothing can match the energy in New York, but I'll admit, there is something special here. I didn't notice it so much as a visiting player, but as Leo reminded me, I had my head up my ass a lot of the time.

My goal going forward is to keep it on my shoulders where it's supposed to be and make a fresh start with the Waves. The weather is definitely better here in the South and Myrtle Beach is a great city. I think, for the first time in my life, I have a chance to be truly happy.

If I don't fuck it up.

Chapter Four

TREY

LEO TEXTED that he's waiting outside so I grabbed Nori's bag and headed down. He was parked right outside the front doors of the hotel where he'd dropped me off a couple nights ago.

I slipped into the passenger seat and placed the bag at my feet.

"Hey," I said as I grabbed my seatbelt and clicked it into place.

"Hey." He drove through the parking lot then turned onto the main road heading in the general direction to Nori's house. "You know you're welcome to stay with me instead of at a hotel, right?"

"I know and I appreciate it, but staying at the hotel will inspire me to find my own place sooner rather than later."

"It's nice to hear you say that."

"Why?"

"Because it means you plan on being here for the long haul."

"Yeah, someone convinced me that if I stop being my own worst enemy, I can have a good life here."

"Must be a very wise man who said that."

I just snorted at that as I keyed Nori's address into Waze and placed my phone in the holder mounted to the dashboard.

"You know you could have had a messenger drop that off."

He gestured to the computer bag between my feet.

"I know, but she said her business depends on this computer and I didn't want to take a chance it would go missing," I said. "Plus we're going out anyway so it's no big deal to swing by and give it to her."

His smirk told me he wasn't convinced that was the only reason, but I refrained from explaining further. It'd be a sure sign there's something more going on. And I don't want to give that impression until I know what that might be.

When I got back to the hotel after the game last night and saw Nori's computer bag, I felt like a total idiot. I called her immediately and asked if it would be okay if I brought it over tonight. She said it would be then we ended up talking for an hour.

I've been in relationships—and I use that term very loosely—with women and didn't talk to them as much as Nori and I have spoken to date. So I have no idea what's going on. Thankfully Leo spoke before I could think about it too much.

"So what'd you do today?"

Today's an off-day before Tampa comes to town for three games starting tomorrow. Then we head to Chicago, for a ten-game stretch away.

"Nothing. Slept mostly. Hopefully I'm caught up now."

"You know my mother says it's not possible to get caught up on sleep."

"Maybe not, but it sure felt good," I said. "Besides, your mother had six kids in seven years, runs a business, and keeps her house spotless. It'd take her years to catch up on sleep if she was ever given the chance."

"That's true."

"We talked about me so much last night I didn't get a chance to ask if your mother's gotten over the fact that you bought a house in Scranton."

"She's not thrilled but it's close enough to Bergen County that she's not giving me the silent treatment." He shrugged. "Although I just closed on the house in January and then had some renovations done so I haven't lived there yet. There's still time for her to lay on a total guilt trip when I do."

"I still can't believe you decided to settle there."

"I love my family and I know how great they are, but now that I've been away at least part time for more than a decade, I feel a little smothered when I'm there all the time." He glanced in his side view mirror before passing the car in front of us. "You know I liked Scranton when we were in college. It's a great city and far enough away from my family to give me some breathing room but close enough to visit regularly. Not to mention you can get a mini mansion for less than I'd pay for a shack in New Jersey and the taxes are a fraction of the price."

We were both quiet as the app's mechanical voice gave directions. Leo turned on his blinker to get off the next exit.

"So tell me about this girl. What should I expect?"

"First of all, you're not going to meet her so you shouldn't expect anything."

"I'm not gonna meet her?"

"Why would you? I'm just dropping off her computer and then we can head to dinner. There's no reason for you to even get out of the car."

"Are you ashamed of me?"

He stuck his lower lip out in a mock pout.

"You're an ass, you know that?"

"Takes one to know one," he said. "But seriously, there must be something special about her that has us trekking to the other side of town running an errand any decent courier could do."

I thought back to when I first laid eyes on Nori. With that pink hair and her violet eyes, she reminded me of an anime character. I'll admit I judged her even as I sat there trying to figure out the pull I felt toward her.

"I know what you've been insinuating since I asked you to drive me to her house, but Nori is definitely not my type."

"Why's that?"

"I'd be surprised if she's five feet tall and she has pink hair. She reminds me of a pixie."

"Did you say pink hair?"

"Bright pink. And she has five tattoos that I noticed. They're all small but still, I'm not

much of a tattoo guy."

"That sounds like your father talking."

I decided to ignore that comment instead of freaking out like I normally would at any comparison between my father and me.

"She's a mural artist and she smells like cinnamon buns."

"And that's a problem?"

"Look, you asked me to tell you about her and I am."

"Don't get your panties in a twist, I just asked a question."

For the next few blocks, the only voice in the car was the one from the app telling us where to go. We turned onto Nori's street and I looked at the numbers on the houses we passed.

"It should be that blue one with the white trim right there."

I pointed to the house in question then checked the address as Leo turned into the driveway just to be sure and unhooked my seatbelt.

"I'll be right back," I said as I stepped out of the car, then reached back in for the bag and closed the door behind me.

I know Leo is just busting my ass, but he's hitting too close to home for me to be amused. There's just something about Nori that I've been drawn to since she sat down in that car next to me. But I definitely don't want to explore it.

I need to focus on getting my shit together and I don't need anyone distracting me from that.

NORI

"AREN'T YOU GOING TO CHANGE?"

Crispin's appalled tone made me chuckle, mostly because I'm not going to give him the answer he wants.

"No. Why?"

He rolled his eyes and let out a dramatic sigh.

"Nori, Trey Youngman is coming here and you're wearing an old pair of leggings that I'm sure at one time were black but now could barely pass as gray. And that shirt…" Pointing at my chest, he shook his head and closed his eyes as a pained look crossed his face.

I held out the hem of my shirt and looked down.

"What's wrong with it? I think it's kind of funny."

"It has a picture of a smiling palette with a dialogue bubble that says 'I arted.'"

"I'm aware of that." I let go of my shirt and put my hands on my hips.

"*Trey Youngman* will be here any second and you're wearing a fart joke for a shirt."

"Who doesn't love potty humor?" I turned to stir my bolognese sauce. "And you can say his full name in any tone you want, but it doesn't change the fact that the man is dropping off my computer and that's it. He's not coming to hang out and be your BFF."

I just finished that sentence when the doorbell rang.

"Oh my God, he's here."

I watched as he ran to the door and stopped to smooth down his shirt. He placed one hand on the doorknob and paused to cup the other over his mouth to check his breath. Seeming satisfied, he turned the knob and opened the door, but his body blocked my view of Trey.

"Hi, I'm looking for Nori."

"I'm Nori's roommate and best friend, Crispin Wells. She's in the kitchen making dinner. Come on in."

The house has an open-concept design so as Crispin stepped aside, I watched Trey enter, looking just as good as I remember.

"It smells great in here," Trey said as Crispin closed the door behind him.

I tapped the wooden spoon against the side of the pan and placed it on the spoon rest.

"Thank you so much for dropping that off," I said.

I walked into the living room and he offered a polite smile as he handed me my bag.

"I'm sorry, I didn't even realize I had it. I like to think I would have noticed today, but I wouldn't swear to it." He slid his hands into the pockets of his khaki shorts. "Did you have any issues getting your note to me?"

"I guess not since you're here." I set the bag on the couch and let out a nervous chuckle. "I went to the stadium and told my story to the gate attendant and she called over a security guard. At first they both seemed to think I was a crazy groupie trying to get to you but I must have convinced them otherwise because the guard agreed to take the note and give it to the locker room manager. I wasn't totally confident he would."

"He gave it to me after the game Monday night but a reporter approached immediately after and I put it on the shelf in my locker and forgot about it. I read it when I was getting dressed for the game yesterday but figured I'd wait to call until I got back to the hotel to confirm I actually had the bag."

"I really appreciate you dropping it off. Thank you."

Trey opened his mouth to say something but Crispin spoke instead.

"Why don't you two discuss this more over dinner, Nori? It'd be a nice way for you to say thank you." He looked at Trey. "She makes an amazing bolognese."

"Oh, no I couldn't intrude on your plans." He hitched his thumb toward the door. "Leo is actually waiting for me in the car. We're gonna grab a bite to eat."

Crispin's mouth dropped open and he practically vibrated with excitement.

"Leo Marakis?" The words were said with a quiet reverence and after uttering them, he held his breath in anticipation of Trey's answer.

"Yeah."

"Leo Marakis is in a car, outside my house?"

Trey nodded and I thought my best friend was going to have a heart attack right then and there.

"Then you both have to stay." Crispin looked at me. "Right Nori? Don't they have to stay?"

His voice was taking on a bit of a hysterical pitch and he looked like he might cry if I said no. As much I want to choke him for putting me on the spot like this, I can't deny him right now.

"Please stay," I said. "There's plenty and it would make me happy to offer a proper thank you."

His honey-colored eyes stared into mine for what seemed like an eternity before tiny crinkles appeared in the corners when he smiled.

"Thank you for the invitation." Trey looked back and forth between Crispin and me. "Let me go get Leo."

As soon as Trey left, Crispin clutched his chest.

"Holy fuck! Both Trey Youngman and Leo Marakis are going to be in this house in the next couple minutes." He walked over to me, placed his hands on my shoulders, and gave me a big kiss. "I owe you big time for this. It's like a dream come true."

It's more like a nightmare for me but I won't mention that and burst Crispin's bubble. There's just something about Trey that I'm drawn to despite the fact that every fiber of my being knows I shouldn't be. I've already been with a carbon copy of him and that didn't end well. It's definitely not something I want to repeat.

But this is just a thank you dinner and then I'll never see him again, so I'll just enjoy tonight with no worries.

"I'm going to go put water on for the pasta."

Chapter Five

TREY

"THIS IS ABSOLUTELY DELICIOUS, NORI," I said as I finished my second bowl of pasta. "It's been a long time since I had a home-cooked meal."

"Thank you. I'm glad you enjoyed it."

Dinner really has been a lot of fun, despite the fact that I've had to fight the urge to stare at Nori the entire time. She looks different in her own space, more relaxed. Having dinner with her and Crispin is like spending time with Leo's family. It's fun and full of teasing. Which is probably why my friend is so comfortable here. That and the fact that Crispin has been fussing over him since he walked through the door.

It turns out Nori's best friend is a huge baseball fan, which doesn't fit in with my first impression of him. I guess it just goes to show that you can't judge a person at first glance. He's a cool guy and definitely knows his baseball.

There's also something about him that's really familiar. I just can't put my finger on why that is though.

His relationship with Nori reminds me a lot of mine with Leo's sisters. Speaking of…

"Can I ask where you got your shirt?"

Crispin choked on his wine and once he stopped coughing, Nori gave him a smug smile and answered my question.

"On Etsy."

I looked at Leo. "Something like that would be perfect for Angie, don't you think?"

"She'd love it," he said.

"Leo's little sister is a graphic artist and also paints watercolors," I explained to Nori and Crispin.

"I'll text you the name of the shop." She picked up her phone. "They sell a bunch of cool stuff."

My phone dinged and I glanced down.

"Got it. Thanks."

I also noticed the time. "We should be going,"

I started stacking empty plates. That's something I wouldn't have done before spending time with Leo's family, but his mom taught me well. Growing up, I had a house-keeper to take care of everything and lacked basic manners and life skills.

Crispin stood. "Nope, this is my job. Rules of the house. Nori cooks and I clean. If I don't, she'll expect me to do something else."

"Let me at least help you clear the table."

At that point, Leo and Nori stood and joined us in our dish stacking.

"Don't make it sound like you're a slave in your own home," she said.

The three of us followed her to the kitchen to place our dishes in the sink. At barely five feet tall, Nori normally looks tiny, but surrounded by three men at least a foot taller, she seems even smaller. I've always been attracted to tall, leggy women, but I gotta say, she's looking pretty ideal to me right now.

Crispin dropped his stack of dishes in the sink, then turned to Leo.

"Come to my office and grab some samples," he said. "I'm convinced the product line I mentioned will be perfect for your hair. It'll add even more shine."

That said, they disappeared down the hall. Once Nori and I were alone, the air in the room changed. It felt a little hesitant and a whole lot charged.

She leaned against the counter and looked across the room, at the floor, then down at her fingernails. Pretty much anywhere but at me, which let me know she was feeling it too.

I should just let it go. I should just stand in awkward silence with her until Crispin and Leo return. But there's just something about Nori that draws me in so I can't.

"Thanks again for dinner. That was the best Bolognese I've ever had."

I was about to add that I've eaten in the best Italian restaurants in New York and around the world, but refrained. I'm trying to turn over a new leaf and even little things like not bragging about something silly like that helps. My therapist would be proud.

"Thank you." Her violet eyes met mine and she offered a shy smile. "And thanks again for bringing my laptop."

I nodded. "So did you get that job?" She drew her brows together and cocked her head. It shouldn't have looked adorable but it absolutely did. "The fairy garden one?"

"Oh yeah. She loved the design. I start in a couple weeks."

"And how's your car?"

She wrinkled her nose. "Not so great. It'd cost more to fix it than what it's worth. So I'm looking for a new one."

"That's too bad."

"Yeah."

Something crossed her face, a note of sadness that went beyond just needing a new car. But that's none of my business. Thankfully Leo and Crispin returned before I felt a need to fill the silence again. Or God forbid, kiss her to see if her lips are as soft as they look.

"Crispin hooked me up," Leo said and held a small brown shopping bag that rattled when he shook it.

The only thing Leo is more obsessed about than his game is his hair. I'm surprised he actually wears a helmet.

"And don't forget to give me a call to set up that appointment," Crispin said. "It would be an honor to work on that hair."

I shook my head and pointed toward the door.

"Let's get going before your head gets any bigger and you can't fit through it."

They walked us to the door and Crispin opened it with a flourish.

"It's been wonderful spending time with both of you," he said.

"Good luck with your fairy mural," I said to Nori as I walked outside.

She nodded and bit her lip, then offered a small smile.

"Good luck with your season," she said.

Leo and I walked down to the driveway and the door closed behind us. Once we got settled in the car, Leo clicked his seatbelt into place and looked at me, a huge smile on his face.

"I don't want to hear how wonderful Crispin thinks your hair is," I said.

"Oh, we'll talk about that later." He started the car and backed out of the driveway. "But right now, I just want to talk about the charge in the air that I'm pretty sure wasn't coming from Crispin and me. Did your whole ride from Fayetteville have that same vibe?"

"You're delusional."

"I'm absolutely right and you know it," he said. "She's adorable. Like a pink-haired pixie, just like you said. And I smelled the cinnamon bun thing, even with all the garlic in the air." When I didn't say anything, he added, "If you're not going to ask her out, maybe I will."

I looked over at him and he burst out laughing. "Yeah, that's what I thought."

I rolled my eyes and turned toward my window.

"You know, you should take it as a good sign that I'm pushing you to a sweet girl like Nori. If you were still a douchebag, I'd never suggest it. So it just shows how much progress you've made."

"Well thank you for that," I said with as much sarcasm as I could muster. "But I don't plan on asking her out. I don't plan on seeing her again. My therapist has told me to work on myself and that's what I'm doing. I don't need any distractions."

"Okay." He drew out the word in a sing-song tone. "But you're wrong about one thing."

"What's that?"

"You will be seeing Nori again. She and Crispin are coming to a game when we get back into town in a couple weeks."

NORI

. . .

CRISPIN CLOSED the door and turned to face me.

"Could you have been more obvious?"

"I don't know what you're talking about."

He breezed by me and walked to the kitchen.

"Please, I'm surprised you didn't pick me up and plop me onto Trey's lap."

"Nori," he said with a sigh. "That man is interested in you whether you want to admit it or not. He couldn't keep his eyes off you."

"It's just the hair. His kind doesn't understand individuality."

Crispin had bent to place a pot in the dishwasher and looked up at me, his brow raised.

"We don't judge like that, Eleanor Mabel Somers."

I clenched my jaw so tightly I was sure my molars were going to turn to dust. Partly because he called me by my full name and partly because I know he's right.

"I know I shouldn't judge Trey without really knowing him, but I can't help it. He reminds me so much of Baxter."

"That's only in your head. They don't look anything alike and from what I just witnessed, he doesn't act anything like Baxter the Bastard either."

He continued to fill the dishwasher, perfectly placing everything to fill it to maximum capacity. For a person who never washed a dish before I moved in here with him, I have to say, Crispin has it down. He makes everything fit just right.

I leaned my back against the counter.

"It's more his aura or the air around him." I shook my head. "I don't know, but the man is definitely upper crust."

He placed the last of the silverware in the dishwasher,

put a detergent pod in, closed the door, and hit start.

"You really don't follow baseball, do you?"

He picked up a towel and dried his hands, looking at me like I'm clueless. Which I suppose I am in this case.

"You've known me for how long and you're asking me that? No, I don't follow baseball."

"Actually." He hung the towel on the stove handle and gestured for me to follow him into the living room. "Trey is as much pop culture as he is baseball." We settled on opposite ends of the couch, facing each other. "His family is Youngman Electronics."

I stared at him, shocked into silence.

"Honey, you need to blink or move or do something that lets me know you're still alive over there."

"See, I was right. The Youngmans are beyond rich."

"Just because he's from that family doesn't mean he's a total dick. Like I said, I didn't get that vibe from him. Not totally anyway. He seems like he's trying to be a normal person."

I tucked my feet under me and shifted farther down onto the couch. None of this really matters because Trey and I aren't interested in each other. We shared a ride, he returned my computer, and I thanked him with a meal. I'll never see him again.

"You're just looking for something to be there between Trey and me so you have an in with the Waves," I said around a smirk.

"I have my own in….Leo. Once I get my hands on that wonderful hair of his and make it more amazing than it already is, he'll be under my spell for life." He sat forward and slapped my knee. "Leo's a pretty good guy, right?" I nodded. "Would he be best friends with Trey if he was as bad as you seem to think he is?"

"I guess not. But Crispin, none of what you're saying

matters. Trey and I aren't interested in each other." He looked up toward the ceiling and mumbled something. I didn't ask him to repeat it, because I'm sure I don't want to know. "And unless he contacts me to paint a mural for him whenever he buys a house, I'll never see him again."

Crispin looked at me and the smug smile on his face put me instantly on alert.

"Actually…"

"What did you do?"

He placed a hand over his chest, trying to look offended, but the smugness won out.

"I didn't do anything," he said around a cheeky smile. "But Leo offered us tickets to a Waves game when they get back to town. How could I refuse that?" He took in a breath and let it out with a shudder. "We'll probably sit in the friends and family section."

Chapter Six

TREY

LEO and I settled into a booth in the back corner of the
bar. It doesn't look like much from the outside, but I
happen to know they serve some of the best deep dish in
Chicago. He's the one who told me about this place, but
since we always played on different teams, Leo and I have
never eaten here together until now.

I just wish it was a celebration instead of a licking of
our wounds after a loss.

The waitress came over immediately with menus and
to take our drink order. Leo got a beer and I asked for
water. We also knew we wanted the extra meat pie so we
ordered that as well and each added on a side salad just to
balance things out.

"You know I always enjoy your company, but don't feel
like you have to babysit me," I said when she left. "I'm sure
there are other guys you usually hang around with. Just

because I'm *persona non grata* doesn't mean you need to give up all your friends and hang out with me."

"You've been with the team two minutes, so it's not like I've given up my whole social life," he said. "And the *persona non grata* thing is changing. I guarantee that by the time we get home next week, you'll be one of the guys."

The waitress returned with our drinks and salads.

Leo picked up his fork and pointed it toward my glass.

"Still on the wagon?"

I shrugged. "If that's what you want to call it."

"How's it going?"

"It's fine. I'm not an alcoholic so it's not like I'm dying for a drink." I shoved a forkful of salad into my mouth and chewed. "It was just a habit that got out of control so I'm taking a break."

My cell vibrated and I pulled it out of my pocket and rejected the call. It immediately rang again and I did the same thing. When it rang a third time, I powered my phone down and slammed it onto the table.

I stabbed at the lettuce until my fork was full. As I went to put it into my mouth, I noticed Leo watching me and stopped, lowering my hand to the table.

"What?"

His eyes shifted to my phone and then back to me.

"Anything you want to talk about?"

I dropped my fork on the plate then pushed it away.

"My father keeps calling me."

"For what?"

"I don't know, I don't answer. When he does leave a message, he just demands that I call him, nothing else."

"You're not curious?" He took a drink of beer and sat back in his chair, his hand wrapped around the bottle.

"A little bit," I said. "But I'm taking a break from my family as well."

It was obvious Leo had a few questions but our waitress returned with the pizza so I was spared for a moment as she set it down and cleared our salad plates.

Leo's family is super close, so despite the fact that he decided to live two hours away from them during the off-season, he'd never go more than a day or two without talking to most, if not all of them. But his family is awesome, not toxic like mine. And it's not just a case of me thinking the grass is greener in someone else's yard. My family is fucked up, but when you shine that up with a heap of money, no one really seems to care.

"For how long?"

"Until I feel more stable as the new me."

"I'm sorry I wasn't around to notice how bad things were getting for you. I mean, obviously I saw what was happening on the field but I didn't realize it was because of your dad."

"I didn't want you to know. Or your family."

I slid the spatula under a slice and shifted it up slightly and decided it had cooled enough to serve. Placing it on a plate, I handed it to Leo then dished up one for myself. We ate that first piece in silence, savoring each bite. I'd just put the last forkful into my mouth when Leo handed me his empty dish. After I filled both our plates again, we picked up the conversation.

"Did your therapist suggest taking a break from your family?"

"No, but when I brought it up, he didn't hate the idea, and he was happy with my reasons."

"Which are?"

"Basically, they make me feel bad about myself and I in turn act like a cocky prick and make other people feel bad." I took a drink of water then traced my finger around and around along the rim of the glass. "Once I feel more secure that won't happen, I'll contact them again. But until then, I'm staying away."

"Do you think they'll show up when we play in New York?"

"I hope not." I shoved a bite of pizza into my mouth, thinking about the question while I chewed and swallowed. "I honestly don't know. But that's a few weeks off so I'm not gonna worry about it right now."

NORI

I SAT CURLED up on the corner of the couch working on a design. A potential client is interested in a wildflower mural for the one wall in her three-season room and I'm playing around with colors on the digital image I created from my original sketch.

It took me a few months to save up for this top-of-the-line Surface Pro, but it's worth every penny. Even with all my software, it's super fast, and the display is amazing. Prior to this, I did things the old-fashioned way. I'd make multiple sketches with different color schemes to showcase at my client meetings. If I had a variety of designs to show, that got pretty cumbersome.

Now I just make a sketch, scan it into the program, and tweak it digitally. I'm able to mix my own colors and select different tools within the program to apply them to my design, which offers different textures and shades. So I can easily save a bunch of options. As a bonus, I add the final color selection to my original sketch and give it to them in a frame at the completion of the project.

"Hello my darling."

I was so into my work, I didn't even hear Crispin come in. He kissed me on the back of the head then walked over to the other side of the room and flopped into the oversized chair and put his feet up on the ottoman.

"I made a garlicky, shrimpy, noodley concoction. It's in the pan on the stove."

His stomach let out a loud growl.

"Great. I'm starving."

"So I hear."

He stood and went into the kitchen. I finished up what I was working on while he made a dish. I'd just set my work aside when he returned.

"This is so ah-mazing." He shoved a big bite into his mouth and glanced at his cell while he chewed. "Do you mind if I put the game on?"

"No, that's fine."

He reached forward and grabbed the remote off the coffee table and changed the channel.

Normally when Crispin goes into sports mode, I zone out and work or read a book. Sometimes I go to my room to watch TV. But I've never actually watched a game with him. Until now.

Once he noticed my interest, Crispin started telling me little facts and explaining things so I knew what was going on. He played baseball until our sophomore year and I regularly attended games back then, but I'll be honest, I never had a clue about what was happening. I was just there to support my friend.

"So they already played this team twice?"

"Yes and they each won one. So whoever wins this wins the series."

"And what does that do?"

"Nothing official, but no one wants to be swept." I

raised my brow. "A sweep is when the team you're playing wins every game in the series."

As I watched the game, I couldn't muster up the same excitement as Crispin. He practically sat on the edge of his seat, plus he yelled at the TV every once in a while, as if they could hear him. Although it was pretty funny when he'd comment on something that happened and the announcer would say the same thing a few seconds later.

During the commercial break, Crispin went and put his empty plate in the sink and dished us each a bowl of *Ice Cream Sammie*. Since Crispin won't accept money for rent or utilities from me, I buy all the groceries, except for the ice cream. I refuse to pay for *Ben & Jerry's* and he won't eat anything else. He says nothing makes you feel better than grabbing a spoon and digging into a pint. The fact that he's actually using a bowl tonight tells me he had a good day.

To serve his every mood, he keeps the freezer stocked with a variety of flavors. Thankfully he shares with me.

When the commercial was over, one of the Waves players stood next to home plate, ready to bat. I have to admit, looking at all these guys in uniform isn't a hardship. No wonder Crispin likes sports so much.

I placed a heaping spoonful of ice cream into my mouth. This is one of my favorite flavors. It's like an ice cream sandwich in a bowl.

The guy that was batting jogged down to first base. I know enough about the game to understand that the pitcher had thrown him four balls and he walked.

"Leo's up next."

Just after he said that, the man in question stepped up to the plate, looking very determined. I jumped when the pitcher threw the ball and it sailed right at Leo's head.

"Leo tends to crowd the plate so the pitchers sometimes push him back."

"By throwing the ball at his head?" I shrieked.

He shrugged. "It's all part of the game."

"These guys are crazy."

I finished my ice cream and placed the bowl on the coffee table then rested back into the corner of the couch, my legs tucked under me.

Leo watched the next ball go by him and the umpire called it a strike. Crispin yelled at the TV, saying the pitch was outside. The pitcher threw the ball over at the guy on first base twice before focusing on Leo again. And this time, Leo swung and hit the ball. It flew into the outfield and just as he got to first base, my phone rang.

I glanced at the caller ID and didn't recognize the number. Normally I ignore unknown numbers, but something told me to answer this one.

"Hello?" I walked toward my bedroom so I didn't disturb Crispin.

"May I speak to Nori Somers?" the woman on the other end asked.

"This is Nori."

"My name is Lisa Cooper. Emily Bishop gave me your number. I saw the Penn State mural you did in her basement and absolutely love it. My husband and I are in the process of renovating our basement and I'd like to hire you to do your magic."

I sat on the edge of my bed and grabbed the notebook I keep on the nightstand. We discussed some basic details and I told her I'd check my schedule and get back to her with dates and ideas in the next couple days.

After we hung up, I made a few more notes then scrolled through my schedule. Spending another weekend in Fayetteville isn't high on my list of things to do, but if this project is as straightforward as Emily's, it'll be easy money. And I definitely need that, especially if I'm going to buy a car anytime soon.

I walked into the living room and settled back on the couch.

"Oh good, you're back. Rios keeps getting into trouble and Trey just got up in the bullpen so you might get to see him pitch." I glanced at the TV. "They'll flash to him while he's warming up," he said in one breath then in the next asked, "Important call?"

"Yeah, it was for another job. Someone who saw the Penn State room at Emily Bishop's house in Fayetteville wants me to do something in the basement they're finishing."

"That's great," he said, one eye on the game. "You better start shopping for a car."

"I know," I said around a sigh. "I just hate the thought of it." He looked me in the eye and pursed his lips. "Don't," I said. "Do not make me cry."

He turned his attention back to the TV and I watched him blink fast, several times. We watched the game in silence for a few minutes and when the pitcher walked the batter, the Waves' manager made his way out onto the field.

The manager, pitcher, and Leo stood on the mound talking, then the pitcher handed the ball to the manager and walked toward the dugout. At that point, the camera panned to Trey, jogging onto the field.

I couldn't take my eyes off the screen.

Instead of looking like Baxter and most of the other guys I went to school with, he looked...Oh. My. God.

They say the clothes make the man and in this case, it is absolutely true. I've only seen him dressed in preppy finery that quite honestly, turns me off. But in his uniform he's completely transformed.

I'd noticed his amazing ass when he got out of the car we shared, but had no idea he's so built. Standing on that mound, he looks fierce and muscular and hot as hell.

I squirmed in my seat.

"You okay over there?" Crispin was watching me with a smug smile and I looked at him and stuck my tongue out. "Now do you understand why I like baseball, and quite honestly all sports, so much?"

I just rolled my eyes and shook my head, but the truth is yes, I absolutely do.

And now that I'm seeing Trey in a different light, I wonder if I can ever go back.

Chapter Seven

TREY

I RESTED against a mountain of pillows, aimlessly flipping through the channels. Boredom on the road, or at home too for that matter, isn't something I have a lot of experience with. Throughout my career, I was usually out partying or spending time with some random woman. But it's a new year and a new me. So here I am, in my room before ten o'clock.

Settling on *Forgetting Sarah Marshall*, I pulled a couple pillows out from behind my head and shifted farther down on the bed.

This is the team's last night in Milwaukee. We leave for Cleveland after the game tomorrow. And I'm happy to say that Leo was right that first night in Chicago. As the days go on, more and more guys are interacting with me and I'm being treated less like a pariah. In fact, we needed a table for six for dinner tonight. So things are looking up.

Instead of focusing on the movie, I stared at the mural

over the couch on the other end of the room. For two days, I've looked at that damn thing and the only thought running through my mind is that Nori would do it better.

Reaching for my phone, I opened the camera, and snapped a picture. Staring at it, I debated whether or not to share it with her. Then I figured it would say more if I didn't than if I did.

I pulled up her number and attached the photo.

> I'm in my hotel room in Milwaukee and this is what I'm looking at. They should have hired you if they wanted it done right. 😊

Before I could talk myself out of it, I hit send.

Dropping the phone on the bed next to me, I turned my attention to the movie. Nori texted back before I had time to get into it.

> That's...interesting. But I guess it does represent Milwaukee.

> It does, but I think you would have come up with something better.

> As much as I appreciate that, you've only seen two of my designs.

> You painted fans in the seats of Beaver Stadium. Details like that make all the difference. But you're the artist so you already know that.

> I'm surprised you noticed that in the tiny picture on my phone.

I did. And if I'm being honest, I've stayed in this hotel many times before and never noticed the murals. So you've broadened my horizons.

Glad to hear it.

Is your computer working okay?

Yes, it's perfect.

I'm happy to hear it's not scarred from the kidnapping.

LOL. No, it's fine.

Are you working on any designs right now?

Yes, a couple. Things have really picked up in the last couple weeks. I have a few *meetings this week.*

That's great. If you can, send me some pictures of the designs you're working on.

Okay.

She's an hour ahead of me so I really should wrap things up. As it is, she's probably wondering why the hell I'm texting. I know that's what I'm thinking.

It's getting late, but I was wondering...will you be attending the game with Crispin when we get home?

Yes, I'll be there.

Even though her response took forever, at least I got the answer I wanted.

Glad to hear it. Then I guess I'll see you sometime next week.

See you then. 

Goodnight.

Shifting back against the pillows, I scrolled back and read through our exchange. Twice. After the second time, I put the phone back on the nightstand, and forced myself to stop acting like a teenage girl.

But as I turned my attention back to the movie, I couldn't wipe the sappy smile off my face.

NORI

WHAT'S THAT LOOK FOR?

"Jesus Crispin. You scared the shit out of me."

"That's because you're sitting there transfixed by your phone." He sat on the other end of the couch, rested his elbow on his knee, and leaned toward me. "I wonder what could be so interesting on that screen. Hmmm?"

I figured I'd divert his attention by bringing up his favorite topic of conversation...himself.

"How was your date?"

He wrinkled his nose then flopped against the back of the couch.

"It was okay." He drew out the last word on a sigh.

"There just wasn't a connection. And he seemed very high-maintenance. I don't want to deal with that."

The scene from *When Harry Met Sally* when Billy Crystal tells Meg Ryan that she's the worst kind of high-maintenance because she thinks she's low maintenance pops into my head. It describes Crispin perfectly. Plus, any guy who's totally out of the closet has to be better than his last relationship. But I didn't say any of that right now. It's definitely not the right time.

"You'll find someone and you'll know when it's right."

"I'm not even looking for *the one*." He used air quotes on those last two words. "I just want to find someone I enjoy spending time with." Looking me in the eye, he added, "Other than you, of course. I want sex during that quality time and sorry hun, but you just don't do it for me."

"Hey, no offense taken. You don't do it for me either."

He let out a long sigh, rested his head against the back of the couch, and looked at the ceiling. "But wouldn't it be much easier if we did do it for each other?"

I scooted over to his side and rested my head on his shoulder.

"It absolutely would."

We sat like that for a long while, in silence, just enjoying each other's company. Crispin kissed the top of my head then shifted away far enough to look me in the eye again.

"Now that that's out of the way, I think we need to circle back around to what you were doing when I got home." He twirled his index fingers in circles then poked me in the chest.

I moved back to my side of the couch and picked up my phone. If I evade the question, I'll be making the texts into a bigger deal than they are. So I decided to spill.

"Trey texted me." A slow smile spread across his face. "Stop that, you look like the Grinch."

"What did he say?"

Instead of telling him, I swiped open my phone and handed it to him.

"Do you want some water?"

Crispin shook his head as he stared at my phone. I stood and walked into the kitchen and filled a glass with water. He was still reading when I got back. Since there's not that much there, I knew he was going over it multiple times.

I sat back on my end of the couch.

"There's not gonna be a test. You don't have to memorize it."

"Holy fuck, Nori. If I wasn't convinced he's into you before, this would do it."

"You're insane."

"Eleanor, guys like Trey Youngman don't reach out like this unless they're interested."

I narrowed my eyes, letting him know what I think about the use of *Eleanor*.

"That exchange was pretty basic. No flirting. No double entendre." Sitting up straight, I added, "Oh and when he asked for pictures, he wanted to see my designs, not nudes."

Crispin bobbed his eyebrows.

"Do you *want* to send him nudes? I'm sure he wouldn't object."

"You're so annoying."

I grabbed the phone out of his hands.

"And you have an admirer."

His sing-song voice made me laugh, despite the fact he's driving me crazy.

"He was probably just bored."

"Yeah." Crispin rolled his eyes. "So he decided to text you and discuss the wall decor in his hotel room."

"Let's just agree to disagree."

He took my hand and ran his thumb against my knuckles.

"Nori, it's been almost two years. It's time for you to get back out there."

I don't disagree with that, but I'm not stupid enough to start with a carbon copy of the last man I was with. But I don't need to rehash that with Crispin. As a picture of Trey standing on that mound in his uniform flashes through my head, I realize that I do need to remind myself of it before I'm in the man's company again.

Chapter Eight

NORI

"I GOT YOU A PRESENT," Crispin said as he breezed into my room.

"Ever hear of knocking?"

"Why? It's not like you're doing anything interesting in here."

He plopped on to my bed and tossed a bag at me. I reached in and pulled out a Waves T-shirt.

"While I appreciate the gesture, I'm not sure this will fit." I held up the shirt then rested it against my chest. The hem fell against the edge of my shorts. "It's so long and boxy. I'll look like I'm not wearing anything underneath."

"We can make it work." He jumped up and gestured toward the shirt I'm wearing. "Come on, take that off. We're going to support the team today."

"You sound like David Puddy in *Seinfeld*."

"Gotta support the team," he said in his best Puddy impersonation. "Put that on or I'll paint my chest."

I laughed, although I'm not totally convinced he's joking.

Pulling my T-shirt with its adorable smiling colored pencils and the words Pretty Sketchy over my head, I replaced it with the less charming Waves shirt. As I anticipated, the hem hung to mid-thigh and the sleeves down to my elbows.

Crispin held his hand over his mouth, but I could still see him laughing at me.

I started to take off the shirt, but he grabbed my hands and stopped me.

"Seriously, we can fix this," he said. "You'll look amazing when I'm done with you."

A half hour later, we were in the car on our way to First Allegiant Bank Park. I have to admit, Crispin worked magic with my shirt. He folded the sleeves up and tied the hem into a knot at my waist so I no longer look like a child wearing her father's shirt.

"Are you excited?" he asked. "This is your first Major League game."

"I'm brimming with anticipation."

"Oh, stop. You'll have a great time. If nothing else, you'll like the food."

"At least that's something to look forward to."

It only took us fifteen minutes to get to the stadium, but the parking garage was insane and it took just as long to find a spot. Then we followed the crowd to the front gate. It's definitely a lot more hectic than the last time I was here.

Crispin led me to the end of the line at the will call window. I thought we'd be there forever, but the line moved pretty fast and before I knew it, he had our tickets in hand.

Thankfully the turnstile we went through had a

different attendant than the one I'd spoken to a couple weeks before. She scanned our tickets and we went inside.

My mouth watered as we walked through the concourse, which boasted an amazing variety of food and drinks. Maybe this won't be so bad after all.

"Do you want to get something to eat or head to our seats first?"

"I'm not too hungry right now so we can just go sit."

"They'll be walking around with certain items like hotdogs, popcorn, and cotton candy, but if you want other things like a burger and fries or the specialty food, I'll run out and get it for you."

"You are a prince among men, Crispin Wells."

"I know."

He put his arm around me and we made our way through the crowd. I thought we'd have a bunch of steps to climb or something, but after walking up one ramp, we went through an opening and then down a few steps. Crispin stopped and pointed.

"We're seat numbers sixteen and seventeen."

I made my way down the row and sat and he settled in next to me.

"The field is so close. I wasn't expecting it to be."

"That's because these are awesome seats." His eyes never left the field as he spoke.

I looked down and watched the players from both teams moving around. Some stretched, others ran sprints, and a few tossed balls back and forth.

"There's Leo."

Crispin pointed to a spot down on the grass. He was lying on the ground with his leg straight in the air and a man was leaning into it, pushing it toward him.

"That doesn't look like very much fun."

"I wouldn't mind it." He looked at me and bobbed his eyebrows.

Over the next several minutes, the players shuffled to their respective dugouts and the stadium had really filled up. A good portion of the seats around us were still empty, but Crispin explained that's likely because they're mostly for the players' friends and family and they'd probably fill in as the game progressed.

He'd just said that when a woman sat next to me. She was bickering with the man behind her.

"They sound just like us," I whispered in Crispin's ear. He chuckled and looked over at them and his eyes widened. "What?"

"Excuse me," he said in the direction of the people next to me. "Are you Leo's twin?"

They stopped talking and looked at him. The girl next to me laughed and looked at the guy.

"No," the guy said. "I'm his brother Chris and this is our sister Angie."

We introduced ourselves and Crispin continued.

"You guys could seriously pass for twins."

"Yeah, my brother Nicky looks the same. Once we reached a certain age, people always mixed us up," Chris said.

Crispin placed his hand over his chest. "I can't believe there's more than one."

"And sometimes it comes in handy looking like Leo, if you know what I mean."

Angie punched him in the arm.

"Please excuse my brother. He's an ass."

Before Chris could defend himself, we were asked to rise for the singing of the national anthem. Then the game started.

Angie and I started chatting so I switched seats with

Chris so he and Crispin could watch the game together. During our conversation, I realized she's the one Trey asked about my shirt for the other night.

"You're the artist, right?"

"Yes, how did you know that?"

I was about to say then remembered Trey mentioned that he was going to buy the shirt for her as a present. So I gave a more vague answer.

"Leo and Trey had dinner with us a couple weeks ago and one of them mentioned it."

She looked at me and blinked then her mouth dropped open.

"Oh my God, you're Trey's girl from the car. The mural artist."

I decided to focus on *mural artist* instead of *Trey's girl*.

"That's me," I said.

"How did you start doing that? I'm always looking for ways to make money using actual paints and brushes instead of my computer."

"It was kind of an accident actually. When I still lived in New York, I worked at a coffee shop and used to draw on the windows and boards for different seasons and events. One of the regular customers approached me and said he and his wife were expecting a baby and asked if I'd be interested in painting a mural in their nursery. He was happy with my work and spread the word." I held out my hands. "And voila, a career was launched."

She shifted toward Chris and slapped his arm to get his attention. "This is Trey's girl from the car."

His eyes widened then he gave me a quick once-over and smiled. "Nice."

I was going to argue that I'm not Trey's girl, but something happened on the field and the crowd went wild. Even if I did speak, no one would have heard me.

TREY

SAM CHERRY LOOKS great tonight and my eyes should be locked on the game but instead I keep looking across the field into the stands. Even if I didn't know where Nori and Crispin would be sitting, I'd still be able to pick her out of the crowd with that pink hair. Although I have to admit, I don't find it as shocking as it did the first time I saw her. In fact, it's kind of growing on me.

I turned my attention back to the game as Sam threw a fastball right at Leo's glove for a called strike one. The batter swung at the next pitch and by the time the crack of the bat echoed to the bullpen, Sam was on the ground.

Everyone in the bullpen stood and moved toward the fence, as if being three feet closer would give a better view. Players, coaches, and trainers surrounded Sam, so the only people who have a chance of seeing anything are the fans in the upper decks.

"Did you see where he was hit?" I asked Shawn Riggs.

I'm happy to say that Leo was right and while I'm not exactly one of the guys yet, at least they speak to me now.

"His hip, I think," he said.

"No, I think it was his leg," Malik added.

Max Abbott thought it hit his knee and Ricky Parrish was convinced it dinged his elbow. I didn't think Sam would still be on the ground if that was the case, but didn't say so.

"Youngman, get loose," Miles said.

I grabbed my glove off the bench and walked out to the bullpen mound. As usual, I

stayed loose between innings but did a few quick

stretches before I started throwing just for good measure. I don't want an injury to fuck things up now that I'm back on track.

It's been an adjustment going from being a starting pitcher to middle relief, but I'm making it work. My goal is to move into the starting rotation at some point, but I know I need to prove myself before there's a chance of that happening. So I need to be able to adjust to throwing without going through my whole routine.

The crowd let out a loud cheer so I figured Sam must be standing.

"They're helping him off the field," Miles said. "So you're up."

I threw one last curveball then walked over and jogged onto the field.

Leo and the other infielders were hovering around the mound as I approached.

"Where was he hit?" I asked no one in particular.

"He took a line drive to the shin," Jimmy Chavez said.

"Shit."

Leo handed me the ball and looked me in the eye.

"You ready?" I nodded. "Good."

He ran back behind the plate. As I placed my foot on the rubber, the other infielders went back to their positions to warm up.

My arm feels good and I'm throwing hard. I just need to get into the right headspace. Tuning out everyone but Leo, I finished my final warmups.

Three innings later I sat on the bench while my team batted. We're ahead 1-0, but I'd feel better with a little bit more of a cushion.

Elmer Jarvis, the Waves' manager approached.

"How are you feeling?"

"Great."

"You have another inning in you?"

"Absolutely."

He looked me in the eye and I met his gaze without blinking. Whatever he saw must have satisfied him because he nodded then walked away.

I sat back and focused on staying in the zone. Unfortunately, I didn't have to focus too long because we only sent four batters to the plate and didn't score any runs. Grabbing my glove, I walked back out to the mound. I just need to get three more outs, then it'll be up to Malik to close it out.

After warming up, I stood at the back of the mound and watched the batter step up to the plate. This guy has trouble with anything inside so I'm guessing that's where Leo will have me throw, with something on the outer half of the plate to mix it up. Instead of giving that another thought, I took in a deep breath and let it out then stepped up next to the rubber to wait for Leo to give a sign, confident that he'll figure it all out. All I need to do is execute his plan.

First he called for a fastball to the inside corner. I went into my windup, reached back, brought my arm over the top, and released the ball. It landed in Leo's glove for a called strike one.

Next, he set up in the same spot, his glove a little higher. I fought to keep my expression neutral when the umpire called it a ball. Leo looked back and said something, probably asking what was wrong with the pitch so he could adjust. He nodded then threw the ball back to me before squatting behind the plate again.

My next two pitches totally missed and I found myself behind in the count. I'll need to throw a strike here, but it can't be something the guy will send sailing into the upper deck.

Leo called for a curveball and as soon as it left my hand, I knew it wasn't good. And sure as shit, it hung right over the plate. Thankfully the batter didn't hit it square so instead of going over the fence, the ball blooped right over Dale Montgomery's head at first base and the guy ended up with a single.

Once the play was over, Leo asked for time and ran out to the mound.

"You okay?"

"Yeah." I kicked some dirt into the hole in front of the rubber and stomped it into place. "I'm good."

"Then let's get these fuckers out so we can go have dinner with Chris and Angie." I nodded. "You got this."

He hit me on the hip with his glove then ran back behind the plate and called for a low cutter. After checking the runner, I gave Leo exactly what he asked for right across the inside corner of the plate. The hitter swung and barely ticked the ball.

We followed that up with a slider to the same location. I know Leo is hoping to get a ground ball here and by slowing things down, we're giving the hitter a better chance of getting his bat on it. Keeping it low will pretty much ensure a ground ball. Unless I screw up again.

I shook that thought away and glanced over my shoulder at the runner. He was off the bag a step too far, so I tossed the ball over to Monte. It was a warning throw more than a pick-off move.

Monte threw the ball back and I placed my foot back on the rubber and focused on Leo's glove. Before throwing my pitch, I checked the runner again. Satisfied, I went into my stretch and released a slider that broke as the batter swung. He got the bat on it just enough to send a ground ball past me to the shortstop side of second base.

Jack Reagan reached down and picked up the ball,

stepped on second, and threw it over to Monte for a perfectly-executed double play. Just what we wanted.

The next batter got into the box. We're starting with a fastball right down the middle. This guy never swings until he sees the first strike so why make him wait?

We followed that with a high curveball, which he fouled back behind home plate.

Leo threw me a new ball and I took off my glove and rubbed it between my hands.

Since I'm ahead in the count, we don't have to offer anything too good, so Leo gave the sign for a fastball just outside. The batter didn't go for it, but I'm still ahead. Again he asked for a fastball, this one just a little high. That pitch was fouled back, too.

When Leo called for the cutter, I knew he was ready to shut this guy down. With my foot on the rubber, I rolled the ball in my hand and set my fingers on the threads. Going into my windup, I reached back and released the ball. As I followed through, I watched the bat sail right over the plate for strike three.

"Yeah!" I yelled as I gave a fist pump and ran off the field.

Chapter Nine

NORI

"I CAN'T BELIEVE how exciting that was," I said as we left First Allegiant Bank Park after the Waves' claimed the win. "My throat hurts from cheering."

"Yeah, you even cheered for the other team," Crispin said.

"Hey, that guy made a great play."

"Rule number one, you *never* cheer for the other team."

"Isn't that bad sportsmanship?"

"Angie, will you explain? Maybe she'll listen to you."

"He's right," she said.

Before I could respond, we came to a crossroads where Crispin and I needed to go left and Chris and Angie were turning right.

"It was so great meeting you," I said. "You have my contact info. Please promise to stay in touch."

"We're meeting Leo and Trey at Barnaby's. Why don't you guys come along?"

"Oh no," I said. "We wouldn't want to intrude."

"Please come." Angie put her hands together like she was praying. "Don't leave me alone with those yucky boys."

I had such a great time talking with Angie at the game and I'd love to continue the conversation, but I really don't want to spend more time with Trey. Seeing him in uniform has flipped a switch inside me and I'm trying hard to hold onto my preconceived notions of him being a typical blue blood jerk. Silly and shallow, I know. But there it is.

Crispin looked at me with wide, pleading eyes. No matter my feeling about sharing another dinner with Trey, I know I have to agree to go.

"Okay," I said. "We'll meet you there."

"Thank you," Crispin said as we made our way to the parking garage.

I slipped my arm around his bicep and squeezed.

"You're welcome."

The restaurant is far enough away from the stadium that it won't be filled with fans from the game. It's a local pub known for its colossal burgers and fresh-cut fries.

Chris and Angie were already seated when we arrived and the hostess led us to their table out on the deck. I sat next to Angie just as the waitress came out to take our drink orders.

I decided to stick with water. I'm a lightweight and don't want to get tipsy and do or say anything to embarrass myself. Angie ordered a few appetizers as well.

"With the way Trey pitched, he'll probably end up doing a lot of interviews so it might take them a while to get here and I know they'll be hungry when they do," she said. "So was tonight really your first time at a Major League game?"

"Yeah. I used to go watch Crispin when he played

when we were younger, but other than that, I've never really done the sports thing."

"As the youngest child, I spent more time at sporting events for my older siblings than I'd like to remember. And I dabbled in a variety of things when I was younger, but by high school when it got really competitive, I was out."

Angie stopped talking when our drinks arrived, but picked up her thought as soon as the waitress left the table.

"But I still went to see my siblings play and as a family, we went to at least one Yankee game every year. I'll admit, that was a lot more fun once Trey started playing for and Leo started playing against them. It's so much better watching when you know someone on the team."

"Is it just the three of you?"

"Oh God no, we come from a stereotypical large Greek family. I have five older siblings, two sisters and three brothers. And I have dozens of cousins."

"Oh wow. I can't even imagine having a family like that."

"And there's Trey, too. He's been part of the family since he and Leo were roommates in college." She shook her head and laughed. "Oh my gosh, I had such a crush on him, which now seems really gross because he's like another brother to me. You must have totally freaked when you got into the car with him."

"Honestly, I didn't know who he was." She stared at me, brows raised. "The driver did though so I knew he was going to play baseball for the Waves. Other than that, I had no clue."

"Wow. That's pretty...surprising." She shook her head then shrugged. "But I guess if you're not into sports or from New York, there's a chance you might not know."

Even though that last sentence was a statement, she raised her voice slightly on the last word, turning it into a question. Not one that needed to be answered, of course. More the I-can't-believe-you're-so-lame-you-didn't-know variety. And *my* next sentence is only going to add to her disbelief.

"I actually lived in New York from the time I was thirteen until a little over a year ago."

"You're from New York?"

Her deadpan expression made me chuckle.

"Crispin and I both are."

"Then how could you not know who Trey is? Besides playing baseball, he was on the *Most Eligible Bachelor* list for a few years, and had a pretty high profile in the city even beyond his family name. That's like not knowing who Derek Jeter is." She looked me in the eye. "Please tell me you know who Derek Jeter is."

I wanted to tell her I didn't just to see her reaction, but couldn't keep a straight face.

"I know who Derek Jeter is."

"Oh thank God."

After taking a long drink of her Sangria slushie, Angie took a deep breath.

"Okay, I'm changing the subject before my mind gets any more blown. How did you end up down here in Myrtle Beach?"

"Crispin moved here a few years ago and kept trying to convince me to move down. I finally decided to take him up on it."

"I'd love to live somewhere warmer." She sighed. "But honestly, I can't imagine being that far away from my family. As crazy as they drive me sometimes, I'd be lost without them. It's tough enough not seeing Leo when he's traveling during the season. And as much as I might fantasize about moving away, I know I wouldn't be happy long-term. Life is too short to not spend it with loved ones."

I wish I understood what she was saying from first-hand experience. The only person I've ever felt truly connected to beside my mother is Crispin. My dad did the right thing after he got my mom pregnant. He spent time with me every other weekend and paid child support, but I always felt like it was more out of obligation than anything else.

Our relationship didn't really change when my mom died and I went to live with him and his family when I was thirteen. My step-mother resented my being there and wasn't very subtle about that fact and he either turned a blind eye or sided with her. I always felt like an outsider and after failing to fit in, I just decided to be myself and let my freak flag fly, which made things even worse.

My half-siblings and I are friendly but they don't really get me. We spent time together when I still lived in New York, but I haven't seen them in person since I moved to Myrtle Beach. At this point, our relationship has narrowed down to the occasional text. When I was younger, I thought maybe we'd get closer as we got older, but it doesn't seem like that's going to happen.

Before I could get too dragged down by those thoughts, Trey and Leo arrived. I tried not to stare as they each gave Angie a hug and kiss and greeted Chris with one of those half-hug, pat-on-the-back things men do.

No one could dispute the fact that Leo is a good-looking guy, but there's just something magnetic about Trey. Especially when he's not looking like a cookie-cutter copy of the guy who broke my heart. Like right now.

Not only is he dressed in jeans and a black T-shirt instead of khakis and a pastel Polo, his jaw is covered with a scruffy stubble, and his hair is still slightly damp. He looks absolutely yummy.

Trey sat in the chair to my right and his clean just-from-the-shower scent surrounded me. It's a vast improvement over whatever expensive cologne he normally wears.

He looked in my direction with a genuine smile.

"Nori, this is a nice surprise."

His bourbon depths look directly into my eyes, seeming to see right through me. His gaze held mine captive and I couldn't blink, couldn't look away. Hell, I could barely breathe as my heart pounded in my chest.

Oh boy.

TREY

OUR WAITRESS APPROACHED with a tray full of appetizers, breaking whatever spell Nori and I had been under.

"I figured you guys would be hungry so I ordered a few things to get started," Angie said. "Do you want to order any more appetizers?"

"You're so smart and thoughtful. That's why you're my favorite sister," Leo said. He ignored Angie's snort of laughter and ordered a drink.

"This looks good to me. But I would love water. Lots of it," I said to the waitress. "Just bring a pitcher so I don't keep bothering you."

"I already know what I want so if no one minds, I'm just gonna dig in to some of these," Leo said and proceeded to fill his plate with wings, calamari, and mozzarella sticks.

Everyone followed his lead and soon the platters were mostly empty.

I was happy to see Nori eating. Most of the women I've

spent time with through the years barely touched food. Of course, they'd want to go to the best restaurants and order the priciest things on the menu, which they'd cut into tiny pieces and move around their plate without taking a bite. Even before my whole lifestyle change that bothered me. Now it'd drive me totally nuts.

The waitress returned with our drinks and as she was taking our meal orders, Nori stood and quickly moved the remaining appetizers onto one platter and stacked the others for the waitress to take.

"Sorry, force of habit from my coffee shop days," she said. "It was always satisfying to consolidate the trays of baked goods throughout the day."

"Oh my God," Angie said. "If our mom was here, she'd kiss you."

"Why?"

"She lives to consolidate like that and doesn't understand why none of us find it as satisfying as she does."

"Our parents own a little deli slash market and I swear she spends her whole day moving things from tray to tray as customers buy things," Leo added. "And she gets mad when we work and don't do it."

"So of course we purposely don't just to aggravate her," Angie said.

Nori asked about the family business and they filled her in on everything from its history to what they carry. My family owns one of the biggest electronics companies in the world, and I'm not as proud of it as they are of that little mom and pop store. Not that I can blame them. It is a great place.

"I didn't hear baklava in that list of items," Crispin said.

"Well duh. That goes without saying. Our mom's

baklava is amazing," Angie said. "But she only makes it for the store on the weekend."

"And it usually sells out by noon both days," Leo added.

"Baklava is my absolute favorite dessert and I haven't had any worth eating since I left New York," Crispin said.

"You and Nori will just have to come up to visit and get some," Angie said. "We're in Jersey, but I promise our mom's baklava is better than anything you've tasted in the city."

Nori looked less than thrilled by that idea, but just smiled, nodded, and shoved a piece of calamari into her mouth.

"And you all still work there?" Crispin asked, obviously looking to change the subject.

"Our brother Nicky works there full-time and he's brought the store into the twenty-first century with a website and online ordering. The rest of us fill in, some more regularly than others," Chris said, then looked over at Leo.

"Excuse me for traveling for work. I'm there off-season when I'm needed."

"You still work there?" Crispin asked. Leo nodded. "Wow, how do the customers react to that?"

"Most customers are either from the neighborhood or have been coming in for years. Trust me when I say, they're not impressed by me. Or Trey."

"*You* work there?" Nori asked.

"It's been a while but yes, I have."

I always loved spending time with Leo's family. They made me feel welcome and I liked who I was when I was with them. That's why I'd fill in at the store even after I started playing for New York. Somehow word got out and the last time I was there, it was a media circus.

"But going forward, Leo will be in Scranton so he won't be around," Angie said with a pout.

"Stop saying Scranton like it's Siberia. I'll be two hours away."

Angie just shrugged.

It still amazes me that no one in Leo's family has ever moved more than a few miles from home. Even his cousins. Some have gone away to school, others travel for work, but they all live close.

"Would you put some nachos and cheese on here, please?" Nori asked, holding her empty plate out toward Crispin. "Be sure to stir the cheese so I don't get a glop of the junk on top."

He took the plate from her and added a handful of nachos.

"Are you sure you want me to stir the cheese? Don't you want me to fold it?" he asked, around a smirk.

"That's why you looked so familiar," I said. "You look like Dan Levy. I'm a huge *Schitt'$ Creek* fan and you remind me of David Rose."

A big smile spread across Crispin's face. "Thank you, Trey. Did you hear what Trey said, Nori?" he asked as he stirred the cheese then heaped a spoonful onto her plate and handed it back to her.

She looked over at me and frowned.

"Please don't say any more," she said. "I'll have to hear about it forever."

I shifted my eyes between them. Crispin's satisfied smirk only made the resemblance that more obvious. I'm amazed I didn't realize it before. But per Nori's wish, I kept my thoughts to myself.

Chapter Ten

NORI

I FINISHED my last French fry and picked up my glass and shifted my straw through the ice to get to the water remaining at the bottom, making a loud slurping sound as I finished it. Placing my glass back on the table, I was surprised when Trey refilled it with water from his pitcher.

"Thank you," I said.

"You're welcome."

My face heated at his soft smile. I have to admit that he's not exactly what I thought he was when we first met. There's no doubt in my mind that cocky, entitled jerk is in there somewhere, but he obviously has reined him in since that first day.

Leaning toward me slightly, he asked, "So how's business? Book any more projects?"

Everyone else at the table was having a discussion about hair, because apparently Leo isn't the only one in his family blessed with a to-die-for mane. But Trey spoke only to me. His low tone and close proximity made things feel more intimate than they should sitting in a public place at a table with four other people.

"Good." My own voice came out husky so I cleared my throat and tried again. "Business is good. As of yesterday, I'm pretty much booked through mid-October."

"That's great."

"Yeah, I'm pretty happy. Things are finally getting steady."

"How do you advertise?"

"Most of my business comes from word-of-mouth. I do have a website, but mostly people go there just to check out my portfolio."

He kept asking questions and I continued to answer, feeling like we're in our own little bubble. His eyes never left mine and he listened intently to my every word.

I recited the story I'd told Angie earlier, about how I was offered my first job in New York, and how it grew from there.

"So if things were going well up north, what made you move down here?"

"Crispin." I shrugged. "He kept asking me to join him and I finally decided it was time for a change of scenery."

I didn't get into details about how I wanted a change because of a broken engagement, but his expression told me he knew there was something behind my decision. Thankfully he didn't ask.

"So you just closed your business, picked up, and moved?"

"Pretty much. I figured if I got it going there, I could do it here, too."

"So how'd you do it? Get started here, I mean."

"Kind of like in New York. I painted a mural in Crispin's shop and got my first booking from that."

"Is it still there?"

"In Crispin's shop?" He nodded. "Yep."

"I'll have to check it out if I go there for a haircut."

"Oh you definitely should go there. Everyone is really good at what they do. It took him a little while, but he finally put together a great team."

"I have no doubt. I'm just not sure I'll feel adequate if I go there after Leo," he said around a smile.

Apparently Leo had been at least half-listening to our conversation because he chimed in.

"You should feel inadequate." He patted the side then the top of his head.

That led to a bunch of smack talk, but they kept it PG-rated for the most part. I'm sure it'd be worse if they were alone.

"As much as I hate to break this up, my back is feeling really tight. Do you mind if we get going?" he asked Trey.

"Oh sure," Trey said. "Did the waitress bring the check yet?"

"I paid when I went to the bathroom."

"I thought we agreed that I'd pay since you're playing chauffeur."

"You can get the next one," Leo said as he stood. He twisted from side to side before putting his arms behind him and stretching back.

We took his cue and stood then walked through the restaurant to the exit.

Once we were in the parking lot, Angie said, "I'm here for the rest of the week. Maybe we can get together again? We'll be going to most, if not all, the games. But other than that, I'm free. I'd love to see your process and just, you know, hang out."

"Oh sure, I'd love that. Let me know what you have going on and we'll make it work."

"Sorry to interrupt," Trey said, coming up next to Angie. "I just wanted to say goodbye."

Angie wrapped her arms around his neck and pulled him in for a big hug.

"You were amazing today," she said. "I'm so proud of you."

She gave him one last squeeze then kissed his cheek and stepped back. It almost looked like he was blushing.

"Thanks." He leaned down and kissed her cheek. "I'll see you tomorrow."

"I'll give you a call," she said then walked away leaving Trey and me alone.

"Thanks for coming to the game today. It was nice having a cheering section."

I chuckled at that. "Trey, most of the stadium was cheering for you."

"Yeah, but it's always nice knowing there are people there who actually know me."

Something flashed across his face when he said that but before I could analyze it, he schooled his features and it was gone.

"I was glad to be there. It was fun."

He nodded and shifted his eyes to my mouth. It was only for the briefest of seconds, but I saw it.

"Well, I better get going. I'm sure I'll be seeing you again since it sounds like you'll be spending time with Angie."

"Sounds good."

He leaned down and kissed my cheek, just like he'd done to Angie. Only he lingered longer than he did with her. It felt oddly sensual for such a chaste kiss and when he pulled back, I missed the warmth of his lips.

"Goodnight." He smiled.

"Goodnight."

I watched him walk away, fighting the urge to place my hand over my tingling cheek.

TREY

LEO PULLED out of the parking lot and turned onto the main road. Thankfully my hotel isn't too far. All of a sudden, I feel exhausted. Probably from a combination of fading adrenaline and all the food I ate.

"Did you get your car shipped down yet?" he asked.

I get my license back next week. We'll be on the road, but it's nice to know I'll be back behind the wheel when I get back.

"No. I think I'm just gonna buy one down here. Something a little more practical."

"Practical? Wow." He glanced over at me and blinked before returning his eyes to the road. "That's great."

"Yeah. Dr. Fisher thought so too when I mentioned it." I shrugged. "I'll be honest, this *new me* thing is a lot easier down here without all the New York bullshit."

"You mean your family?"

"Them and all the usual crap that's there."

He just nodded at that and we drove the next few miles in silence. But as we pulled into the hotel parking lot, he said, "So, you and Nori looked pretty cozy tonight."

Honestly, I'm surprised he waited this long to say anything. When I didn't comment, he continued.

"It's pretty obvious you like her. You gonna do anything about it?"

"Probably not." I rubbed my eyes then looked over at him. "Even if I did, what could possibly come of it? I don't know anything about normal relationships and I'd just fuck it up."

He pulled around to the hotel entrance and I unbuckled my seatbelt.

"Maybe, maybe not. But you'll definitely never know if you don't at least try."

"Thank you Dr. Marakis."

I opened my door and stepped out.

"I'll be here at nine tomorrow. Max is gonna work on my back to loosen it up before I warm up so I need to get here a little early."

"See you then."

After slinging my bag over my shoulder, I closed the door. Leo pulled away and I walked through the automatic doors.

When I got into my room, I tossed my duffle on the floor next to all the other bags I haven't emptied yet. I really need to hire a realtor and find a real place to live. Hotel life is getting old.

I was so exhausted on the short ride here, I thought I'd fall to sleep immediately, but after tossing and turning, I decided to listen to a book. Reaching for my iPad, I powered it up, and opened the last audio book I was listening to, but couldn't get into it. My mind kept wandering and I ended up rewinding to listen to sentences over and over.

Instead of continuing to waste my energy going back and forth in the book, I decided to investigate what I couldn't stop thinking about. Nori.

I brought up a search engine and typed in her name. Her website came up first, so that's a good sign. I'm no expert, but her site looks really good. It's organized well and easy to navigate. I looked through her designs, enlarging them, then magnifying to see specific details. She really is very talented.

After going through her designs a second time, I clicked on her *About Me* page. It didn't include any real personal information, just offered an abbreviated version of the story she'd told me earlier about how she got into mural design. What really drew my attention was her picture. I almost didn't recognize her with blonde shoulder-length hair. My first thought was that it looks better pink, which shocked the hell out of me.

Resting the iPad on the pillow next to me, I rolled onto my side and continued to stare at the picture. I wasn't lying when I told Leo that I have no idea how to be in a real relationship. Most of the people I grew up surrounded by got married more for alliance than love. After the ceremony, they basically did whatever they wanted, as long as they were discreet.

The women I dated—and I used that term *very* loosely —expected nothing from me other than a good time and to be seen with me. Even if they did want something more, they weren't going to get it.

I know I was a cocky prick. Hell, if I'm being honest, I knew it then, I just didn't care. And while I'm working on it, a lifetime of bad habits don't just disappear. It's something I have to stay conscious of all the time. At least I have Leo and his family as role models so I just act how they would in any given situation. Not that I've told him that.

Shifting farther down into bed, I pulled the blanket up over my shoulder.

I have a video call with Dr. Fisher tomorrow after the game. Maybe I'll ask him what he thinks about the whole Nori thing.

With that decision made, I closed my eyes.

Chapter Eleven

NORI

I SAT STARING STRAIGHT AHEAD, my pencil poised over the blank page. I'm supposed to be creating sample sketches for a project I just booked, but nothing is coming to me. Instead, my mind kept wandering back to last night. More specifically to Trey.

That kiss on the cheek affected me way more than it should have. I'm not some blushing virgin from a historical romance novel. But, when he moved toward me, my heart pounded so hard, he could probably hear it. And when his lips touched me and then lingered, my entire body felt like it was on fire even as it broke out in goosebumps.

The Waves have a day game today and Angie invited me over to Leo's later for dinner and to go swimming. Since the Marakis clan is pretty tight with Trey, it only seems logical that he'll be there. I'm not sure how I'll react when I see him.

Angie asked me to bring my computer and sketches so I can show her how I work. Hopefully I'll be too engrossed with that to notice him.

Giving up on getting any work done, I opened my computer and gave in to the urge I've been fighting since Crispin told me who Trey's family is. The Youngmans are to New York what the Kennedys are to Massachusetts. Even though I never paid attention to society news, I'd have to be totally out of it to not know the name.

I typed Trey's name into the search engine and page after page of articles filled the screen. Since I'm a firm believer that every picture tells a story, I clicked on the images tab.

Holy shit.

While there was a good assortment of pictures of him in uniform, in most of them, he's wearing a suit or black tie with a big-boobed, long-limbed accessory on his arm. Blonde, brunette, redhead, he doesn't seem to discriminate as long as they have certain measurements.

I'm not a big fan of formal wear, but I have to say he looks amazing in custom-made clothing. He just doesn't look very happy. Mostly he looks cocky and entitled, and very tense, especially in the family photos. Every smile looks forced and none reach his eyes.

The Trey I initially met that first day in the car only showed a trace of this one's cockiness. And I'll admit that in my encounters with him since then, he seems different. I'm not sure if that's because it's true or because I've developed a ridiculous attraction to him.

It's been two years since I broke up with Baxter. Crispin keeps telling me I need to get laid once in a while to avoid getting obsessed with the first pretty face that interests me. Unfortunately, I'm not into casual hookups so that hasn't been an option. The thought of getting intimate with someone I don't know well freaks me out. And there hasn't been anyone I've wanted to get to know better since I moved down here. Until now.

Grabbing my bag, I put my computer and sketchbook inside and placed it next to the couch. Crispin is still at work and I don't have anything to do until later.

I picked up the remote, turned on the TV, and did something I've never done before. I flipped the channel until I found the Waves game. Since he pitched last night, I probably won't see Trey play today, but I want to get more familiar with the game.

Before I could second-guess that or talk myself out of watching, I placed the remote back on the coffee table and settled in to watch.

TREY

SITTING IN LEO'S OFFICE, I booted up my laptop and found Dr. Fisher's email with the link for our meeting today. Clicking on it, I sat back and waited for him to let me in. Seconds later, his image filled my screen.

After getting the pleasantries out of the way, he got right to it.

"So how've you been doing since we last spoke?" He looked down, I'm assuming to check his notes from our last session. "That was about a month ago. You were living in North Carolina playing Triple A ball. It seems there've been some changes to your life since then."

Dr. Fisher took a well-earned vacation last month so we

didn't have our weekly appointments. He did ask me to email him updates anyway and also gave me contact information for his associate in case I needed to talk to someone. Which I didn't. I'm more self-aware than I was just a few months ago when I started meeting with him and am able to work things out for myself a lot of the time.

"Yeah, I got called up to the Waves right after we spoke, so I'm here in Myrtle Beach now."

"And how's it going?"

"The first few days were a little rocky, but now it's good. I'm pitching well and getting

along with the other players."

"Your friend plays for them as well, right?"

I nodded. "Leo. It's great having him with me again. And his brother and sister are here this week so it's like a family reunion."

"Speaking of family. Have you spoken to your father yet? In your email you said he called but you didn't answer."

"No, he's actually been calling more frequently too, but I'm still sending him to voicemail." I looked directly at him. "I'm in a good place right now but I know it's fragile. I don't want him messing with that. If it was something really important he'd leave a real message instead of just barking at me to call him."

He looked down again, probably to take notes.

"So tell me about your move to Myrtle Beach."

"It all happened pretty fast. After a Sunday night game in Fayetteville, the coach called me into his office and told me I was moving up and they were expecting me at First Allegiant Bank Park for the next day's five o'clock game. I had less than twelve hours to pack and figure out a way to get there."

"I'm surprised they didn't arrange that for you."

"At the time I was too, but…" I trailed off thinking about my time playing for the Fayetteville Waves. "I didn't exactly make friends there. So no one volunteered to take me."

"So what did you do?"

"I called a ride share."

He chuckled. "Well that makes for quite a story."

"Yeah, I ended up pitching that night and the local media mentioned it in their coverage

of the game."

I thought back to that ride. How I kept looking at Nori like she was some anomaly I needed to figure out.

"Is there something more you wanted to say about that?"

"I ended up sharing the ride with someone. A woman." His brows rose, but he didn't speak. "The driver asked if it was okay and I said it was because the man wouldn't stop talking. I hoped that someone else in the car would act as a buffer so I wouldn't lose my shit."

"And did it work?"

"For the most part."

"And what about the woman? Did she speak?"

"No, she just sat there drawing in a notebook. The sound of her pencil on the paper kind of grated on my nerves but I didn't say anything." He nodded at that. "Turns out she's an artist." Again his brows rose, urging me to continue. "I asked, although it was kind of obvious. Her hair is bright pink and she was drawing."

I told him the rest of the story, about how I ended up with Nori's computer bag, and how Leo and I ate dinner with her and Crispin when I dropped it off. And how they came to the game yesterday and Angie invited them out with us afterwards.

"So you've been with this young woman on three occasions now. Is there something about her that you want to discuss?"

"I think I like her." Shaking my head, I added, "I don't know. She's not my usual type, but there's just something about her."

"Did your usual type make you happy?" I just looked at him through the screen. "Trey, is there something specific you want to ask me?"

"Leo thinks I should ask her out."

"And what do you think?"

"I don't know. I'm not sure now is the right time."

"Why do you say that?"

"I'm just getting settled down here and finally feel like I'm acting like a normal human being instead of the jerk I was my whole life. I don't want to jeopardize that. And I also don't want to hurt her. She seems really sweet."

"Why do you think you'd hurt her?"

I snorted. "Seriously Doc? What do I know about having a real relationship?"

"If you're thinking in terms of relationship instead of just going out and having a good time, I think you already know."

He looked down again and this time I saw his pen moving as he wrote his latest observation down.

"So you really think it'd be okay if I asked her out?"

"Trey, I think you're doing great. If I'm being honest, you seem to have had some sort of breakthrough since I spoke to you last. We've been talking for six or seven months now and there've been subtle changes over that time, but today, you just look different. That bored, cynical expression you always wore is nowhere in sight. You seem more relaxed and the fact that you're actually considering this woman's feelings is new." He leaned back in his chair and tapped his pen on the notebook like I've seen him do countless times. "I think this move was good for you. Playing for this team is good for you. And maybe this woman will be good for you, too. But you won't know unless you take the chance."

Chapter Twelve

NORI

"THIS IS SO NICE," I said to Angie as she led me through the house and opened the French doors out onto the patio.

The water in the kidney-shaped pool reflected the late-day sun giving the whole outdoor area a cozy feel. I'd expected to see the guys out here, but they're nowhere to be found. I wasn't going to ask, but as if she read my thoughts, Angie offered an answer anyway.

"Leo and Chris ran to the store to pick up some fresh steaks to grill," she said. "Trey is in the office on some kind of call, but he should be out soon. Have a seat. I'm dying to see your stuff."

We settled next to each other at the table and I emptied everything out of my laptop case.

"Ooh, it's the fancy Surface Pro. Do you like it?"

"I love it. It's the best investment I've ever made." I turned it on and flipped through to my designs and handed the computer to her.

She swiped through a few pages then pinched and expanded her fingers to magnify something before moving to another picture.

"So you sketch your designs by hand first then upload and work on them digitally?"

"Yes." I opened my book and flipped to the sketch that corresponds with the design she's looking at and turned it so she could see. "I've tried creating it from scratch right on the computer but I didn't like it as much. It took me some time to tweak this method but I have a system down now. Once I finalize my sketch, I scan it into the program, then I can play with the colors. See?" I reached over and flipped back and forth between two images, explaining how I used to do it all on paper. "Now I just change it on the screen and show that to my potential clients. It also streamlines the process because I can make changes right in front of them and get verbal approval without having to set up multiple meetings."

"This is so awesome. Do you mind if I look through your sketches?"

"Not at all." She set down the computer and pulled the book in front of her. "Those are just the designs I'm working on. Once a client approves colors for their mural, I color my original sketch and frame it for them."

"That's such a great idea and they probably love it."

She continued to flip through the book and I looked around Leo's yard. It's a decent size, but nothing too obnoxious, kind of like the house. And I love the pool and patio area.

Crispin has a great outdoor space but isn't interested in installing a pool. I'd love one but since it's not my house, I don't really have much to say about it.

Angie sucked in a startled breath pulling my attention back to her.

Shit. I forgot those were in there.

Her eyes darted back and forth between the pages and me as she flipped through all my sketches of Trey. She lingered on the last one for what seemed like forever before meeting my gaze.

"Wow." She shook her head. "Just wow. I don't know what else to say."

"Please don't say anything and forget you saw them," I said around a nervous chuckle.

"Why?"

"Because it seems kind of stalkerish to have sketches of a professional baseball player in my book."

"No, it'd be stalkerish if you had random pictures of him in your phone that you took because you were following him around." She flipped through the pages again. "These are works of art and they're amazing. When did you draw them?"

"I did all but the last one in the car on the ride we shared. The light was hitting his face perfectly and I couldn't resist."

Angie looked at me and chuckled.

"I think that's the first time I heard a woman say she couldn't resist *drawing* Trey.

Usually it's something else." She bobbed her eyebrows.

My face heated because I've definitely thought those kinds of things too, especially after last night.

"What about this last one?"

"What about it?"

"You said you drew all but the last one in the car."

"Oh, I did that when I got home later that day. When he smiled at me…" I trailed off remembering the moment, then shook my head. "It was a really great smile and I wanted to capture it." She closed the book and I grabbed it and the larger one and shoved them in my laptop case. "Please don't say anything to Trey."

"I won't, I promise."

"Thank you." I sat back in my chair.

"But Nori, that smile you drew—" She looked so serious, I was afraid to hear what she would say next. "That's the real Trey, and he doesn't show it to many people."

Before I could ask her to expand on that, the topic of our conversation emerged through the patio doors.

TREY

DID you ever walk into a room and get the feeling people were talking about you? Yeah, that's how I felt as I approached Angie and Nori.

Growing up the way I did and doing what I do for a living, it's something that happens to me quite a bit, but I've never been as intrigued as I am right now.

"Ladies. What are you two up to out here?"

"Nori was just showing me her designs and how she creates them," Angie said.

I looked at the laptop case sitting on the table then over at Nori.

"Be sure to keep that bag with you at all times. I don't want it going home with me again."

She lost her deer-in-the-headlights look and smiled.

"I'll be sure it doesn't."

"You know, if this was a movie, you two would have had the best meet-cute ever," Angie said.

"What do you mean?" Nori asked.

"You know, the scene in a movie when the couple

meets for the first time? You can't beat sharing a ride together then having the guy end up with the girl's computer bag so they have to get together again."

"And don't forget the amazing bolognese dinner he got when he dropped it off," I said.

A blush spread across Nori's cheeks making her look even more adorable.

"Since we're done looking at these, I'm gonna put this bag in the foyer and bring out

some drinks," Angie said.

It's almost like she's purposely leaving us alone. I mentally shrugged. I'll take it.

Sitting in the chair Angie just vacated, I looked at Nori's T-shirt and smiled.

"Art is My Favorite Sport. Cute."

She looked down at her shirt then back at me.

"I thought it was appropriate for today's company."

"I'm surprised you didn't wear that to the game."

"Crispin made me wear the Waves shirt."

I nodded in understanding then looked around.

"Speaking of, where is Crispin?"

"He had an issue at the salon. A leaky pipe or something, so he has to stay there until the plumber fixes it. He'll be swinging by to pick me up when he's done."

"You haven't gotten a car yet?"

"No, but I've searched online and I'm going to look at some tomorrow."

I was going to ask her why she's been putting it off so long but figured it was none of my business. Leo and Chris returned before I could ask the question anyway.

After dinner, Angie convinced Nori to take a swim. I nearly swallowed my tongue when I first saw Nori in her bright yellow bikini. It's pretty conservative as far as two-piece suits go, but it highlights the curves her clothing only hints at.

"You better be looking at Nori because if you're staring at my sister like that, we're gonna have a problem," Leo said. When I continued to clear the table without commenting, he continued. "I got this. Why don't you go cool off?"

I handed him my stack of plates. Even if I didn't want to get a closer look at Nori in that suit, I'd be crazy to pass up a chance to get out of clean-up duty.

Pulling my T-shirt over my head, I tossed it on the lounge chair and walked toward the diving board. Nori's eyes widened when she caught sight of me. Angie glanced over her shoulder to see what she was looking at and frowned.

"Trey Youngman, you better not splash me," she said.

"Or what?"

"I don't know, but you're staying here tonight so I'm sure I'll think of something."

History has taught me that Angie, and all Leo's siblings, can be super creative when seeking revenge. So instead of doing a cannonball like I'd originally planned, I bounced twice on the edge of the board and executed a perfect dive.

Once I joined them at the shallow end of the pool, Angie talked about today's game then asked questions about some of my new teammates.

"Leo's been playing with some of those guys for a couple years now. Why haven't you asked him?"

She put her hands on her hips and raised one brow.

"Because whenever I bring up the opposite sex, he goes into big-brother mode."

I crossed my arms over my chest. "You're not ever getting involved with a ballplayer."

"If it was up to you guys, I'd never get involved with anyone."

She stormed across the pool and up the steps. Well, as much as you could storm through water anyway.

While her brothers' overprotectiveness is something Angie has complained about for years, something tells me that little show was more about getting Nori and me alone than real anger. Now I just have to figure out how to take advantage of the opportunity I've just been handed.

I've never asked a woman out in a normal way. If I'm being completely honest, it's a little nerve-wracking. Is it possible for your hands to sweat underwater? I wiped them against my board shorts anyway and cleared my throat.

"I'm actually glad we have a minute alone."

Nori shifted her eyes in my direction. I can't help but notice that she's avoided looking at me since she gawked while I was on the diving board. When she didn't say anything, I continued.

"I have a game tomorrow, then we head to the West Coast for ten days. But I was wondering, would you be interested in getting together when I get back?"

Her eyes rounded and she blinked. Three times.

"Oh. Um I—" She looked down at the water and trailed her index finger through it.

This is the first time in my life I've felt unsure of the answer when asking a woman to spend time with me. Hell, most of the time I never even officially asked. Women were just *there*. Always available.

But Nori isn't like any of them and I have no idea what she's thinking.

"We could go out to dinner and to a movie or whatever you want."

Her violet eyes met mine and seemed to see right through to my soul. I fought the urge to look away.

"Why?"

That wasn't what I was expecting her to say, but it's definitely better than a no.

"I'd like to spend more time with you, get to know you better."

The corner of her mouth kicked up at my words and she glanced down at my mouth before meeting my gaze again.

"I think I'd like that."

"Yeah?"

"Yeah."

I let out a relieved breath.

"Great. I'll text you some dates I'm free so you can let me know if either of them work. If not, we'll figure it out."

"Sounds good."

We stood there, staring into each other's eyes and more than anything, I wanted to kiss her. Without letting go of her gaze, I took a step forward. Just as I started to lower my head, Crispin arrived and things got pretty lively behind us, reminding me that we're not truly alone.

Letting out a frustrated chuckle, I looked over my shoulder at the rest of the gang before meeting Nori's smiling face.

"We should probably go join the party before they come looking for us," I said and gestured for her to walk up the steps ahead of me.

As I followed her out of the pool, I felt light and hopeful and content. They're not feelings I'm very familiar with, so it took me a minute to assign words to them. And it amazed me that, at the moment, they seem to be replacing the anger, frustration, and cynicism that usually fill me.

Maybe Dr. Fisher is right. Maybe I can truly change and be happy.

Chapter Thirteen

NORI

I PULLED into Leo's driveway and shifted Crispin's car into park. He graciously let me borrow it today so I can take Angie to the beach. Speaking of Angie, she came running out wearing a cute cotton sundress and flip-flops.

"Hey."

She settled into the passenger seat and clicked her seatbelt into place.

"Do you want to throw that in the backseat?" I asked, pointing to the tote bag resting between her feet.

"No, I'm good."

I put the car into reverse and backed onto the street.

"What's Chris up to today?" I asked.

"I have no idea, but he's probably just as happy we're not spending the day together as I am." She shook her head. "Like I said, I love my family, but sometimes we need a break." Shifting to face me, she added, "I planned on coming down here by myself to just chill. I'm twenty-eight-freaking-years-old, I should be able to plan my own vacations. But my parents are so old-fashioned, and hate the idea of a 'woman traveling alone.' I fought them for a good while but in the end, they made me feel so guilty over the fact that they'd be worrying about me, I asked Chris to come."

I was about to say that I wouldn't mind having that issue, but figured it'd sound condescending.

"Well, I'm glad we can have a girls' day before you leave tomorrow."

"Yes!" she said. "I just want to chill with my toes in the sand."

Leo lives pretty close to the beach so it wasn't too long before I pulled into the parking lot. We got out of the car and grabbed the chairs, umbrella, and cooler I brought along then made our way to the sand. As soon as we reached it, Angie kicked off her flip-flops and dug her toes in.

"You know, I only live a couple hours from the Jersey Shore and I go there often, but there's just something about the beach down here that's more soothing."

She bent down and picked up her flip-flops and we walked a few feet down then to the right and found a perfect spot. We set up our chairs and put the cooler and our bags on them then worked together to set up the umbrella.

"Whew! I better start exercising more if sticking an umbrella in the sand makes my arms burn," Angie said.

After pulling off her sundress, she plopped into the chair not seated under the umbrella and twisted her hair into a knot on top of her head. I looked at her perfect curves and laughed as I stripped down to my bikini.

"Crispin has trouble doing that and his arms are like

steel." I sat across from her, making sure to keep my legs in the shade. "And you look amazing."

Pulling sunblock out of my bag, I sprayed it over every inch of my body then put some on my hands to cover my face. I held the can out toward Angie.

"Want some?"

"I'm good for now."

I tossed it back into my bag then opened the cooler.

"Want a drink?"

"What'd you bring?"

"Iced tea, water, and Crispin's last bottle of hard lemonade." I looked over at her. "Sorry, I'm not much of a drinker so I didn't even think about packing this with alcohol."

"I'll have an iced tea for now."

I grabbed two bottles of iced tea out of the cooler and tossed one to Angie. Sitting back in my chair, I twisted the cap off and took a long drink then rested the bottle in my lap and shifted my chair closer to the umbrella pole to stay out of the sun.

"Why do you have to stay under the umbrella if you just coated yourself with SPF one million?"

"It's SPF 70 and because this skin doesn't stand a chance against that sun." I pointed between me and the sun then took another drink.

"Gotcha." She took a drink then rested her head against the back of the chair.

We sat there in silence just enjoying the sound of the ocean and the feel of the breeze.

I really like Angie. It's a bummer that she lives in New Jersey. I don't have a close girlfriend here in Myrtle Beach. Then again, I didn't have one back in New York. Not really. There were females I hung out with occasionally, but since junior high, Crispin has been my best friend.

Two guys slowed as they walked by and one lowered his sunglasses. Angie shook her head and he held his hands out and flashed a panty-melting smile. She shook her head again then shifted her chair slightly to better face me.

"I don't intend to speak to anyone with a penis today. I've been surrounded all week." She glanced over her shoulder then back at me with a sly smirk. "No matter how hot they are."

Thank God she's committed to keeping this get-together girls only because I'm not in the mood to deal with guys either. Not guys trying to hit on me anyway.

"Since we're on the subject of guys," Angie said. "You know I have to ask about you and Trey." She bobbed her eyebrows.

"There's not really anything to tell."

"Please. I knew there was something there the first time I heard your name mentioned. It was written all over his face. And then when I saw you together, there was no question. The man can't keep his eyes off you."

My face heated and it has nothing to do with the temperature outside.

"He's just trying to figure me out. You should have seen the look on his face when we shared a ride here." Hoping to get her off the subject of Trey and me, I decided to change it to their history. "So how did Trey get so tight with your family?"

"Well, you know he was Leo's roommate in college, right?"

"Yeah, they mentioned it at dinner."

"For the first month, Leo couldn't stand Trey and complained about him all the time. Then, the next thing you know, they were best friends. Trey spent the holidays with my family and the summer between their freshman and sophomore years."

She took a moment, seeming to be deciding how much information to disclose then continued.

"His family is extremely rich but didn't offer him support beyond money. I think he liked spending time cramped into our house because it's stable and we're very close. My mom treated him just like one of us. He had chores, worked at the store, and had to clear and wash the dinner plates. And surprisingly, he didn't complain about any of it. In fact, he seemed to crave it."

"You know that I had no idea who he was when I first met him, but I'll admit to doing some cyber-stalking since then. I know that what's in the media isn't always true but I have to say, the guy you're describing is totally different than the one I've read about."

"I agree. Especially once he started playing for New York and was even more a part of the city's social scene. I'd read these stories about him and see pictures and it was like they were of and about a different person. But like you said, the media tends to spin things however they want. Plus, we all act a certain way when we're with certain people." She looked toward the water.

My cell beeped and I pulled it from my tote.

I just wanted to say hi before heading to the stadium. I'm not available for relief tonight so I won't be playing at all. But I will be starting tomorrow since Sam Cherry is out for a few weeks. So send positive thoughts my way. ☺ Have fun at the beach.

Even though you don't need them, I'll send good vibes your way.

I appreciate it. How did the car shopping go?

> I didn't go today. Crispin is going with me tomorrow.

> Good luck to you too. I hope you find what you're looking for.

I doubt I will so I'll have to settle for something that works for me. Honestly, if I was made of money, I'd fix the Jetta no matter how much it costs. But I'm not, so here we are.

> Thank you.

> Enjoy the rest of your day. TTYL.

> You too.

I reread the texts, my heart more affected than it should be by the short exchange. I don't know when I stopped thinking of Trey as an entitled jerk, but somewhere along the line he started seeming like a normal guy. Maybe it was seeing him in the uniform. I felt my mouth curl up into a smile at that last thought. The man does look amazing in his uniform.

"Something funny happening over there?"

Slipping the phone back into my bag, I looked at Angie and shook my head.

"Was that Trey?" she asked.

"It was. He just texted to say hi and to tell us to have fun at the beach."

"I'm sure he didn't mention me at all." She chuckled. "But see what I mean? The guy in all those articles would never text just to say hi. He's always been a great guy and after everything that happened last year, he's finally working on being his true self all the time."

"What happened last year?"

"That's his story to tell. Just be sure to give him a chance. He's worth it, I promise." She

stood. "I'm gonna go cool off. Wanna come?"

"No, I'm good for now."

I watched her run into the water then swim out and tread water, bobbing in the waves. I'm sure I could Google and figure out what Angie's talking about, but she's right, it's his story to tell. And if we get to the point where he's comfortable to tell it, I'll definitely listen.

TREY

"ARE YOU PSYCHED ABOUT STARTING TOMORROW?" Leo asked.

"Psyched, scared shitless. Take your pick."

I shoved the last bite of pizza into my mouth. After today's game, Leo and I decided to order in instead of going out. We're sitting on the balcony of my room and I looked out at the water as I chewed. After I swallowed, I noticed he was staring at me.

"What?"

"I don't think I've ever heard you admit you're scared about anything."

Honestly I've never admitted that to anyone, not even myself. I'd just mask my fear as anger or cockiness then bulldoze my way through things. That or drink and treat everything like a joke.

"Things are different now." I shrugged. "I feel like people are waiting for me to fail so if I have a bad day I'll end up back in Fayetteville."

"I'm not sure they'd pull the trigger for one bad outing."

"But I don't know that for sure." I grabbed another slice and took a bite then thought about that while I chewed and swallowed. "Baseball is the only thing that's kept me sane my whole life. I know I fucked up through the years but it's always been important to me. When I got sent down, it was like a knife to the heart. And I'll admit it was also a huge blow to my ego."

"Yeah, but now you're good. You're talking to Dr. Fisher and getting all the shit from the past out of your head for good."

I nodded and finished my pizza then took a long drink of water.

I'm not sure what deity is responsible for rooming me with Leo in college, but it's one of the best things that could have happened to me. He's been my best friend and voice of reason for more than a decade now. His whole family pulled me into the fold and showed me how real families interact. Because of them, life was good when I played in college. I don't know how I let myself get sucked into my own family drama and all the other shit when I played in New York.

I guess at this point it doesn't matter. It's not like I can go back and change anything. All I can do is focus on moving forward with my head on straight. Playing for the Waves is like a godsend for that. Besides the fact I'm hanging out with Leo regularly again, I'm out of the city and far enough away from my family that I can ignore them. I even blocked my father's number so I'm not tempted to answer his phone calls.

"What are you doing for the rest of the night?" Leo asked.

Leo has a date with a woman he spends time with

whenever he's in San Francisco. Surprisingly, I was asked to do things with my teammates, but decided to take a rain check. I'm exhausted and need to be at my best for tomorrow.

"I'm just gonna relax. Maybe listen to a book or watch a movie then get to bed early."

He wiped his face then crumbled up the napkin and tossed it into the empty box along with his paper plate. Standing, he picked up the box.

"I'll throw this in the garbage in the vending room on my way down the hall."

"Thanks. Have fun tonight." I waggled my eyebrows.

Once he left, I went inside and turned on the TV. Nothing really caught my attention so I grabbed my iPad from the table. But instead of pulling up a book, I started searching for a new car. I officially have my license back and if I want to take Nori out when I get back, I should have some way to do it.

Chapter Fourteen

NORI

I BENT down and dipped my roller in the pan then rolled off the excess before covering the walls with a fresh coat of *Fancy Pink*. The color has enough tint that it adds some warmth but is light enough so the colors I'll layer on top will pop.

Today is my first day of work on the fairy mural. I'm hoping to get as much done as possible this week while Molly and her family are away on vacation. First step is this base color. Once that dries, I can sketch on my design, which will take at least a full day. After that, the painting begins, which takes the longest since I do it in layers to add depth, so I have to wait for each layer to fully dry before adding another.

Since this wall was already painted white and I'll be putting so much detail over it, I don't think I'll have to do a second coat. But I'll decide that once this first one dries. I covered the last of the white paint, then stood back and inspected my handiwork.

Once I was satisfied I didn't miss a spot, I rested the roller in the pan and headed for the kitchen to wash my hands. After I removed the worst of the paint splatter, I dried my hands on a paper towel and wiped off the rest.

Grabbing my lunch from the refrigerator, I walked outside and settled onto a lounge chair. Molly's house is beautiful, the perfect combination of style and comfort. Since this part of the patio is covered, I'm out of the sun so I don't have to worry about getting burned. Plus in the shade there's a nice breeze so I decided to just hang out and read a book until it's time to sketch.

I went inside and threw away my trash then grabbed the paperback I keep stashed in my purse for just this purpose and headed back outside. But despite the good book and ideal setting, I just couldn't get into the story. My mind kept wandering to Trey and I found myself rereading passages over and over until I just gave up.

Closing my eyes, I took in a deep breath through my nose and let it out through my mouth just like I learned in yoga class. After repeating that three more times, I opened my eyes and looked out at the blue sky and fluffy clouds and took a moment to just be.

Unfortunately my cell phone rang, putting a stop to that. I glanced at my caller ID and frowned. My sister usually just texts. She rarely calls.

"Hey Eloise. Is everything okay?"

"I can't take it anymore," she said in a wobbly voice. "He treats me like a child just because he paid my tuition." She sniffed. "And my other bills."

I don't have to ask who she's referring to because the *he* in question wanted to do the same thing to me. Which is why I quit college and moved out of his house before my nineteenth birthday.

"What happened?"

"Garrett asked me to marry him and I turned him down. Daddy freaked out and told me it's time for me to grow up and be responsible."

"Oh."

"Then he said that since he still pays my way that he's still in charge of me and that he insists I call Garrett and tell him I'll marry him."

Her voice got louder and shriller with each word and she said *he* with such vehemence, it sounded like a curse.

"Did you try to have your mom talk to him?"

"She's on his side," she whined, then started sobbing.

I rested my head back against the lounge chair and closed my eyes, trying to figure out what to say. Eloise has always seemed to enjoy living in her little bubble, which is one of the reasons she never understood why I had such a difficult time there. She asked me more than once if my life wouldn't just be easier if I didn't push back so much. I always said that then I wouldn't be myself. Maybe now she understands. But probably not.

This isn't the first time Eloise has started to rebel and then fallen into line when things got tough. She's twenty-four-years-old and has never worked a day in her life. Our father still fully supports her financially. He pays for school, her apartment, her car, and gives her an allowance. And she wonders why he believes he can control her?

She finally settled down enough that I thought I might be able to understand what she was saying.

"So what do you want to do?" I asked.

"I don't know." She blew her nose. "Would I be able to come down there and stay with you for a little while? Just until I figure it out."

"Oh uh…" I scrambled for what to say. "You know I don't have my own place. I live with Crispin."

"Do you think he'd mind? Honestly, it'll just be for a little while."

I pulled the phone away from my ear and fought the urge to throw it in the pool. As satisfying as that would be, instead I put it back into place.

"Let me talk to Crispin and I'll let you know."

"Thank you so much Nori, you're the best."

Once we hung up, I texted Crispin.

Eloise just called. She's rebelling again.

This too shall pass.

Not this time. Not yet anyway. She asked if she can come down to stay for a bit.

Seriously?

Would I kid about something like that?

So what'd you tell her?

That I'd talk to you.

Oh sure, make me the bad guy.

Someone has to be.

Are you really gonna tell her she can't come?

What do you think I should do?

I texted Eloise and told her she's welcome to come down—no matter how begrudgingly—and to let me know her flight details when she has them.

That settled, I went back into the house to start sketching. Hopefully I'll get pulled into the fairy garden and forget that Hurricane Eloise is coming to town.

TREY

LEO STOOD and tossed the ball back to me and I walked toward the back of the mound. Taking off my glove, I rubbed the ball between my hands, trying to figure out what to do here. I've been off just a fraction all night, but it's been enough that I'm getting behind in the counts and batters are getting hits they shouldn't. Thankfully I'm backed by amazing fielders and they've helped hold San Francisco to two earned runs.

Somehow I've managed to limp my way into the sixth inning but I'm near the hundred-pitch mark so I know if I don't get this guy out, I'm getting the hook.

There are two outs and a full count. I can do this. I *need* to do this.

Shoving my hand back into my glove, I stepped back toward the rubber and waited for the sign. Leo's asking for a high fastball and I reached deep down for every bit of strength I have inside me and went into my windup. As I followed through, I watched the ball land in Leo's glove right behind the swinging bat.

In the dugout, I grabbed a Gatorade and sat at the end of the bench to watch the rest of the game. After scoring a run in each of the first three innings, our offense has pretty much been shut down. So after three batters up, and down just as quickly, we moved into the seventh inning with Ricky Parrish on the mound.

The next three innings went by in slow motion and there were times I could barely watch. But at the bottom of the ninth, when Malik threw his last pitch, we were still ahead 3-2 and I had my first win as a Wave.

After giving the obligatory interviews, I took a shower, and found Leo just outside the locker room.

"I'm starving. Where are we headed?" I asked.

"A bunch of the guys are going to a little steakhouse the groundskeeper told Jack about."

"The groundskeeper?"

"He's a local and Jack asked."

"Gotcha," I said. "Steak sounds great."

That's how I ended up sitting at a table with nine of my teammates, in between Leo and Jack Reagan. Jack is not only a Waves legend, but he also kicked my ass most of the time I pitched against him. But now that he's my teammate, I don't have to worry about that anymore.

"How's the arm feel?" Leo asked. "It's been awhile since you've thrown that many pitches."

"It's okay now but I'm sure I'll be feeling it a little tomorrow."

"You did great today." I heard from my left.

My eyes widened at Jack Reagan's words. Great isn't the word I'd use to describe my performance on the mound earlier. I gave a passable performance and managed to squeak by.

As if he read my thoughts, Jack added, "They're not all perfect days. I'll admit I've seen you throw better, but you kept your head in the game and figured out how to get the job done. Sometimes that's more important than hitting every spot every time. Because days where it's just not working come along more often than not and the guys who can stick it out are the ones you want out there."

Monte bumped Jack's arm with his elbow and leaned into him to speak directly to me.

"Listen to this guy. Expecting his first baby and he's all full of fatherly advice."

"You're right about the advice," Jack said with a grin. "But you're wrong about one thing." He pulled his phone out of his pocket and swiped it open and held it out for Monte to see. "I'm expecting babies, as in two."

"Are you shitting me?" Monte asked.

"I shit you not."

"Did you know about this?" Monte yelled to Dan McMullen, who was sitting directly across the table next to John Kasprzyk.

They both looked at the phone Monte held up. Dan nodded and offered a smug smile.

"What the hell?" Monte asked. "Why's McMullen in the loop and I'm not?"

"I just got permission to officially share the news. Hannah's dad was on location with limited communication and she wanted to make sure he knew before I told anyone besides my dad. She texted just as we got seated that she finally got a hold of him."

More drinks were ordered to celebrate. I toasted with

my water then half listened to him answer everyone's questions.

"Thankfully she's due in November so I'll be home for a few months before I have to report to spring training. We'll figure everything else out after they're born, once we see how it's going. Right now all I'm worried about is taking care of Hannah and having two healthy babies."

It's funny to see Jack in domestic mode. He had quite a reputation as a ladies' man back when I started playing and didn't seem inclined to change that.

Then one day he did.

Since she works for the Waves, I've met Hannah and she seems nice. She and Jack don't seem like an obvious fit. But I saw them together once and you'd have to be blind to miss their connection.

That last thought made me pause. It's the same thing Angie said about Nori and me.

Our steaks arrived, putting an end to all the talk of babies. As I started to eat, there's one question I was dying to ask Jack. A few bites in, I figured it was now or never.

"Can I ask you something?"

"Mmm Hmm."

"When you met your wife, did you know she was the one for you?"

He finished chewing then swallowed and took a long drink of beer.

"Actually we worked together for years and I didn't see her as more than a coworker, then one season we ended up working closely together. I don't know what it was, but all of a sudden, I saw her as something more and that was it. It sounds cliché and corny, but you just know. You just have to trust yourself enough to go after her and not totally fuck it up."

And therein lies the problem.

Chapter Fifteen

NORI

I OPENED the door and found my sister standing on the porch.

"Eloise." I looked around. "How did you get here?"

"I flew down, silly." She gave me a big hug then pulled back and patted my head. "Oh my God, your hair. I almost didn't recognize you."

She entered as I stepped aside carrying her purse and one small suitcase. As I went to close the door, she said, "I have more bags in the car."

I ran out to the red Mercedes convertible and found two suitcases in the backseat. I managed to drag them out of the car, stack one on top, and wheel them into the house without Eloise's help, which hadn't been offered anyway.

Closing the door behind me, I looked around the living room but didn't see my sister. Rolling the bags behind me I walked toward the office and stopped outside my room when I saw Eloise sitting in the middle of my bed propped up against the headboard scrolling through her phone.

"I figured this was your room because it's more girly," she said when she spotted me. "This bed is so comfy."

"I'll put these in the office for you."

"But there's just a couch in there."

"It has a pull-out bed."

She flashed a pouty bottom lip and blinked her eyes repeatedly. If I did that, I'd look ridiculous but somehow she manages to look adorably sad. Then again, if I stepped on a flight, no matter how short, I'd have dark circles under my eyes, wrinkled clothes, and my hair would be a mess. Eloise looks like she just walked off a runway.

I walked away before I got sucked into her vortex. Crispin will kill me if I give in and let her stay in my room.

After placing her bags in the office, I went back into the living room. As I passed my room, I spotted Eloise still lying on the bed, now staring at the ceiling.

I settled back onto the couch and picked up my sketch-book. Opening to the page I was working on before Eloise arrived, I tried to get back into it. If she wants to lie in bed and pout, I'm not gonna stop her. I have work to do.

I'd barely added to my sketch when Eloise emerged from the bedroom. I finished shading what I was working on then closed the book and looked over at her.

"Where's Crispin?" she asked.

"At work."

"Oh."

She wrinkled her nose. Apparently, the thought of someone actually having a job is both

foreign and distasteful to her. Which reminds me.

"Eloise, I thought you were going to let me know your travel plans so I could pick you up."

"Well, I was going to do that but decided I'd start being

the new independent me." She smiled and shimmied in the chair, obviously proud of herself. "So I made my own reservations online, took a cab to the airport, flew down here, picked up my rental, and followed the GPS here. All by myself."

"That's great, but how did you pay for everything?"

"My credit card."

Which is exactly what I figured, but there's one big problem with that.

"You mean the credit card dad gave you?" She nodded. "The one he pays for?" Again she nodded, obviously still not seeing an issue. "El, how are you being independent if you're still using a credit card dad pays for?"

"Well, how else was I supposed to get down here? I mean, I didn't want to ask you. I know you're not exactly financially secure."

I rubbed my eyes then shifted to sit against the armrest, ignoring her last comment.

"That's something you need to figure out and save for before you actually take the leap."

"Everything just happened two days ago. How could I have possibly done any of that?"

Instead of answering, I asked a question of my own.

"So what's your plan?"

"I was hoping you could help me figure it out while I'm here."

That's what I was afraid of.

"Okay, how much money do you have saved?"

I'll overlook the fact that any money she has is from the allowance our dad gives her.

She drew her brows together as she thought about the question. "I have a couple thousand in my checking account and maybe five hundred on me. Then of course there's my trust fund. The rest of that's finally available to me in September when I turn twenty-five. I can probably live off my credit cards until then."

"Eloise, living off credit cards dad pays for and money he gives you isn't being independent. You need to get a job to earn your own."

Before she could answer, Crispin came walking in. Eloise jumped off the chair, ran over, and jumped into his arms.

"It's so good to see you," she shrieked. "It's been forever."

"Eloise! What a surprise! I had no idea you were going to be here."

He gave me the evil eye as he set her back on her feet.

"I was just telling Nori about how I got here all by myself."

"That's awesome," he said.

Eloise absolutely loves Crispin and thinks they're best friends. He finds her semi-amusing at times and intolerable others, but he puts up with her for my sake. So her time here should be interesting.

He settled next to me on the couch and Eloise sat back down in the chair.

"So what did I miss?" Crispin asked.

"Not much. Eloise just got here a little while ago. We were actually just starting to discuss her plans now that she's striking out on her own. You'll probably have some good pointers for that."

Crispin also comes from an affluent family and they've been semi-estranged for years. His parents don't agree with his "lifestyle" and his father even offered him a big chunk of change to marry a woman and "try to look normal." Because you know, it's all about how things look.

At any rate, Crispin turned him down and went on

with his life. Which was a little easier because he had both emotional and financial support from his grandmother.

"You have a degree, right?" Eloise nodded. "Have you done any internships?"

"No, I didn't really have time."

It took her almost six years to get a Bachelor's Degree and she didn't work during that time, but she didn't have time to do an internship? This is not going to be easy.

Two hours later, Eloise grudgingly went to sleep on the pullout in the office and my head was pounding. I rubbed my temples and like the knight in shining armor he is, Crispin appeared in front of me holding out a glass of wine.

"Thank you."

I took the glass from him and took a big drink. Even though I'm not much of a drinker, I do like wine and maybe it will help my headache.

"So that went nowhere," Crispin said as he sat on the other end of the couch. "It was like talking to a brick wall. That girl just doesn't get it."

"You know, when she called me the other day, I figured the issue would go away. Either my father would give in or she'd reconsider Garrett's proposal. I didn't expect her to show up here without warning."

I finished my wine and Crispin grabbed the bottle off the coffee table and refilled my glass. After topping off his, he shook the empty bottle, and stood.

"We're going to need another."

"I probably shouldn't. It's been a long time since I had a drink. My tolerance is probably zero at this point."

He walked to the kitchen and pulled another bottle out of the wine cooler. I heard him remove the cork before returning to my side and placing the wine on the coffee table.

"You're not going anywhere tonight and don't have to be anywhere tomorrow. Get your wine on and relax."

"She has no life skills." I blew out a breath and rested my head against the back of the couch. "If I thought she was serious about getting out from her parents' control, I'd have no problem helping her but I don't think she is."

He topped off my glass and spoke in a soothing tone.

"Just let her have her little temper tantrum vacation here and don't worry about trying to sort out her life. If she wants to fix things, she'll have to figure it out and let you know her plans. Then maybe you can help."

I took in three deep breaths and let myself sink deeper into the cushion.

"I know you're right. I just don't want to turn my back on her if she needs help." I looked at him. "What would I have done if you weren't there for me?"

"Two totally different situations. First of all, you always worked and earned your own money. So when you decided to leave, you weren't using a credit card or the allowance your father gave you to support yourself." He shook his head and took a drink. "Besides, I got help from Nanny so I was just paying it forward."

"You still are."

"That's because, as you tell me all the time, I am a prince among men."

He flashed one of his dazzling smiles.

"Yes you are."

I shifted sideways and curled up against the armrest of the couch. My head has stopped pounding and I'm feeling a little buzzy. Thank you, wine.

Crispin turned on the TV.

"What do you want to watch?"

"Something fun and easy that doesn't make me think too much."

"Ooh, *The Wedding Date* is on."

We sat there, curled up on opposite ends of the couch, watching Debra Messing and Dermot Mulroney fall in love. My favorite scene—the one where the characters are dancing to *Sway*—had just ended when my phone chirped. I reached over and found a text message from Trey.

You still up?

Yes.

Can I call you?

Sure.

I stood and Crispin gave me a knowing look.

"I'm going to my room. See you tomorrow. Good night."

"Tell Trey I said hi," he said in a sing-song voice.

TREY

I PULLED into the driveway next to a white Honda Accord and turned off the engine. I've been waiting for this night since I asked Nori out in Leo's pool nearly two weeks ago. For a person who never really had to wait for anything, that seemed like forever.

As I approached the door, I was surprised to feel a slight fluttering in my stomach. I don't ever remember being nervous for a date. Both Leo and Dr. Fisher think all these new things I've been feeling are good signs, but it's still a bit unnerving.

I rang the doorbell and stepped back. A few seconds later, the door opened and I froze. Nori stood on the other side of the threshold looking absolutely stunning in a long sundress. Its deep purple color makes her eyes look even more violet and she's wearing some kind of chunky-heeled sandal that brings the top of her head a couple inches closer to my chin.

"Nori," I croaked.

Holy hell, I haven't heard that voice since my pre-teen years. I cleared my throat and tried again.

"Nori, you look beautiful."

"Thank you." She brushed her bangs off her forehead and smiled. "You look great too."

Angie had given my wardrobe a makeover during her visit, saying I needed to get rid of the "rich prick" attire I've been wearing my whole life. And I have to admit, she may have been right. Last time I wore something she picked out, Nori kept looking at me and the same thing is happening right now.

"Are you ready to go?"

"Let me just grab my purse."

Leaving the door open, I enjoyed the sight as she walked over to the coffee table and picked up her purse. Her heels have put an extra little wiggle in her walk that's really quite nice.

I stepped back and she walked onto the porch then closed the door behind her, giving the knob an extra turn to make sure it was locked.

She looked up at me with a smile. "Ready."

As we made our way down the sidewalk, I pointed toward the Honda.

"Is that your new car?"

"Yeah."

"Nice."

She looked at the car and wrinkled her nose.

"Yeah."

"Don't you like it?"

We approached my car and I opened the passenger

door. She thanked me before sitting down and fastening her seatbelt. Once she was settled, I closed the door and jogged around the car and got behind the wheel.

"Leo told me about this great place right on the water, Aqua Blue. Have you ever been there?"

"No, but Crispin has and he loved it."

"I thought we'd start there and then see where the night takes us."

"Sounds good."

She looked around the car.

"Now *this* is a really nice car. And judging from the new car smell, I'm guessing you just got it."

"This is actually just the second time I've driven it. I picked it up when I got home last night."

"New team, new car?"

"Something like that." I glanced over at her. "So what don't you like about your car?"

Again, she wrinkled her nose. It's probably the most adorable thing I've ever seen.

"Nothing really." She sighed. "It's a long story."

"Tell you what. How about if, over dinner, you tell me yours and I'll tell you mine?" Her eyes widened at my words. I didn't mean for them to sound so suggestive. Instead of apologizing, I forged on. "Hey, we have to talk about something, right?"

"I guess so." She pointed her finger at me. "But you're going first."

"The rule is always ladies first."

She looked at me out of the corner of her eye, trying to see if there was a hidden meaning behind my words. Why the hell is everything I'm saying sounding like a double entendre? I better get my shit together if this date is going to go well.

I turned left into the parking lot and circled around to

the front door. The valet approached and I stepped out, handed him the fob and a twenty dollar bill, and took the ticket. Another valet had opened the door for Nori but I reached for her hand to help her out. Her hand looked so tiny in mine, but she has a firm grip.

Nori and I stepped inside and approached the hostess, who greeted us with a friendly smile.

"Welcome to Aqua Blue. My name is Cindy. How can I help you?"

"We have a reservation for Connery."

She looked down at her tablet.

"Yes, I have you down for two in one of the nooks." I nodded. "Perfect. Follow me."

We followed her along the edge of the main room and into an alcove with a table set for two.

I pulled out a chair for Nori and after she sat, I took the seat across from her.

"Ken will be your waiter. He'll be over shortly," Cindy said as she handed us menus once we were settled.

We thanked her and she left us alone, then Nori looked at me over the flickering candle in the middle of the table, one eyebrow raised.

"Connery?"

"It's my first name. I figured it's less recognizable than Youngman."

Another new thing. When I went out in New York, it was usually to be seen and the women I spent time with would expect nothing less than the preferred seating. But tonight I just want to be anonymous and alone with Nori.

She blinked. "I never really thought about the fact that Trey is a nickname. But I guess it is."

"It is." I smiled. "What about Nori. Is that short for something?"

She sucked in a quick breath and looked down at her

menu. Interesting. Whatever her name is, it must be really good. Before I could bug her to tell me, Ken approached.

"Hi, my name is Ken, I'll be your waiter tonight. Can I start you off with a beverage?"

"Water with lemon, please," Nori said.

"Water's good for me too."

"Perfect," he said. "We have two specials tonight. First, there's a garlic crusted sixteen ounce New York strip steak. That's served with sour cream and butter mashed potatoes, broccoli, burgundy onions, and a Cuban avocado salad. And second, we have seared diver sea scallops over fresh potato gnocchi, colossal lump crab, bacon, capers, haricot vert, and grape tomato in a spicy truffle tomato sauce. Our catch of the day is grouper and that can be prepared grilled, broiled in a lemon butter and caper sauce, or blackened. Would you like me to put in any appetizers to get you started while you decide on your main course?"

I looked over at Nori.

"Leo told me the shark bites are amazing so I definitely want to get an order. Maybe we can get a couple things and share?"

"Everything looks so good, but I'd love to try the seafood bruschetta."

"And we might as well round it out with an order of calamari. Anything else?" Nori shook her head. "That's it."

"Excellent," Ken said. "I'll put those appetizers in and be back shortly with your drinks."

I already looked up the menu online and know what I'm getting so I'm able to watch Nori study hers. Her hair kept falling in her face as she looked down and she'd push it back with her index finger. It still amazes me how such a tiny woman has such a big presence.

She looked up and caught me watching her just as Ken returned with our drinks.

"Do you have any questions about the menu?"

Nori shook her head. "I think I know what I want."

"What would you like?" he asked.

"I'm going to go with the scallop special," she said.

"And you, sir?"

"I'll have the seafood paella."

"Can I get anything else for you right now?"

"No, I think we're good," I said.

"Your appetizers will be out shortly."

Nori looked out the door to the main restaurant then around our little nook.

"It's so pretty in here. I love the colors and they have some unique artwork," she said, then took a sip of water.

I leaned my forearms against the table, shifted forward, and looked her in the eye.

"Don't think you're going to distract me from the question that I asked."

Chapter Sixteen

NORI

I WAS in mid-swallow when he said that and I choked on the water. Thankfully I was able to get it under control pretty fast. I took another quick drink to soothe my throat.

"Oh, what was that?"

"Your name? Is it short for something?"

I thought about telling him it wasn't, that my name is just Nori, but it'd be easy enough for him to check if he really wanted to. I have no idea if this date will lead to something more, but just in case, it wouldn't be good to start off with a lie.

"My full name is Eleanor."

"Eleanor?" He shifted his eyes away from mine to look at a spot just above my head as he seemed to consider the word. Looking me in the eye again, he said. "I like it."

I glared and pointed my finger at him, just like I do to Crispin.

"Don't ever use it. *Ever.*"

Trey threw his head back and laughed and I sat frozen staring at him. I thought his smile was amazing, but his laugh totally transformed his face. Studying his every feature, I took a mental picture so I could sketch him later.

He stopped laughing then took a drink. After setting his glass down, he met my gaze again and said, "So I'm guessing you don't like the name Eleanor."

I wrinkled my nose. "It makes me sound like I'm ninety."

"Is it a family name?"

"No, my mother said she wanted a 'classic' name, but one that could have a fun nickname. So at least she didn't call me by my given name very often."

"If it makes you feel any better, I'm not thrilled with my full name either. Especially since two other people have it. So I usually just stick with Trey since it's mine alone." He seemed so serious when he said that last sentence but then he looked at me and smiled. "But enough talk about names. We've both managed to create identities with our nicknames. Let's talk cars."

"Yours is really nice. The seats are so comfy."

Honestly I figured he'd drive some fancy sports car, so the Mercedes SUV was kind of a surprise.

He nodded. "It's definitely a change from what I've driven before, but I like it."

"What did you have before?"

Ken arrived with our appetizers, pausing the conversation. We each took a sampling of the appetizers before picking it up again.

"Most recently a Porsche 918 Spyder."

That definitely makes more sense.

"So what made you get a new one?"

"*That* is a long story."

I speared a shark bite with my fork and held it up.

"Well we have appetizers and entrees to go, so I think we have time."

"Yes we do," he said around a smile. "But this sharing thing goes both ways."

Popping the bite into my mouth, I thought about that while I chewed. I'm kind of curious. Not that I'm surprised he'd buy a new car, but it sounds like there's a story behind it. So I'll play.

"There's not much to tell with my car. It's a nice car. I like it. But I was really attached to my other car."

He seemed to think about that as he finished chewing.

"What kind was it?"

"A Volkswagen Jetta." He nodded and took a drink and even though he didn't specifically ask, I decided to tell him. "My mom bought it brand new in 2005. It was her first new car and she was so thrilled she was finally able to afford it. When she died, I inherited it." I shrugged. "So the only thing wrong with my new car is that it's not my old one."

"Oh wow," he said. "I'm so sorry."

I hadn't expected him to say that or have such a sincerely sympathetic look in his eyes. It kind of threw me off. I took a long drink of water to give myself a moment to regain my composure.

"So what about you?"

"Last year, my life got a little out of control and my game suffered. Because of that, I got sent down to Triple A, which really pissed me off, so I spiraled even more. I was acting like a rebellious teenager, doing stupid things, acting like I was invincible. One of those dumb things was seeing how fast my fast car could go. The cops stopped me a lot. The first couple times they let me go with warnings, either because of baseball or my last name. After that, when I did get tickets, my father made a few calls and they went away."

The person he described sounds more like the Trey I'd imagined him to be than the one I've spent time with. But what he said didn't really explain the new car purchase.

"So did you get into an accident or something and needed a new car?"

"No, thank God. I was very lucky I didn't hurt someone." He shook his head and looked up at the ceiling before meeting my gaze again. "My father wouldn't help out with the last few tickets I received and I ended up having a hearing. I was being my usual cocky, entitled self and the judge gave me the stiffest sentence. I lost my license for six months. I actually just got it back a few days ago." He let out a self-deprecating chuckle. "At this point, it's too late to make a long story short, but I'll wrap it up. After all that, I got my head out my ass and decided to make some changes in my life. I figured a more practical car was a good idea."

I nodded, acknowledging his words, and finished my last shark bite just as Ken approached with fresh glasses of water. He cleared our empty plates and promised our entrees would be out shortly.

"Well, I'm sorry you went through such a hard time, but I'm glad it got you to where you are today."

And I really mean that, because there's no way I'd ever go out with that other Trey.

"Me too." Then, as if he read my thoughts, he added, "Because I know the old me would never have a snowball's chance in hell with someone as amazing as you."

I got lost in his bourbon-colored eyes as they stared into mine, letting me see the truth of his words. This man is totally different than I'd first thought and I'll admit, I'm getting pulled in.

TREY

NORI'S PHONE RANG, breaking whatever was going on between us. She looked over at her purse and pulled out her cell.

"I'm so sorry, I thought I turned the ringer off."

She rolled her eyes then sent the call to voicemail. As she was lowering the ringer volume, it rang again. Letting out a little frustrated groan, she sent that call to voicemail, too.

"Do you need to answer that?"

"No, it's just my sister."

"Are you sure it's not important?"

"Positive. She's down here visiting while she has a quarter-life crisis." She rolled her eyes. "Crispin is probably telling her something she doesn't want to hear and she's calling to complain."

She didn't seem to want to talk about her sister, so I changed the subject.

"So how long have you and Crispin known each other?"

"Since seventh grade." A sweet smile crossed her face. "I met him my first day at a new school and we had the most bizarre conversation and somehow became best friends."

"What was the conversation about?"

"Well, it wasn't really a conversation so much as snarky comments."

She stopped talking as Ken approached with our entrees. Once he was assured we had everything we needed, he left us alone again in our little alcove.

"This smells so good," she said as she picked through her plate, speared a piece of crab, and popped it into her mouth.

Closing her eyes, she smiled and let out a long groan that made me thankful I was sitting down. I'd love to hear her make that noise when we're really alone, and imagined what I could do to her to make that happen. I watched her lick her lips then shifted my attention to my own plate before things really get out of control over here.

"So what were the snarky comments?" I asked after we each put a good dent in our meals.

She looked over at me and that same sweet smile crossed her face.

"When he saw my name, he told me that nori is what's used to wrap sushi, not a name. And I told him that Crispin sounds like a cereal."

"Seriously? You became inseparable after that?" She nodded. "That definitely could have gone another way."

"I know, but for whatever reason, we just started laughing and that was it." Her smile faded and she shook her head. "Honestly, I don't know what I'd do without him."

"I feel the same way about Leo."

"Angie said you two were roommates in college."

"We were and we hated each other for the first month. And the thing that really sucked about that was that we not only lived together, we had all the same classes, and we were on the baseball team too. We were together all the time."

"So what changed?"

"He heard me fighting with my father and I guess he felt bad for me."

"Why?"

"That is too heavy of a story for a first date," I said. "And we've already talked about some pretty serious stuff."

She dropped the subject and we finished eating. When Ken came to check on us we both declined dessert and he cleared the table. After I paid the check, we stood and I placed my hand on her lower back and followed her outside.

Before I handed my ticket to the valet, I looked over at the beach and the fiery sky as the sun set.

"Would you like to go for a walk on the beach?" I asked.

Nori looked over at the beach then up at me and nodded.

"I'd like that."

As we approached the sand, she kicked off her sandals and I toed off my deck shoes then bent down to pick up both. I held them with my middle and index fingers then reached out with my other hand. She placed her hand in mine and I wove our fingers together and led us down toward the water.

"The sunset is so beautiful. What amazing colors."

Once we were a few steps beyond the tide, we just stood there, holding hands, looking at the sky. That's something I never would have done before last year. I didn't like quiet or taking time to just be. Dr. Fisher says it's because I wasn't happy with my life and didn't want to slow down enough to think about that.

"Have you ever painted a sunset mural?"

She looked up at me and by some silent agreement, we started to walk along the edge of the water.

"No, but I'd like to." She smiled.

"Once I get a house maybe I'll let you have your way with it."

"Have you started looking yet?"

"One of my teammates gave me the name of the realtor he used last year so I'm gonna give her a call and at least give her my wish list so she can start looking."

"What's on your wish list?"

"Nothing too crazy. Something like Leo's would be nice. Although I'd love to be on the water."

"I'd love to be by the water, and I definitely want a pool."

I stopped and turned to face her.

"So if I get something on the water with a pool, you'll come to visit often?" I asked, trying to keep the question playful so she doesn't totally freak out by how serious I am.

"Don't forget that I'll be there often anyway creating a mural on every wall."

We both laughed at that, but then we both just stopped and stood there, staring into each other's eyes. I squeezed her hand.

"Thank you for coming out with me tonight."

"I had a great time."

My eyes shifted to her mouth and I took a step closer. I took it as a good sign when she didn't move back. I rested the hand holding our shoes at her lower back and slowly leaned down to brush my mouth against hers. I'd meant it to be a quick kiss, a thank you for a nice dinner. But once I felt her lips against mine, I couldn't stop.

I kissed her once, twice, three times, before pulling her against me and opening my mouth over hers. Nori raised up on her tiptoes and leaned against me as her arms circled my neck. Her lips parted and the kiss turned into something much more.

Wrapping my hand around the back of her neck, I wove my fingers into her silky hair and kissed her like I own her. Our tongues teased, tangled, and tasted. Consuming, devouring, savoring. Moving deeper then retreating as sparks zinged between us and the kiss burned hotter.

Dropping our shoes into the sand, I wrapped my hand around her waist and pulled her closer. Her hips pulsed forward, brushing my erection and I groaned deep in my throat as I feasted on her mouth. I was about to pull her tighter against me, but somewhere in my lust-addled brain, I heard the sound of a squawking seagull and remembered we're standing on a public beach.

I softened the kiss then slowly pulled back, reluctant to break contact. Loosening my grip, I lowered her until she stood firmly on the sand. As I straightened, she unlocked her hands from around my neck and rested them against my chest for just a second before letting them fall away as she took a step back.

She bit her lip and looked up at me through her lashes, flashing a shy smile. I know I have a sappy smile on my face, but I don't care. That was one of the best—make it *the* best—kisses I've ever experienced. Before I could give in to the temptation to repeat it, I reached down, picked up our shoes and shook off the sand.

"Let's go," I said and held out my hand.

Nori took it and I leaned over and kissed the top of her head then led us back to the car.

Chapter Seventeen

NORI

THE RIDE HOME was filled with an easy, comfortable silence. I looked down at our joined hands resting on the console. His is so much larger but somehow fits mine perfectly. And it seems like he fits me perfectly, despite my first impression.

I'll admit that when I accepted the date I wasn't sure what to expect, but I had a great time. Dinner was really nice and I especially enjoyed myself during our walk on the beach afterwards.

That kiss.

Wow.

I realize it's been a long time since I've been kissed but I'd certainly remember something like *that*. I'll admit it's making me wonder what other things would be like. Between the way his tongue stroked against mine and the impressive erection I felt against my belly, I'd say he definitely has a *lot* of potential.

Thankfully we pulled into my driveway before I could think about that too much.

Trey removed his hand from mine, shifted into park, and turned off the car. Unbuckling his seatbelt, he shifted to face me, resting his elbow against the headrest of my seat.

"I had a really nice time tonight, Nori."

"So did I."

"Would you want to do it again, maybe later this week?"

Using his index finger, he tucked my hair behind my ear then stroked his thumb along my cheekbone. His touch felt so good and I turned into it, like a cat craving attention.

"I'd like that."

"Yeah?"

"Yeah."

He flashed one of his sweet smiles then leaned forward and kissed me. It wasn't quite as heated as the ones on the beach, but that didn't make it any less potent. I wasn't ready for it to end and when he pulled back, I fought the urge to clamp my hands on either side of his head and drag his mouth back to mine.

As if he read my thoughts, he said, "We better stop that before things get out of hand here." Smiling, he added, "I'm pretty sure Crispin is looking out the window."

I shook my head and laughed. "I wouldn't be surprised."

He sat back, putting some much-needed space between us.

"I know you're not into baseball, but I'm pitching Wednesday night and was wondering if you'd want to come to the game. I really liked you being there the other night and I know you enjoyed the food at the stadium."

I saw the vulnerability in his eyes and also realized his last comment was thrown out to deflect from that.

"The food *is* awesome."

"Crispin and your sister are welcome to come, too."

"Just Crispin."

"So you'll come?"

"I'd love to."

"While you're being so agreeable, how about dinner after the game, too?"

"Sounds good."

"Great," he said then nudged his head toward the house. "But I better let you get

inside before Crispin starts flicking the porch light on and off like Leo's parents used to do when his sisters came home from a date."

I laughed at that, mostly because I could totally see it happening.

Trey got out of the car, walked around the back, and opened the hatch. I heard it slam and a second later, my door opened. I took his proffered hand and stepped out.

We walked to the porch and he handed me my sandals.

"Thank you for tonight," he said.

"Thank *you*. I had a great time."

He leaned down and gave me a quick kiss then stepped back.

"I'll call you tomorrow after my game."

I watched him make his way back to his car before opening the door and stepping into the house. Closing the door, I turned around and screamed.

"Why are you standing there like a stalker?" I asked Crispin.

"You guys were out there an awful long time," he said

with a knowing smile. "And your lips look all red and swollen."

I walked into the living room and placed my purse on the coffee table then looked around. Crispin is one thing, but there's no way I'm going to discuss this in front of Eloise.

"Please, she's been in her room for hours." He rolled his eyes. "It shouldn't surprise you that she didn't like what I had to say."

Sitting on the couch, I dropped my sandals on the floor then tucked my feet up underneath me. Crispin sat on the other end, legs crossed.

"I don't think she'll ever get it."

"Oh no." Crispin waggled his index finger. "You just got home from a date with Trey Youngman and you two were out in the driveway steaming up the windows." He bobbed his eyebrows. "You are not going to try to sidetrack me with talk of Eloise. You need to tell me every single detail of what happened tonight."

No matter how close Crispin and I are, I'd never tell him the personal stuff Trey disclosed or give specific details of anything that happens between us.

"We went to dinner at Aqua Blue and he reserved one of those private alcoves you talked about after you went there."

"Ooh, nice touch."

"The food was amazing and we had a really good conversation. Then we went for a walk on the beach."

"So what did you talk about?"

"Just usual first date stuff."

"You're not going to give me anything, are you?" I shook my head. "Fine," he said with a sigh. "Do you still think he's a jerk?"

"No, he actually seems really great."

He nudged his head in my direction. "And how about those puffy lips? Were they worth it?"

I felt my face heat remembering our kisses.

"Yeah, they were worth it."

He leaned forward and squeezed my knee.

"Good."

Before things got too serious, I said, "I guess he had a good time too because he not only asked me to go out later in the week, he also asked me to go to watch him pitch Wednesday night and go out to dinner afterwards."

His eyes rounded.

"And of course you asked if your best friend in the world could come along."

I stood and picked up my purse and shoes.

"Of course I did."

"That's why I love you so much."

"Consider it payment for making you endure Hurricane Eloise."

He threw back his head and laughed.

"Goodnight, Crispin."

My phone buzzed just as I reached my room. Closing the door behind me, I pulled my phone from my purse and swiped it open.

> In case I didn't say it enough, thank you for tonight. I had a great time.

> I had a great time too. Looking forward to Wednesday.

> Me too. Sweet dreams.

> You too.

I sat on the edge of my bed and re-read the messages.

Trey Youngman is definitely turning out to be a pleasant surprise.

TREY

I THREW the last of my warm-up pitches and stepped to the side of the mound as Leo fired the ball down to second base. Oskar Marquez caught the ball then tossed it over to me. Sticking it in my glove, I took off my hat and wiped my face with my forearm.

It's the bottom of the sixth and we're winning by two runs. The bottom of Baltimore's order is up this inning and if I can hold the lead, the bullpen will start the seventh ahead.

Looking up into the stands, I spotted Nori and Crispin. She looks absolutely adorable in the jersey I sent to her earlier today. Well, actually Hannah Reagan sent her all the swag but I'm the one who asked her to, so I'll take at least some credit.

As the batter got into the box, I stood at the top of the mound and waited for Leo's sign. We've been working the corners all night, but now that each guy has seen me at least a couple times, it looks like we're mixing it up and starting with a high curveball.

I put my foot on the rubber, found the right grip on the threads, then went into my windup. As I released the ball, it started out high then fell into the zone, and took a dive toward the plate just as the batter swung. Next was a low fastball to the center of the plate that just missed for a called ball.

Going with another fastball, Leo set the target letter

high. I gave him exactly what he wanted but the batter managed to get the bat on it, sending a little blooper into center field. Dan McMullen had been playing deep but somehow he managed to snag the ball in the web of his glove in a perfect basket-style catch. I tipped my hat his way as he threw the ball in to Jack Reagan.

One down, two to go.

They put in a pinch hitter next. He stepped up to the left side of the plate and Leo gestured to Jimmy and Monte to be ready for a bunt. Then he gave me the sign for a high fastball inside. If this guy is gonna try to lay one down, we're not going to make it easy for him.

That pitch landed right in Leo's glove for a called strike one.

The batter moved up in the box and a half step away from the plate. So of course, Leo called for a pitch high and outside. My fastball still has some zip this late in the game and the batter didn't get the bat square and ended up popping it up straight ahead.

It was too far off the plate for Leo to catch so it was up to me. I ran off the mound, knowing I'd have to grab in the air or I wouldn't have a play. When it was obvious I wasn't going to do that if I didn't dive, I reached my arm out and threw myself forward, keeping my eye on the ball the entire time. It landed in my glove and I squeezed it tight as I landed on the grass and skidded to a stop.

Leo grabbed my hand and pulled me to my feet.

"Nice play."

"Thanks."

I handed him the ball and he ran behind the plate and got a new one from the umpire. He tossed it to me and I walked back to the mound. When I turned around, I saw Leo jogging toward me then realized Lenny Gill was coming out.

"You okay?" Lenny asked.

"Yeah, why?"

"Your arm is bleeding."

I turned both of my arms and saw that he was right. Blood was running all along my left forearm.

"I'm fine."

"Do you want me to get Max out here to clean and bandage it?"

"No." I smiled. "He can do that when I get back in the dugout after we get this guy out."

He nodded, slapped me on the shoulder, and jogged back to the dugout.

I must have cursed myself with what I said to Lenny because the next guy was all over the first pitch and sent a frozen rope into right-center field. That brings the top of the order and the tying run to the plate.

Blowing out a breath, I looked to Leo for the sign. We're starting with a curveball again. After checking the runner, I gave him exactly what he wanted. The batter fouled it back behind the plate. When the next pitch was called strike two, I breathed a sigh of relief. Just one more strike and I'm out of this.

We're going with another fastball. The batter hit a ground ball just to my left. I turned and watched Oskar shift over and get into position to catch it, but the ball took a weird hop and he just managed to knock it down. Unfortunately both runners were safe.

So with runners at first and third, the go-ahead run walked up to the plate.

Leo ran out to the mound.

"Tough break."

"Yeah."

"We'll get this guy. He stands so far back, he can't

reach the outside of the plate. So that's where we're going." I nodded. "I just wanted to give you a minute."

"Thanks, but I'm good."

And as he ran back behind the plate, I realized that I wasn't just saying that, I really am good. I'm not feeling pissed off or out of control, like I would have in the past. I'm not freaking out at Oskar for not making the last play. I'm just focused and confident that I can keep throwing strikes.

Just like he said he would, Leo gave the sign for an outside fastball. After checking the runners, I zeroed in on his glove and threw the ball directly to it for a called strike one. The batter fanned at the second pitch and managed to catch it with the end of the bat. It bounced foul, just to the left of home plate.

For the next pitch, Leo wanted an inside slider. The batter made contact with the handle of the bat and hit a chopper right back at me. I snagged it with my glove and tossed the ball over to Monte for the third out. Jack and Jimmy each patted me on the back as they passed on their way into the dugout.

I walked down the steps into the dugout and grabbed a water. Max Riggsby approached with the first aid kit as I sat on the bench.

"Let me clean your arm," he said as he settled next to me.

I held out my arm and let him do his thing. Now that my adrenaline is starting to fade, it stings like a son of a bitch. But at least I managed to keep a cool head, do my job out there, and get off the field with a lead.

Now it's up to the bullpen.

Chapter Eighteen

NORI

"FOR SOMEONE who's not a sports fan, you were sure into that game," Crispin said.

"That was so nerve-wracking. I almost couldn't watch."

The Waves ended up winning by one run but it wasn't an easy victory. Once Trey was done, the bullpen almost blew the lead. They used two relief pitchers in the seventh inning and ended up putting the closer, Malik Walters, in with one out in the eighth.

Crispin was super patient explaining everything that was happening on the field. He didn't even roll his eyes once at any of my questions.

Now we're waiting for Trey and Leo to meet us at O'Leary's, a cozy little pub across town from the stadium. I followed Angie's lead and ordered a bunch of appetizers so they're here when they arrive.

"That's baseball," Crispin said and took a drink of sweet tea. "Like Yogi said, 'It ain't over 'til it's over.'"

I spent the first thirteen years of my life living a half hour from the Yogi Berra Museum, so even I know who Yogi is and didn't need him to clarify.

"Well it's annoying. How do you handle it?"

"It's all part of being a fan, so I guess you'll find out." His gaze shifted to my shirt then met mine again. "I still can't believe you now have your very own Waves wardrobe. Trey has practically branded you with his gear."

I received a big box of Waves gear yesterday, including the Youngman jersey I'm currently wearing.

"You're just jealous that Leo didn't send you anything."

The two of them have developed quite a bromance over the past few weeks. They first bonded over baseball and a love of Leo's hair but apparently they have a lot in common.

Crispin scrunched his face and gave me a sarcastic laugh, but before he could comment, the topic of our conversation arrived.

"Trey should be here in a little bit," he said as he sat next to Crispin. "The reporters had a lot of questions for him and then Max wanted to bandage up his arm."

Our waitress arrived with the appetizers and set them down in the middle of the table, then took Leo's drink order.

I picked up two plates and handed one to each of the guys.

"That game was a nail-biter," I said. "You guys are killing me."

"Yeah, I don't imagine it was easy to watch. Unfortunately, it happens," he added as he filled his dish.

"So I've been told. But I'm new to all this, so you guys need to give me a break."

"I'll tell the team," Leo said around a chuckle then shoved a mozzarella stick into his mouth.

Trey arrived then leaned down and gave me a quick kiss before sitting next to me.

"Sorry I'm late," he said and held up his arm. "Max acted like I have a compound fracture instead of a few cuts on my arm."

I looked at the bandage covering his entire forearm.

"Better to be safe than sorry, I guess."

"I guess."

I handed him a plate and nudged my head toward the appetizers.

"Help yourself."

"Thanks." He smiled. "I'm starving."

He filled his plate and dug in.

Leo's cell buzzed and he checked the text message then held up his phone for Trey to see.

"My new countertop is installed," he said. "The house just might be ready for me to move in when the season is over."

"Nice," Trey said. "I still can't believe you're going to live in Scranton."

"Yeah, you and my whole family. But I like it there and it seems like the right move."

"Are you keeping your place in Bergen County?"

"Angie would kill me if I got rid of it. She's basically claimed it through squatter's rights."

The waitress approached for our dinner orders. Since I ate a ton of stuff at the stadium and we have a bunch of appetizers, I just ordered a side salad. But the guys got full meals, even Crispin who ate just as much as I did at the game.

Over the next hour, we finished the appetizers and dinner, and the conversation flowed seamlessly. Leo talked more about his house, Crispin mentioned his plans to expand the salon's services, and Trey encouraged me to share pictures of my latest mural. Each topic was discussed at length and before I knew it, all the plates were empty.

"I know Crispin is going exactly where you are, but I was hoping I could drive you home," Trey said after he paid the check. "It'll give us a chance to talk more and we can plan our date Friday night."

"Oh sure."

I glanced over at Crispin, who was having his own conversation with Leo, but of course, he heard what Trey said. He flashed me a smug smile and waggled his eyebrows. He's thrilled that I'm actually going out with someone and the fact that it's Trey Youngman makes it even better.

We all stood and made our way outside.

"See you tomorrow," Leo said. "Bye Nori."

"I'll see you at home," Crispin said and walked to the other side of the parking lot with Leo.

I said goodbye to them both and followed Trey to his car. He opened the door for me and I got in. He jogged around the back then got behind the wheel and turned to face me.

"Hi," he said with a sweet smile then leaned over the console and kissed me before turning and clicking his seatbelt into place.

It's amazing how even the shortest, softest brush of his lips against mine makes me break out in goosebumps.

"That shirt looks nice on you."

I looked down at the jersey then back at him.

"Thank you again."

"You're very welcome." He started the car and backed out, then pulled out of the parking lot and onto the main road. "I'll admit, it was a little distracting though, seeing you up in the stands in my jersey."

Thankfully it's dark in the car so he can't see my blush.

"It seemed like you managed to focus on the game just fine. You were amazing. I was on the edge of my seat again."

"Yeah, it was touch and go there those last few innings," he said. "But enough about the game. Let's discuss Friday night. The game starts at five o'clock so hopefully it'll be done around eight. Since I'm not playing, I won't be held up afterwards and should be able to pick you up around eight thirty. Does that sound okay?"

"Yeah, that'll work."

"Great. Dinner again or is there something else you'd like to do?"

"Dinner sounds good."

"Anywhere special you'd like to go?"

"I'll leave that up to you since you're the celebrity."

He chuckled. "Is that what I am?"

"Well, you're definitely more recognizable than me," I said. "And you guys seem to know where to go to avoid being mobbed."

"It's surprisingly easy down here." He shrugged. "Although, if I'm being honest, I never really tried to avoid it in New York. So it may have been just as easy up there."

I wasn't sure what to say to that, so I just remained quiet. From what I saw online, he *was* out and about quite a bit when he lived in New York, but of course, what's reported probably doesn't tell the whole story. But I don't think we've known each other long enough for me to pry into his past too much.

He asked me about my schedule in the upcoming weeks and I told him about the projects I have lined up. Before I knew it, we were pulling into my driveway. He unhooked his seatbelt and turned to face me.

"Thanks for coming tonight," he said.

"Thanks for inviting me."

"Just to be clear, you have an open invitation. Anytime you want to attend a game, just let me know."

"I'll do that."

I smiled and Trey's gaze shifted to my mouth. The atmosphere in the car changed and Trey's eyes burned as he drank me in. Somehow his eyes turned darker and seemed to glow at the same time.

"Nori." He whispered my name, his voice low and sexy.

We both moved at the same time, and our lips collided in a hungry, desperate kiss.

Our mouths melded together, opening and closing, as we feasted on each other. He groaned deep in his chest and wrapped his arms around me, pulling me closer. I twisted my fingers into his hair and held on tight.

Trey's tongue twirled against mine and he added a slight suction that I felt in every erogenous zone in my body. I squeezed my thighs tight to ease the throbbing ache between them and fought the urge to climb over the console and straddle his lap. I don't think I've ever felt this kind of desperate passion and it's equal parts exciting and terrifying.

His hand moved down the curve of my waist to my hip and squeezed. Our breathing turned ragged as he plundered my mouth, claiming me in a way no one has in a long time, if ever. I was so lost in his kiss, I actually whimpered when he slowed it down and pulled back. He made a noise that sounded like half-moan, half-chuckle against my mouth.

"This is too fucking good. If I don't stop now, I don't know that I'll be able to."

He moved back, his hands leaving my body in a wake of goosebumps.

For two years, my libido has lain dormant and this man

awakened it with nothing more than his magnetism and a few amazing kisses.

"Thank you." I kissed his cheek and pulled back before I could do more than that.

"What for?"

"Just—" I searched for a word, but only one came to mind. "Everything."

He smiled. "Come on. Let's get you inside before I forget about my good intentions."

Chapter Nineteen

TREY

I PULLED into the driveway next to a little red Mercedes. Grabbing the summer bouquet off the passenger seat, I stepped out of the car and walked up the sidewalk to the porch and rang the doorbell.

A minute later the door opened and I was surprised when it was neither Nori nor Crispin standing on the other side of the threshold, but a tall, curvy woman with brown eyes and long brown hair. Her eyes widened and I knew immediately that she recognized me.

"Hi, I'm here for Nori."

Her eyes widened even more when I said that but she quickly recovered and stepped aside.

"Of course you are," she said in a voice as fake as her nails. "Come on in."

I stepped inside and she closed the door behind me then placed her hand on my bicep and squeezed.

"I'm Nori's sister, Eloise."

"Nice to meet you. I'm Trey."

She flashed a knowing smile that at one time I would have found sexy, but now realize it's just fake, and think it kind of makes her look constipated.

"I know just who you are Trey Youngman." Again with the smile.

Thankfully Nori appeared before I had to respond.

"Sorry about that," she said, her eyes shifting to Eloise, who slowly released her hold on my arm. "I had a bit of a wardrobe malfunction and had to change."

She's wearing another sundress, this one pale pink, and a little shorter than the one she wore for our last date.

"No worries, especially since I'm earlier than we originally planned." I held out the flowers. "These are for you."

"Thank you, they're beautiful." She took the bouquet and held it to her nose. "Mmm, and they smell great. Let me put them in some water."

I followed Nori to the kitchen and watched her open a top cabinet and look up. There were three vases on the top shelf and there's no way she'll be able to reach them without standing on something.

Walking up behind her, I asked, "Need some help?"

She looked over her shoulder at me and smiled. "Please. I think these will look nice in the blue one."

I reached over her head and grabbed the vase she pointed to. She took it from my hands and went to the sink to fill it with water.

"So where are you kids headed?" Eloise asked.

"We're just going out to dinner," Nori said.

"What time will Crispin be home?"

"I'm not sure."

Eloise stuck her bottom lip out. They must teach that

in prep school because I swear every woman I've ever spent time with does it. Except Nori. But she's not like anyone else I've ever known.

"So I'll be here alone again."

That whiny voice must be taught, too. I've heard it before as well.

Nori's shoulders tensed but her voice sounded even as she arranged the flowers in the vase.

"Aren't any of your friends around?"

"No."

"I'm sure you'll be fine."

I made the mistake of looking directly at Eloise. She batted her eyelashes and flashed the pouty lip. I shifted my eyes back to Nori, who placed the last flower in the vase and was adjusting the arrangement.

"These are so pretty. Thank you," she said.

"You're welcome. The colors reminded me of the fairy mural."

She smiled up at me. "They do."

After changing the placement of two flowers, Nori stood back and nodded, then picked up the vase, carried it to the living room, and placed it in the middle of the coffee table. She grabbed her purse from the chair.

"Ready?" she asked and walked toward the door.

Eloise shifted her gaze between us, that bottom lip still jutting out. It's pretty obvious she's looking for an invitation, and as much as I'm looking forward to this date, I'd extend one if I thought that's what Nori wanted. But that doesn't seem to be the case.

We said goodbye to Eloise and I followed her out. Opening the passenger door, I held Nori's hand as she settled into the seat then let go and closed it. She was clicking her seatbelt into place as I got behind the wheel.

"Sorry about that. I would have been out of my room to open the door, but I took a drink of orange juice and spilled it down the front of my dress, so I had to change."

"It's not a problem. I just hope I didn't throw off your timing since the game finished earlier than I expected."

We won again, this time 1-0, and the game was a pitcher's duel so it went by really fast. It was scoreless into the eighth but Jimmy Chavez managed to get his bat on a fastball and sent it into the upper deck in left field. Otherwise, we probably would have gone into extra innings and I would have been late for our date.

"No, I had the game on so I saw that it was moving fast and made sure I was ready."

The fact that she watched the game made my chest fill with warmth. I know she wasn't a baseball fan prior to meeting me and now she not only comes to the stadium, she also watches the games on TV.

"You're turning into a true fan."

She laughed at that.

"Yeah, who'd have thought?"

I merged onto the highway then realized I never told her where we're going.

"We're heading to Sophia's."

"Ooh, I love Italian."

"I do love the fact that you like to eat."

"Food is one of the best things in life."

I started to say something then thought twice, but she called me on it.

"Most of the women I know don't eat. I don't understand it."

"They just don't eat in front of *you*. That's how my sister is. She'll eat before a date so she doesn't eat on it. It doesn't make sense to me either."

Since she mentioned Eloise, I figured I'd ask about her.

"So how long is Eloise here for?"

"Who knows?" Nori shook her head. "But I'm ready to shove her in my trunk and drive her back myself."

"I never would have thought she was your sister. You don't look anything alike. You also don't act anything alike."

"We're actually half-sisters. Same father. She looks like her mother and I look like mine. I was also raised differently, well until my mother died."

"How old were you?"

"Thirteen." I wanted to ask what happened but didn't quite know how. Nori must have sensed my question because she answered it anyway. "She had pneumonia that went untreated and then there were complications."

"I'm sorry."

"It was a big shock," she said. "And then I had to go live with my father, which was an

even bigger shock."

"Why's that?"

"My mom and dad came from totally different worlds. They met when he was at Princeton and she was a waitress at a local diner. I'm sure it was supposed to just be a fling for him but then she got pregnant with me."

"So what happened?"

She shifted slightly to face me and shrugged.

"Well thankfully they never got married. That would have been a disaster. But he did 'do the right thing,'" she said, using air quotes with those last four words. "He sent monthly child support and spent time with me every other weekend, but I wouldn't say we've ever been close. Maybe if we'd had more alone-time together, but my brother Clay is only two years younger than me, so he had a wife and family before we really got to know each other."

I got off the exit and turned right. We're about ten minutes from the restaurant so I figured I'd ask more about her story.

"So how did it go when you moved in with them?"

"To say it was a culture shock is an understatement. My first thirteen years were spent in a small Jersey town being raised by a mother who worked as a legal secretary. We weren't wealthy by any means but had everything we needed. Plus my mom was very affectionate and open. We talked about everything. My father lives in Long Island in a McMansion where kids are supposed to be seen and not heard. They're not very affectionate and don't really talk. Their way of dealing with anything is to throw money at it."

It sounds like Nori's family and mine aren't so different. I suppose the fact that she had thirteen years of a normal life is why she's so down to Earth and not like the people I grew up around.

"For the first couple years, I tried to fit in, be the perfect daughter. But my step-mother was less than thrilled that I was there and made things difficult, and my father didn't really pay attention. So I decided to just be me and at least be happy...or as happy as I could be considering the situation. Needless to say, that made things even worse, so I just spent a lot of time either out of the house or in my room. And I counted the days until I could leave."

I turned in the parking lot of the restaurant and backed into a parking space. I'm loving learning more about Nori, but we'll have to pause the conversation until we get seated.

NORI

.   .   .

WE SAT at a private table near the back of the restaurant picking at a charcuterie board.

"This right here is my idea of a good time," I said as I popped a green olive into my mouth. "I could eat this for every meal."

Trey smiled as he chewed and swallowed.

We'd stuck to just this for an appetizer since a salad is included with our meals, and I'm hoping to have enough room to have cannoli for dessert. Plus I spotted some of the entrees at the other tables as we walked through the restaurant and the portions are huge.

"So, you were living with your father counting the days until you could leave. Where did you plan on going?"

I pointed at him with a prosciutto-wrapped breadstick.

"I think I talked enough about myself on the ride here. It's your turn."

I've never told anyone that much about myself, but it just seemed right to share with him. But now that we've taken a break from the topic, I want to move onto something else.

"What do you want to know?" he asked.

"Do you have any siblings?"

"A younger brother, Max."

"Are you close?"

"Not really." He shrugged. "My father always played us against each other so as far back as I can remember, there was a rivalry between us more than anything."

"That's too bad."

"I never really noticed how bad it was between us until I met Leo's family. He's so tight with his siblings and Max and I just don't have that. I could never really count on him and I don't totally trust him. Honestly, I feel more comfortable with Leo's family than I do with my own."

"Does he work with your father?"

"Yeah, he's the heir apparent to the throne."

"Did your father expect you to work there too or was he supportive of your baseball career?"

He took a long drink of water and seemed to be mulling over how much to tell me. I'll be happy with whatever he's willing to share and told him so. When I said that, I was rewarded with one of his sweet smiles then he spoke.

"I'm sure he expected me to follow in his footsteps when I was born but when I was about seven-years-old, he decided that I'm an idiot and wasn't good enough to work there."

"What?" I cringed at my shrieky voice and toned it down for the next word. "Why?"

"I'm dyslexic."

So many emotions flashed in his eyes when he said the word that I couldn't sort them all out before he shuddered them. I have a feeling that's a fact not many people know that about him and I'm truly touched that he told me.

"That doesn't make you an idiot."

"To my family, especially my father, it does. I had trouble reading and my grades were terrible. I wasn't diagnosed until I was ten so for those three years, he just thought I was either lazy or a moron. Those are his exact words. Of course, I didn't know there was something wrong either. But I did know I wasn't lazy. I tried and I studied but it didn't do any good."

"Who finally diagnosed it?"

"My fifth grade teacher figured it out pretty fast so I don't know why no one else did."

The waitress approached with our salads and she cleared away the now-empty charcuterie board. I figured

Trey would use the interruption as a chance to change the subject so I was surprised when he continued.

"The teacher recommended a special school where I could get help but my parents didn't want me to go there. They did hire a tutor for me though."

"Did that help?"

"It did." He shrugged. "Just knowing the issue was a help and the tutor showed me how to cope with and manage it."

"Were things better with your father after that?"

"Not because of academics, but that's around the time I started doing really well in baseball. He loved the fact that I was one of the best, if not *the* best on the teams I played on...even if he never came to a game. After that, he never bugged me about my grades or cared what I did in school as long as I was eligible to play baseball. I played on the most elite travel teams and took the best lessons money could buy. And I really loved the game, so it wasn't exactly a hardship."

"Do you still?"

"Love the game?"

"Yeah."

He didn't even hesitate to answer.

"I do." He finished his last bite of salad. Once he swallowed, he added, "That's why I'm so angry with myself that I let him get into my head and almost ruin my career. I mean, don't get me wrong, I take full responsibility for any issues I had and the shit I did, but now I know that my relationship with my entire family is unhealthy. They make me feel bad about myself and then I do stupid things."

The waitress approached again and refilled our water glasses then cleared our empty plates. She said our entrees were almost up and she'd be out with them shortly.

Trey reached over and placed his hand over mine.

"How about we spend the rest of the meal talking about something a little lighter. We can get to know each other more as time goes on instead of spilling it all out at once because it sounds like we both have some pretty heavy shit in our past."

"That sounds like a good plan."

Chapter Twenty

TREY

WE SAT in the car in the restaurant parking lot, a bag of leftovers and cannoli in the back seat.

"This place is amazing," she said. "And not for nothing, but they could serve a quarter of their portions and it would be a full meal."

"Agreed. It's not very often I take home leftovers."

"Thank you for getting the cannoli to go."

"I know you were looking forward to it."

I started the car, but before I pulled out, I wanted to ask her something and I want to be facing her when I do it. Shifting so I could look directly at her, I took her hand in mine and entwined our fingers.

"Nori, this dating and relationship thing is all new to me so I'm going to need you to let me know if I ever do or say anything that upsets you or makes you uncomfortable."

"Okay." A sweet smile crossed her face. "But just in

case you're wondering, you're doing great so far. Perfect, in fact."

"I appreciate that." And I really hope she still thinks that after this conversation. "Tonight has been great and I was hoping we could spend some more time together. Alone. The problem is that you live with Crispin and now Eloise and I live in a hotel."

Her eyes widened as she seemed to understand where I was heading.

"My room is a suite so there's a whole sitting area with a TV and even a mini kitchen. It's not like I'm staying at a pay-by-the-hour no-tell motel."

She laughed at that and I relaxed a little bit.

"So I was wondering if you'd come back to my place so we could spend more time together. Maybe talk or watch a movie."

"I'd like that."

"Yeah?"

"Yeah."

After that, we took what seemed like the slowest ride known to man back to my hotel. I found a parking spot then used my keycard to let us in through a side door. It's the entrance I've been using not only because I see less people but also because the elevator right inside brings me only a few doors from my room.

Once we got to my floor, I led her down the hall, and opened the door, stepping aside for Nori to enter in front of me. She looked around then glanced over her shoulder at me as I closed the door.

"This is really nice. At least you have more than a bed and a bathroom since you're staying here long term."

"Yeah, it's not too bad, but I'm definitely ready for my own place." I gestured for her to have a seat on the couch. "Would you like a drink?"

"No, thank you. I'm good."

Sitting next to her, I grabbed the remote off the end table and switched on the TV. Flipping on the guide, I scrolled through.

"Just yell if you see something that interests you," I said.

She pointed to the screen. "Oh that. I love these home shows. They crack me up."

I put on the show she requested and we sat there watching in silence until the commercial break.

"Why do they crack you up?"

"To start the show, the people introduce themselves and share their background and budget and it's ridiculous." Using a fake voice, she said, "'I'm a part-time basket weaver and my husband restrings toy ukuleles. Our budget is one million dollars.'"

"Is it really that bad?"

"Close to it," she said. "And then, they'll find the perfect house that checks nearly every item of their wish list and they'll be like, 'I don't know. I really don't like that blue paint in the kitchen' or 'the light switches are almond and we really wanted white.'"

"You're obviously very passionate about this."

"Crispin and I have no life and tend to watch marathons of these types of shows. Sometimes we make bets or play drinking games about all the stupid things the people say."

The show ended and another one was coming on. I shifted closer to Nori and put my arm around her shoulders. She sat forward and at first, I thought she was moving away from me, but then she settled back and tucked her legs up underneath her and I realized she just took her sandals off. Setting her head against my shoulder, she rested her arm across my stomach.

I've never just hung out with a woman like this before and I'm really enjoying myself. Just being with Nori is nice.

The people on the show weren't quite as ridiculous as Nori had described but I see what she's talking about. I'm not sure how a couple who owns one food truck can afford a half million dollar house, no matter how successful it is, without another income.

He didn't like the color of the carpeting in the extra bedrooms and she wasn't thrilled with the curtains. Obviously they have to say something negative about the houses to make it interesting, but you'd think they'd find something not so silly. I wouldn't want to look like a total idiot on TV.

About halfway through the show, Nori shifted her head and looked up at me.

"See what I mean?"

"I understand now." I kissed her forehead. "And you can rest assured, when I look at houses, I won't pick on the carpets or paint, or the curtains for that matter. It seems to me like they're things you'd change anyway. I mean, unless you find something perfect, and what are the chances of that?"

"Which house do you think they're gonna pick?" she asked.

"Personally, I'd go with the second one, but I think they'll go with number three. He was obsessed with that garage. How about you?"

"I think they'll go with the first one. She liked all the land. None of the other houses had that."

"So what do I get if I'm right?"

"What do you want?"

I pretended to think about it, but I knew my answer as soon as she asked.

"A kiss."

"Okay."

"What do you want if you win?"

"Can I let you know?"

"Sure."

We settled in to watch the end of the show. They dragged it out and made us wait for an answer but in the end, I was right. The couple picked house number three.

Nori shifted back slightly to look at me, but kept her hand resting on my stomach.

"Are you sure you didn't see this one before?"

"I've never seen this show before. Call it beginner's luck."

She smiled and looked down at my mouth before shifting her gaze up to meet mine again.

"I guess it's time to pay up."

I was going to tell her that she didn't have to, that I was serious when I said we could just come here and hang out, but more than anything, I wanted to kiss her. And it looks like she really wants to kiss me too.

That's another thing I like about Nori, she's so open and honest. I never have to worry that she's playing some kind of game.

Shifting sideways, I slid my hand along her neck to the back of her head and slowly pulled her closer. I dragged my nose along hers and kissed her softly once, then again just a little harder. I tilted my head then opened my mouth over hers and she eagerly followed my lead.

The open-mouthed kisses are deep and wet and hot as hell, but I want more. Pulling her closer, I slipped my tongue inside to tangle with hers and she met me stroke for stroke. Her fingers dug into my shirt and I hoped she kept her hand there because if she moved it down a couple inches, she'll feel the erection that's throbbing against my zipper. It amazes me how hot she gets me with just a kiss.

Then again, the kisses we've shared haven't been *just* anything.

I'd only asked her for a kiss and if we keep doing this, it's gonna go way beyond that, so I slowed things down and pulled back. I waited until she opened her eyes and met my gaze. I offered a small smile as I fought to get my breathing under control.

Her eyes are glazed and I can feel her tight nipples against my chest. It's nice to know I'm not the only one affected.

NORI

"NORI?"

Trey's worried voice broke me out of my trance and I realized I was just sitting there, clutching his shirt, staring at him. I cleared my throat.

"Yeah?"

"Are you okay?"

I nodded and shifted my gaze to his mouth then back up to his eyes.

"I think you kissed me senseless."

His chuckle was low and sexy and full of promise and I want to find out exactly what he could deliver. I don't usually take the lead in situations like this, but if I don't at least let him know what I'm thinking, I have a feeling he'll stop.

I moved my hand slowly up his chest, enjoying every rippling muscle along the way. Cupping his jaw, I rubbed my thumb across his cheek, loving the feel of the soft stubble. His questioning gaze met mine and I smiled.

"Would you mind doing it again?"

"Nori." This time my name came out as more of a groan.

He covered my hand with his then kissed each of my knuckles before placing a kiss right in the center of my palm and laying it flat against his chest. I felt his heart pounding and was happy to know I'm not the only one affected here.

"While I'd love to do that, I'm not sure I'll be able to stop."

"Then don't."

"Are you sure?"

"Yes."

I slid my hand down his stomach toward the erection tenting his pants. He grabbed my wrist and placed my hand on his shoulder, pulling me forward and against his chest. I took it a step further and shifted my leg over to straddle his lap.

He sucked in a sharp breath, then wrapped his fingers around my bare thighs and squeezed. His hands are so large, I'm sure if he extended his thumbs, they'd brush right against my clit. My core clenched at the thought. Trey moved his hands to my ass and pulled me right against his hard cock.

I let out a long low groan and rubbed myself against him. It's been a long time and he feels so good. With one hand still on my ass to hold me in place—as if I'm going anywhere—he slowly moved the other up my back and twisted his fingers into my hair, holding me still as he ravaged my mouth.

That's the only word I could think of to describe what he's doing to me...*ravaging*. He's devastating me with the feel of his mouth against mine. Destroying me with every stroke of his tongue. Ruining me for every other man.

Trey's fingers squeezed my ass, shifting me forward to pulse against his erection. The hard ridge fit perfectly into my cleft and rubbed against my clit. My moans and whimpers got louder and more frequent. Clutching his shoulders, I forced myself to stop before I come without doing more than dry-humping him.

He slipped his hand between us and squeezed then molded my breast to his palm. When he pinched my nipple between his thumb and forefinger, I felt the zing all the way down in my sweet spot. I thrust against him again to try to ease my throbbing need. I'm so wet and achy and my clit is pulsing, so it won't take much more of this to push me over the edge.

Breaking the kiss, Trey looked at me with his darkened honey eyes, his fingers still teasing my nipple and the hard ridge of his erection rubbing me just right. I closed my eyes and, between panting breaths, let out a low groan.

"Nori, let go. Just let it happen." He leaned forward and tugged on my lobe with his teeth then whispered in my ear. "I want to watch you come." His words and the warmth of his breath made my nipples tighten even further.

He looked at me again then squeezed both hands into my ass and held me tight against him. I couldn't hold back anymore and thrust like a wild woman until I felt the telltale tingles concentrating in the tiny bundle of nerves between my thighs before spreading through every erogenous zone in my body.

"Trey." I dug my fingers into his shoulders and thrust even faster. "Trey, I'm…I'm…" I ended that sentence with a long keening cry as an intense orgasm crashed through me.

TREY

Nori blinked and looked at me, eyes wide and a little bit dazed. I shifted forward on the couch and kissed her forehead.

"Wrap your arms around my neck."

Once I felt her arms lock into place, I gripped her hips. Holding her tight, I stood and she wrapped her legs around my waist. I walked into the next room and she released her hold on me as I placed her on the bed. Kneeling between her thighs, I gripped the edge of her dress, then dragged it up and over her head and tossed it onto the floor behind me.

I've been with actresses, models, and socialites, but sitting there in a pale pink cotton bra and panty set, Nori is the most beautiful woman I've ever seen. For someone so tiny, she's surprisingly curvy, and I'm torn between going slow so I can explore each sweet dip and swell and taking her hard and fast before I get blue balls.

"This peep show needs to go both ways, you know."

Nori's normally husky voice sounds even more sexy, throwing fuel onto the inferno already raging inside me. I ripped off my shirt and threw it behind me then reached around and unclasped her bra and slipped it off, giving it the same fate.

The moment my mouth opened over her breast, she let out a soft moan and dug her fingernails into my shoulders. I sucked, teased, and tasted her nipple with my lips, tongue, and teeth, while squeezing, rolling, and twisting the other with my fingers.

Letting go with an audible pop, I put my hands on her waist and followed as I pushed her back on the bed so I could settle between her widespread thighs. Moving to her other breast, I gave it the same treatment, loving each and every one of the sexy little sounds coming out of her mouth.

She raised her hips, rubbing herself against me.

"Trey…"

With one final squeeze, I let go of her breast and trailed my hand down her stomach and shifted back just far enough so I could slip my fingers inside her underwear. She seemed to hold her breath as I moved down, down, down and let it out on a soft pant when I finally rubbed along her slick seam. Dipping my middle finger inside, I swirled it around her swollen clit and her hips jerked up off the bed.

I twirled my tongue around her nipple once more then pulled back and found Nori watching me with heavy-lidded eyes, that at the moment look more dark blue than violet.

Shifting my hand, I slipped my finger inside her and slowly moved it in and out, then back up to circle around her clit. She bent her knee and dropped her leg to the side, as I repeated that motion over and over again…in and out then circle, in and out then circle, in and out then circle.

"Trey." My name came out on an agonizing moan.

"Tell me what you want, what you need."

"You. Just more of you."

I circled her clit one last time and moved my hand up to remove her panties. Before I could do that, Nori reached forward and unbuttoned then unzipped my pants. Reaching inside, she wrapped her fingers around my cock and slowly stroked. I closed my eyes and clenched my jaw tight. It's been a while and she has me so worked up, if I don't stop her I'm going to seriously embarrass myself.

She swirled her thumb around the tip and that was nearly my undoing.

"Nori…"

Grabbing her wrist, I pulled her hand away then looked into her eyes and offered a pained smile.

"That feels *way* too good."

As I shifted off the bed, my pants fell to my ankles and I stepped out of them. Bending forward, I slid my index fingers into the waistband of her panties and slowly pulled them down her legs, then tossed them to the floor.

She's so wet, she's glistening and I have to fight the urge to drag my tongue through the plump lips her perfectly trimmed blonde landing strip leads to. But, while I'd love to taste her, my cock is ready to burst.

I was about to remove my boxer briefs when I remembered protection. Looking around the room, I tried to remember where I put the condoms. Since I haven't needed them, they're probably in the bottom of a bag somewhere.

"Trey? Is everything okay?"

"Everything is perfect. I just need to remember where I put the condoms."

"Oh." Her eyes shifted around the room, then landed on the nightstand. "They're not in there?"

I shook my head and tried not to panic. That must have helped some blood flow back to my brain because I suddenly remembered where I saw them last.

"I'll be right back."

I dashed over to the closet and grabbed my duffle. Ripping open the zipper, I turned the bag over and shook, emptying its contents out onto the floor. The crushed box was one of the last things to fall out.

"Yes!"

I grabbed the box and walked back over to the bed and tossed it onto the pillows. When I pulled my underwear down and kicked them to the side, my dick bobbed against my stomach. Nori's eyes widened and she licked her lips.

Reaching over, I grabbed a condom out of the box and tore it open with shaking hands. As I rolled it down my aching length, Nori bit her lower lip and watched.

"I'll make this as good as I can, but I swear, no matter what happens, we'll take it slower next time."

"Next time?"

"Oh you can bet there will be a next time. There are too many things I want to do to you. There's no way I'll get them all done in one shot."

She smiled at that as I crawled up and settled between her thighs. Bending her knees, she put her wet heat right next to the tip of my dick. I reached down and lined myself up then thrust forward, and went...nowhere.

"*Holy fuck!*" I groaned. "You're so tight."

I pressed forward and slowly slid inside. It was the most exquisite kind of torture.

"You feel so good," I panted as I slipped in, inch by slow inch, giving her body time to adjust.

She shifted her ass down, pulling me in a little farther. That put me in far enough that I could move back out then forward again with a slow thrust. Over and over, in and out I moved, going in a little more each time. Nori arched her back and wrapped her leg around my waist, pulling me in balls deep.

I don't want to hurt her and if I start thrusting the way I want to, I can't guarantee that I won't.

Wrapping my arm around her waist, I said, "Hold on."

She tightened her grip on my neck and stayed with me as I flipped us over so she was on top. We both groaned when she slid down onto me and rested against my pelvis.

"Oh God, Trey. It's so good." She sat up straight, looked down at me, and rocked back and forth. "So good."

"Nori." I didn't even recognize my own voice when I said her name. It sounds harsh and hoarse and desperate.

She placed her hands on my chest and leaned forward slightly as she moved back and forth, faster and faster. I groaned as her inner walls fluttered and tightened against me. Her breasts bobbed up and down with her every thrust and I reached up and pinched her nipples between my thumb and index finger, then tugged, using her momentum to add to the sensation.

"Trey...that feels...I'm gonna..."

Her thrusts became more and more frantic and I moved my hands to her hips holding her against me, letting her take what she needed.

"Nori, I can't..."

I fought to hold on, but it just felt too damn good. My balls tightened and I sucked in then blew out huge breaths of air, trying to hold off the inevitable. And then I felt it. Nori quivered around me as her orgasm built. She let out a long groan and I saw the look of pure bliss on her face just before her inner muscles clamped around me then squeezed and I let go and came so hard, I saw double.

Chapter Twenty-One

NORI

I COLLAPSED onto Trey's chest, trying to catch my breath. I've never experienced anything like that in my life. Even now, tiny aftershocks have me clenching around his cock that's still semi-hard inside me. Trey's heart pounded against my ear and his hands still gripped my ass.

We stayed like that until his heartrate slowed and my breathing returned to normal. Trey trailed his hand up and down my back in long, soothing strokes and I love the feel of his touch. But now that I'm coming down from my orgasmic high, my legs are starting to cramp. I shifted a little bit, trying to get more comfortable.

Trey kissed the top of my head and moved his hands to my waist.

"I'm gonna roll us over so I can go take care of this and you can stretch your legs."

He shifted us onto our sides and gave me a quick kiss and pulled back, then leaned in and kissed me again, this time a little longer. Before things could heat up too much, he pulled back, flashed an adorable smile, and shook his head.

"I'll be right back."

I appreciated the sight of his ass as he walked to the bathroom. Once he disappeared inside and closed the door behind him, I rolled onto my back, reached my arms up over my head, straightened my legs out, and stretched. It's been a long time since some of my muscles got a workout like that and I know I'll be feeling it tomorrow. But it was definitely worth it.

Feeling the loss of his warmth, I moved under the covers. The bathroom door opened and Trey walked back to the bed just as I settled against the pillows. And I gotta say, watching him move toward me is an even better sight than when he walked away.

He slipped under the covers and settled his head on the pillow next to me. His bourbon eyes skimmed down my body before meeting mine.

"Are you okay?" I blinked then frowned. "I didn't hurt you, did I?"

I have no idea why that made me laugh, but it did. And not just a small chuckle, but a full belly laugh.

"Hopefully that's a no."

He raised his voice slightly on the last word turning his sentence into a question.

"I'm sorry. No, you didn't hurt me." I nibbled at my bottom lip and looked up at him. "I thought what just happened was pretty amazing."

Trey's mouth curled into a slow, sexy smile.

"Yeah, it was." He rested his hand against my lower back and pulled me closer. "You're pretty amazing." That's not what I was expecting him to say and I had no idea how to respond so I just blinked. "Don't look so surprised."

"I am surprised." I shook my head and shifted my gaze to his chest. "This whole thing…you...us...it's all surprising to me."

"Why?"

I looked into his eyes again.

"When we first met, I just assumed you were a certain kind of person, but you're not. And it's equal measures refreshing and surprising."

"Oh, what kind of person did you think I was?"

He asked the question in a playful tone, but I felt his muscles turn to steel under my hand.

"Like just about every guy I graduated high school with, cocky and entitled."

Something flashed in his eyes, embarrassment maybe? Regret? From what I saw online, it seems like Trey was exactly that way when he lived in New York. Or at least that's how he acted. The fact that Leo is his best friend tells me that deep down, Trey was always a good person. He's only now letting people see that.

He shifted onto his back and pulled me close. I wrapped my arm around his waist and rested my head against his shoulder.

"I'd be lying if I said that's not me. I mean, it's the way I've always been."

I tilted my head back and looked at him.

"But you're not like that now."

Trey stared straight ahead and I watched a muscle in his jaw tick as he clenched his teeth. His eyes stayed locked on the ceiling as he spoke.

"I told you how my life kind of got out of control last year, but honestly that was just the way I lived. For some reason, it just caught up to me at that point in time." He turned his head and met my gaze. "I'm trying to change, but I'll admit my first instinct is usually to be the prick I was my entire life."

Moving back, I rested my fist against his chest, propped my chin on it, and waited for him to look at me. It took a few seconds, but he finally shifted his eyes in my direction.

"If that were true, you wouldn't have let me share your ride to begin with."

"I only agreed to share the ride because that driver kept talking and asking me questions and I hoped another person in the car would take his attention off me."

"Really? You seriously thought some other random person was going to shift the driver's attention off you? The man was a die-hard baseball fan so unless, I don't know…" I trailed off, then named the only really famous, living player that came to mind. "Derek Jeter got into the car, it stands to reason, he'd still pay attention to you."

The corners of his mouth kicked up in a self-deprecating smile.

"It seemed like a good idea at the time."

"It also doesn't explain why you asked me about my art, then took my card."

"At first, I asked because you caught me staring at you," he said around a chuckle.

"And if I'd caught you staring say a year ago, would you have cared?"

He looked at the ceiling again and tilted his head from side to side.

"Probably not."

I raised up on my elbow so I could fully face him.

"Trey, I don't know who you were before, but I like who you are now. And I really hope to get to know you a lot better."

TREY

IT'S amazing how such a tiny woman could pack such a big punch to my heart. From the moment I saw her, I knew she was different. There was just something that drew me in, even though I fought against it.

"I appreciate your faith in me and I'm hoping to get to know you a lot better, too," I said. Reaching out, I tucked a strand of hair behind her ear and stroked her cheek with my thumb. "My schedule during the season is crazy but, if you're willing to work with me, I think we'll be able to manage some quality time together."

She settled back against my shoulder and rested her arm on my stomach. I kissed the top of her head and pulled her tighter against me.

"I think we'll be able to work something out," she said. "I know you're going somewhere tomorrow but I haven't looked at the schedule to see where or how long you'll be gone."

"I'm going to Tampa tomorrow. I'm there for three days then go to Houston for three more. Then there's an off day for travel to Milwaukee and I'm there for four days before coming back here for a ten-day stretch."

"Your schedule is so exhausting. How do you handle it?"

"Besides all the travel, it's been pretty easy for me because I don't have a family or people I've missed while I'm on the road. Until now." I felt her smile against my chest. "I love what I do and the crazy schedule is part of the game."

She made a humming sound but didn't say anything else. I felt her warm breath against my chest as her breathing slowed and became more steady. Instead of fixating on all the doubts trying to invade my brain, I decided to just enjoy the moment.

I'm actually kind of surprised at how comfortable I am with her in my bed. After the sex, I mean. This kind of intimacy isn't something I know anything about, but I think I'm willing to learn for Nori.

She shifted closer and slid her leg over mine, settling into place with a sleepy murmur. I love her sexy little sounds and look forward to hearing more of them.

I closed my eyes and relaxed against my pillow. I just dozed off when Nori jumped up and startled me awake.

"What time is it?"

"I don't know," I said, looking around half-dazed, trying to blink the clock into focus. "It's ten after eleven. Why?"

The blanket fell to her waist when she sat up and she grabbed it and pulled it back up, but not before I caught sight of her perfect breasts and rosebud nipples.

"I should get going."

"Why?" I asked again, rubbing my eyes, still only half awake.

"Because."

I chuckled. "That's not much of a reason."

"Trey." She dragged out my name with an exasperated sigh.

I shifted up to sit back against the headboard.

"I was hoping you'd stay.'"

"But you're going tomorrow."

"Not until noon. Maybe we can have breakfast, then I'll drop you off?" Then I realized that even though I'm free in the morning, maybe she's not. "Unless you have to be somewhere."

"No, I don't have any appointments tomorrow."

"So will you stay?"

"If you're sure."

I took her hand in mine and kissed her fingertips.

"I'm positive."

"Okay." She offered a shy smile. "But I should let Crispin know I won't be home."

"I'll go grab your purse."

I got out of bed and walked into the living room and grabbed her purse from the coffee table. Her eyes never left me as I walked back toward her. Resting my knee on the bed, I leaned forward and kissed her.

"Keep looking at me like that and I won't be responsible for my actions."

After handing her the purse, I slid under the covers and settled back into my pillow.

She pulled out her cell then her thumbs flew across the screen. A few seconds later, it

dinged and after she read Crispin's response, she smiled and shook her head, then texted again before tucking the phone back into her purse. After setting the bag on the bedside table, she turned to face me.

"Everything okay?"

"Yeah, Crispin is just being his usual self."

I shifted onto my side and held out my arm.

"Come here."

She turned and settled back against me. I wrapped my arm around her waist and curved my body around hers, big spoon to her little one. At first she held her body a little stiff but slowly relaxed against me. I rested my head right behind hers, breathing in her sweet, cinnamon scent and drifted off to sleep, feeling more at peace than I've been in my entire life.

Chapter Twenty-Two

NORI

I PUT the finishing touches on the gigantic tiger I've been working on for most of the day and moved back to check my work. Reaching down, I grabbed the brush out of the white paint and climbed the ladder to add a little more contrast toward the top. I leaned back as far as I could without falling off the ladder and was satisfied with the change. Those few streaks of white added the pop that was missing. I stepped down off the ladder and pulled the rag from my back pocket and wiped the paint from the brush.

I'm spending three days in Fayetteville covering the walls in the Cooper's newly-finished basement with all things Clemson University. Yesterday I painted the base coast and sketched out most of the design. So far today I painted the outline of the stadium and the entire tiger.

Right now I need a break, but may work a little more later if my hands, arms, and shoulders aren't too tired. If not, I'll start again fresh tomorrow.

The Coopers went to Orlando for a long weekend, leaving me alone to complete the project. Their home is beautiful and it certainly isn't a hardship to be here for any length of time. I do feel guilty about leaving Crispin alone with Eloise, but this project was booked before she decided to make her surprise visit.

As I suspected, she hasn't been spending her time down here wisely. Crispin and I have tried to help her figure out a plan...both alone and together...but it's no use. She just doesn't get it and I honestly don't think she ever will.

Eloise has "friends" everywhere and she's spent quite a bit of time here with her local gang. Besides that, she's been shopping. The office is now filled with bags and boxes she's accumulated during her time here. All bought with the credit card our father pays for. At this point, if she's not going to change her ways, I really wish she'd just go back to New York. But of course, I'd never come out and tell her that.

After cleaning my brushes and putting the lids back on all the paint, I decided to take a quick shower. Stepping under the spray, I put my head back and shivered as the cold water cascaded down my body. Even though the basement is air conditioned, I worked up a sweat today and it feels good to cool off.

I turned the lever toward hot and warmed up the water then washed my hair. Thoughts of Eloise filled my head as I washed the last of the paint off my hands and forearms. I'd always hoped we'd be closer but that doesn't seem to be in the cards. We're just too fundamentally different. I suppose the best I can hope for is that we'll be friendly.

At least that sounds better than what Trey has going on with his brother. I never felt like I was in competition with Clay and Eloise. My stepmother wasn't thrilled that I lived with them, but thankfully I didn't live in a total *Cinderella* situation or anything. She just treated me like an unwelcome guest instead of as part of the family.

My stomach growled, reminding me I worked through lunch and now it's dinnertime. I turned off the water then grabbed the towel from the rack and quickly dried off before wrapping it around my chest. Stepping out of the shower, I stood in front of the vanity and brushed my hair. Leaning closer to the mirror, I looked at the blonde roots peeking through at my part. I need to decide what I'm doing with my hair before it gets any worse.

As silly as it was, the thing that put the final nail in the coffin of my relationship with Baxter was the pale pink streaks I put in my hair. Despite the fact that he always told me he loved my artistic vibe, he found it embarrassing when I actually expressed myself creatively.

After we broke up and I moved down here with Crispin, I told him I needed a change and had him cut my shoulder-length hair into a pixie cut and dyed it all bright pink.

Funny enough, the new hairstyle seemed to help my career. Apparently people like the artist painting their walls to have a funky look. Crispin says it's because I started giving off a kick-ass vibe once I changed my hair and it draws people in. Whatever the reason, I'm just happy business is getting more steady.

I slipped into a cami and a pair of shorts then went downstairs to figure out what to order for dinner. Lisa left a bunch of takeout menus on the kitchen counter for me and I flipped through the stack and decided to order pizza. That way, I'll have leftovers for breakfast and lunch tomorrow. I also added an order of boneless wing bites so my order meets the minimum requirement for delivery.

Since it will be about an hour before the food gets here, I grabbed my laptop and headed down to the basement.

Settling onto the oversized chair across from my mural wall, I studied the part of the design I completed so far.

I like it.

The tiger is such a vibrant color and the shading I added has given it a 3D effect that's pretty powerful. I'm really excited to see what it will look like when it's all finished.

I propped my feet on the ottoman and pulled my computer onto my lap. Just as it booted up, my cell rang. I smiled when I saw Trey's name flash on the screen and swiped to answer the call.

"Hi."

"Hey," he said. "Am I catching you at a good time?"

"Yeah, I'm either taking a break or quitting for the night. I haven't decided yet."

"How's it coming along?"

"I was just sitting here critiquing it."

"And?"

"I like what I've done so far."

"Can I see? Or are you one of those artists who doesn't share their work until it's totally done?"

"I can text you a picture."

"I have a better idea," he said. "Let me call you right back."

The call disconnected and a few seconds later he called through FaceTime. I swiped to answer and Trey's smiling face filled my screen.

"Hello again."

"Now I can not only see your mural, I get to see your beautiful face, too."

"And I can see yours."

"I definitely have the better end of that deal."

"That's a matter of opinion," I said. "So how's Milwaukee?"

Trey pitched a winning game yesterday in Houston and today is the team's day off to travel to Wisconsin. He won't be pitching again until they get home and Crispin and I plan on going to that game.

"It's Milwaukee." He chuckled.

"Do you have plans for tonight?"

"Just dinner with some of the guys. Nothing crazy. How about you?"

"I ordered a pizza and wing bites. They should be delivered in about an hour. And like I said, I may or may not paint some more. It depends on how my hands feel."

"Speaking of painting, let me see what you're working on."

I turned the phone and directed it at the wall across from me.

"Can you see it?"

"Holy hell, Nori. That looks amazing through the phone. I can't imagine what it looks like in person."

I turned the phone back around so I could see his face.

"Thanks. I'm happy with it so far. I really love that orange. It's one of my favorite colors."

"You really are great at what you do."

I felt my face heat at his compliment.

"Ditto."

We sat there staring at each other through the small phone screen. He looks as good, and definitely more relaxed, than when I first met him. Part of that is due to his longer hair with less product and the light stubble covering his jaw. But there's also something in his eyes that's more welcoming and less cynical.

"Speaking of what I do, are you and Crispin still planning on coming to the game Friday night?"

I nodded. "Crispin works until seven so we probably

won't make it for the first pitch, but we'll be there as soon as we can."

"I really can't wait to see you."

"You're seeing me right now."

"I'd like to be within touching distance."

His words were relatively innocent, but said in that intimate tone and paired with his sexy smirk, my body reacted. Before the other night, it had been two years since I had sex and I didn't even miss it, which totally boggled Crispin's mind. But after spending one night with Trey, it's like a switch was flipped on my libido. After we had sex that first time, we did it again in the middle of the night, and in the shower the next morning.

And then he left.

Thankfully I've been busy or I probably would have driven to Tampa or Houston, or even Milwaukee to get a fix.

"What time will you be home Thursday?"

"Late."

I kind of already knew that, but had hoped he'd give a different answer.

"So I guess I won't see you, within touching distance, until after the game Friday."

"Maybe we could get together Friday morning or early afternoon if you're not doing anything."

"I have two meetings and one is a follow-up where we'll be deciding on colors, so that will probably be a couple hours."

"So the in-person stuff will have to wait until after the game. It'll give me something to look forward to." His phone made a noise and he shifted his eyes down then back up to me. "The guys are ready to go."

"Oh, okay."

"I'll call you tomorrow after the game."

"Sounds good." I smiled at him, way too pleased with his words. "Have fun at dinner."

"Enjoy your pizza."

We stared at each other for a few heartbeats before I heard a noise in the background. He turned his head toward the door and yelled "I'll be right there" then looked back at me.

"I'll talk to you tomorrow. Sweet dreams."

With one final smile, his image disappeared from my screen.

I rested the phone against my chest.

Plans for Friday night and a promise he'll call tomorrow?

It seems I've stumbled into a relationship with Trey Youngman.

TREY

I FINISHED my water and looked around the table. If you'd told me a few weeks ago that I'd be regularly spending time with these guys—or any of the Waves besides Leo for that matter—off the field, I wouldn't have believed it. But these outings have become the norm more than the exception during the past couple road trips and I really enjoy them.

There were guys I hung with on the road when I played for New York, but it was different. I never felt like I belonged, like I do here. Although I'll admit, a lot of that was probably my own fault.

Other than Leo and me, these guys are all either

married or in Rusty's case engaged, which is what the conversation is about at the moment.

"We figured Ivy dumped you since she hasn't been around," Jack said.

"No, my mom is all about us getting married sooner rather than later and they've been huddled up at the house in the Keys getting a plan together."

"Will Finn be the best man?"

Dan asked the question with a smirk so I figured there's an inside joke there somewhere. I have no idea who Finn is and before I had to decide if I was going to ask or not, Leo filled me in.

"Rusty's fiancée has an Irish Setter named Finnegan. He's the coolest dog you'll ever meet."

"I'm sure Finn will be in the wedding somehow," Rusty said around a chuckle.

"It's like there's something in the water at First Allegiant Bank Park," Leo said to me. "There've been a bunch of weddings the past few years."

"Dan started it," Jack said, pointing to his best friend.

"Guilty. And I agree, there must be something because no one ever thought this guy would settle down." Dan pointed back at Jack.

"I won't even argue with you on that because I was one of the people who thought that," Jack said. "But when it happens, you can't fight it."

"And yet you did," Dan said.

Jack punched him in the arm then looked across the table.

"But now I pass on my hard-won knowledge to those smart enough to listen. Like Monte and Rusty over there."

"Hey, I never fought things with Karen. She's the one who needed convincing to give us a chance." Jack raised his brow and smirked. "Keep your comments to yourself, Reagan."

Jack laughed and saluted Monte with his beer then finished it in one long chug.

"At first Ivy was a little reluctant to get involved because of our parents." Rusty looked at me and added, "My mom and her dad are married. When Ivy and I got involved, they were dating so it's not like we were raised together or anything. In fact, we barely knew each other."

"Tell them *how* you ended up getting together," Dan said.

"My game was in the shitter and I decided to get away for All-Star week since you know, I wasn't involved in the all-star activities since I sucked. Sam, my now step-father, told me I could stay at his house in the Keys. Ivy was also looking for somewhere to hide out for a few days so without telling anyone, she and Finn drove down to stay at the house. Once she realized it was occupied, she was going to leave but a hurricane hit. So we were stuck there together for a few days." He smiled. "And that's all it took."

Leo looked at me.

"That's as good as your story with Nori."

"I didn't know you were involved with someone," Rusty said.

"It's *very* new," I said.

"So how'd you meet?" Jack asked.

This is not the type of conversation I've ever had with any of my teammates, but it's actually kind of nice getting to know the guys beyond what they do on the field. Which is the only way I knew all my other teammates, besides Leo and some guys we played with in college.

"When I got called up, I ended up taking a ride share from Fayetteville to the stadium. Nori's car broke down and she was looking for a ride to Myrtle Beach, too. The driver asked if I'd mind sharing the ride with her. I didn't realize the driver gave me her computer bag when I got out and ended up returning it to her a couple days later." I shrugged. "One thing led to another."

To take the spotlight off me, I asked about how the other guys met their significant others. I already knew how Jack and Hannah got together and just heard about the start of Rusty's relationship. Dan and his wife had been involved in college and years later, he wanted her back and hired her to be his live-in physical therapist after an injury.

Jack met Monte's stepson at a benefit he attended then invited him and his mom to a game. Apparently it was love at first sight for Monte and two years later, he finally convinced her to give him a chance. They got married last year, so I guess it all worked out.

Since Leo has been busting my ass about Nori since he first heard about her, I decided to put him in the hot seat. All these guys are in long-term relationships and seem to be of the mind that everyone should be.

"And what about you, Leo? What's your relationship status?"

"I'm fine being single, thank you very much."

Jack snorted. "Famous last words."

I can't argue with that. Just a couple months ago, I didn't think I wanted a relationship, yet here I am in one with Nori and missing her like hell.

And I wouldn't want it any other way.

Chapter Twenty-Three

NORI

THE STADIUM IS PACKED TONIGHT, but according to Crispin, that's normal when Boston or New York are in town. Tonight it's the former. We didn't get here until the middle of the third inning, but from what I heard the woman in front of me say, the game has been moving fast.

According to Crispin, Trey is doing well. I have no clue how he can tell that from the myriad of numbers on the scoreboard, but I'll take his word for it.

The Waves hitters got out pretty quickly so I didn't have to wait long to see Trey. My eyes drank him in as he walked out to the mound and started throwing warm-up pitches. I always thought he looked good in his uniform, but that's been multiplied by a thousand since I now know what he looks like out of it.

The first batter got up and swung at the first pitch. I almost screamed when he hit a line drive right back at

Trey's head, which he thankfully caught. I have no idea how, but he did.

"I think that took a few years off my life."

"It's fun watching your reactions."

"I'm glad you're enjoying yourself, because half the time I feel like I'm about to have a heart attack watching these games."

Crispin chuckled then wrapped his arm around my shoulders and pulled me to him to give me a kiss on the top of my head.

"Welcome to baseball."

The next batter got into the box and the first pitch was called a strike.

"Wow, Trey is throwing hard tonight," Crispin said. "That one was ninety-five."

They all look fast to me, but what do I know?

The next pitch did something that seemed to defy gravity and the batter took a big swing and missed. Another straight pitch followed that and the umpire called it strike three. The batter looked back at him and seemed to be arguing and the crowd booed.

"That was right on the corner," Crispin said. "And it was harder than the last fast ball, ninety-seven."

"How do you know that?"

"I'm a savant," he said.

"You're something all right."

He directed my attention out to the scoreboard in left field.

"Watch that box in the lower right-hand corner. It'll flash the speed of the pitch."

The next pitch was slower...I saw the number eighty-five in that box...and did that thing where the ball dropped toward home plate. The batter missed it for strike one.

After that, Trey threw two balls. He walked to the back of the mound and took off his hat, then dragged his arm over his forehead and scratched his head before putting his cap back on. I've seen him do it before, usually after he throws a ball. I guess it helps him figure things out.

He reached down and picked up a little bag then dropped it back on the ground.

"What was that?"

"What?"

"That little bag Trey picked up."

"Rosin. It helps with grip."

Whatever it does, it must have worked, because the next pitch was called a strike.

The crowd started cheering and clapping. It got so loud, I have no idea how the guys on the field could concentrate.

Leo ran out to the mound and said something to Trey, who just nodded. Once Leo was back behind the plate, the batter got into the box.

I watched Trey throw the pitch and saw the batter swing sending the ball flying out into the outfield. The thing is, it was too far in for the outfielders to get it and too far out for the infield to catch. Or so it seemed.

Jack Reagan somehow got far enough out onto the grass that he was able to dive and catch the ball. The crowd went wild and Crispin and I joined right in.

Trey looked up at me as he walked toward the dugout. I was still clapping like an idiot and he smiled up at me.

Oh my heart.

Sitting back in my seat, I sucked in a deep breath and let it out slowly. One of the women in front of me shifted in her seat to face me.

"We haven't met yet, but I'm Hannah Reagan." I

shook the hand she held out. "I was going to introduce myself when you got here but figured I'd wait until Trey was off the mound."

"Oh hi, I'm Nori Somers," I said, then introduced her to Crispin. "I guess we have you to thank for these great seats."

She smiled and pushed her glasses back into place with her index finger. The frames are yellow with tiny pale blue flowers. I love the look and told her so.

"Glasses are kind of my thing. I have a huge assortment of frames so don't expect to see these again any time soon," she said around a chuckle. "As for the tickets, you're welcome. If there's anything you need just let me know. More shirts or whatever."

"No, I think I'm good, but thank you. I appreciate it."

The woman next to her had turned to half face us and Hannah introduced her as Sabrina McMullen, Dan's wife.

"It's nice to meet you," she said. "Dan has a lot of good things to say about Trey. I guess they've been hanging out on the road."

Other than Leo, I have no idea who Trey has been hanging around with, but I don't need to share that, so I just smiled and nodded.

Sabrina's eyes shifted to Crispin.

"Crispin Wells," she said. "Don't you own Haven?"

"I do."

"I have an appointment there next week with Franco. One of my patients said he's amazing." She looked up and shook her head. "And trust me, I need all the help I can get. I have no idea what's going on with my hair since my son was born a couple years ago, but I'm seriously ready to shave it off."

Her hair is in a French braid, but I don't see anything

seriously wrong with it. I'm sure whatever is going on, it can be fixed at Crispin's salon.

"No need to take such drastic measures. Although you could totally rock the bald look, your bone structure is perfect," he said with a wink. "But seriously, put yourself in Franco's hands and you'll be golden. He's a hair whisperer."

We alternately chatted and paid attention to the game. I didn't engage as much when Trey was on the mound because, quite honestly, I can't keep my eyes off him and ogling apparently takes all my concentration.

After the sixth inning, the relief pitchers came in, so I could relax a little. There still isn't a score so hopefully the Waves offense does something soon or the game will go into extra innings, and I don't want that to happen. I'm really looking forward to seeing Trey "within touching distance."

"I'd like to tell you the games get easier to watch, but I'd be lying," Sabrina said.

Hannah nodded. "I worked for the Waves for a decade and watched hundreds of games before Jack and I got involved and I was fine. Once we got together, I was a nervous wreck sitting here."

"I've never been a sports fan so this whole thing is new to me. I never understood how people could get so into it, but now I know."

The rest of the game went by as if in slow motion, but it must have actually been pretty fast because only three batters got to the plate for each team in the seventh, eighth, and half of the ninth innings.

Leo was up first in the bottom of the ninth. He got hit on the leg so the Waves had a guy on to start things off. They put in a runner for him because, according to Crispin, he doesn't run fast.

Oskar Marquez was up next and he bunted, getting the runner over to second. That brought Dan McMullen up with one out. After fouling off a bunch of pitches, he hit a ground ball between shortstop and third base that was knocked down in the grass. Jack Reagan was up next and he got hit on the elbow, loading the bases.

After that, Boston changed pitchers. While he warmed up, I looked down and spotted Trey and Leo outside the dugout leaning against the railing. Trey glanced over his shoulder and looked up at me. Even though I couldn't see his mouth, I could tell he was smiling and I smiled back.

"Ouch." Crispin rubbed his bicep.

"What's wrong?"

"I was sitting too close and got singed by all that heat Trey was throwing at you."

I punched his arm, but can't deny it. I'd kind of melted just from that look.

It's been a long road trip. Once this game ends, I have no idea how we're going to make it through dinner without jumping each other. Our conversations have been getting increasingly steamier so we're pretty primed at this point.

The designated hitter Phillip Riddle was up next and he took the first two pitches, which were strikes. Then thankfully, he hit a long fly ball into centerfield, which was far enough out that the pinch runner on third base was able to tag up and score, ending the game with a 1-0 Waves victory.

We said goodbye to Hannah and Sabrina and slowly made our way out of the stadium.

"Look at you, bonding with the other team wives," Crispin said as we finally got into his car and out of the crowd.

"You're such a smartass."

"And that's why you love me," he said. "But seriously,

they were really sweet. And they obviously knew that you and Trey are dating."

"Yeah, I guess they did," I said then looked at him. "What do you think that means?"

"Oh honey, I told you when Trey sent you that big box of Youngman shirts that he was branding you as his. It's the same thing."

Logically I feel like I should rebel against that but honestly it makes every fiber of my being want to shout with joy.

TREY

I FINISHED the last of my fries then wiped my hands with the napkin, crumpled it up, and tossed it on top of my empty plate. Sitting back, I took a drink and listened to the conversation going on between Nori and Leo. They're discussing paint colors for his house in Pennsylvania and backsplash options for the kitchen.

Shifting closer to Nori, I rested my arm across the back of her chair. She looked at me and smiled. I sucked in a sharp breath at the primal wave of possessiveness that flowed through me.

Nori frowned. "Are you okay?"

"Yeah, just moved my arm a weird way."

She seemed to accept that as truth then turned back to Leo and commented on something he'd said. I want to keep this relationship honest, but there's no way I could tell her what had actually startled me. That at that moment, I realized I want her to be mine in every way possible.

I remember seeing a clip from *Fifty Shades of Grey* where

Christian said to Ana, "You're mine." At the time I laughed because not only were the words unthinkable to me, the intensity with which he said them seemed ridiculous.

But now I totally get it.

Somehow, within mere weeks, I've gone from considering Nori to be some sort of anomaly to someone I don't ever want to live without.

"Maybe I'll be able to convince you to take a trip to Pennsylvania to paint a mural for me," Leo said to Nori.

"What design would you want?" she asked.

"I don't know, I'd have to think about it."

"Well when you decide, we'll discuss it."

"Don't think I won't hold you to that. You and Trey can come stay for a few days and he'll give you a tour of our old college town."

She glanced over her shoulder and smiled at me.

"That'd be fun."

The waitress approached to see if we needed anything else.

Since we were all done eating, I spoke for everyone and said, "No, just the check."

She told me she'd bring it right over and cleared some empty plates before leaving.

Leo looked over at me with a smartass smirk and I shot him a warning look. I don't care if he busts me when it's just us, but I don't want him embarrassing Nori. The fact that he knows I care makes him smile even bigger.

The waitress returned with the check and I handed her my credit card without even looking at the total. I'd told Nori I wanted to be within touching distance, but now that I am, it's not enough. I really need to be alone with her.

After I added a tip and signed my name to the receipt, I looked at Nori.

"You ready to go?"

She looked around the semi-cleared table, over at Crispin and Leo, then at me.

"Yeah sure."

We both stood and said our goodbyes and I rested my hand against the small of her back as she walked out of the restaurant ahead of me. I opened the passenger door for her and she got into the SUV and was clicking her seatbelt into place as I settled behind the wheel.

More than anything, I want to kiss her, but I'm afraid if I do, I won't be able to stop. So instead, I started the car and pulled out of the lot. I'd just merged onto the highway when I realized I never asked her if she wanted to go back to the hotel with me. I just assumed she would, and you know what happens when you assume.

"I was heading to my hotel, but I can take you home if you'd rather."

From the corner of my eye, I saw her turn her head to look at me.

"No, I wouldn't rather."

I glanced over at her and nearly ran off the road when I saw the heat in her eyes. My knuckles turned white as I gripped the steering wheel and fought the urge to push the gas pedal to the floor.

It felt like hours later that I saw the sign for our exit, but it couldn't have been more than ten minutes. The air in the car is so charged with sexual tension, it's amazing the windows aren't fogged.

I veered off the highway and took the few turns that led me into the lot of the hotel then pulled into a parking spot. Nori met me at the front of the car and I grabbed her hand as we took the few steps to the side door. After three attempts, I finally got my card to swipe correctly and opened the door.

We stepped into the elevator and before the doors even closed, I had Nori pinned up against the wall with my mouth covering hers. Moving my hands down to cup her ass, I lifted her and she wrapped her legs around my waist. I groaned against her mouth as my erection settled against her hot core.

Our mouths opened and closed over each other as we each fought for dominance of the kiss. Her fingers dug into my shoulders as she pulled me closer and met my tongue stroke for stroke.

I could have gone on feasting on her mouth forever but I felt the elevator stop and ended the kiss with a gentle nip of her lower lip. As the doors opened, I stepped back and pulled her into my arms then let her slide down my body and didn't let her go until her feet were firmly on the floor.

We walked at a surprisingly controlled pace down the hallway to my door, which I managed to open with just one card swipe. Nori walked into the room ahead of me then let out a screech when I bent down and tossed her over my shoulder fireman style.

I carried her through the living room and into the bedroom. She'd been clutching my shirt so when I tossed her onto the bed, she dragged it halfway over my head. I tugged it the rest of the way off and launched it behind me.

Crawling between her widespread thighs I kissed my way up her stomach and grabbed the hem of her shirt then pulled it up over her head. Tangling the material around her wrists, I trapped her hands together and pushed her arms against the bed.

Nori blinked up at me with wide eyes but her flared nostrils and the sexy little nibble she gave her bottom lip let me know she's as into this as I am. Thank fuck because stopping right now just might be the end of me.

I licked at her lip until she released it then took it between my teeth and gently tugged before slowly letting it go to smile down at her.

"I don't have to be at the stadium until three o'clock tomorrow and I intend to spend as much time as possible between now and then driving you wild."

Chapter Twenty-Four

NORI

I FELT a rush of moisture between my thighs and attempted to squeeze them together to ease the sweet ache his words had created. But since the man in question wedged himself between them, all I did was squeeze him tighter against me. Not that I'm complaining.

After letting my bottom lip go—and seriously, who knew having your bottom lip nibbled was so hot?—Trey kissed his way down my neck. His lips, teeth, and tongue found every sensitive spot along the way and when he licked and nipped at the pulse beating wildly at the base of my throat, the sound I let out was a cross between a whimper and a groan.

His low, sexy chuckle sent warm breath across my bare chest, leaving goosebumps in its wake.

"What do we have here?"

Taking the edge of my bra cup in his teeth, he pulled it

down to expose my hard nipple, the cool air making it tighten even further. His tongue gave it a few quick licks before he opened his mouth over my breast and sucked. My hips bucked off the bed and I looped my still-bound hands around his neck.

He kissed his way across my chest to the other side and gave it the same treatment. With both bra cups pulled down, my breasts were pushed up against each other, as if they were offering themselves up for him to feast on. And feast he did. He moved back and forth licking, nibbling, and sucking, driving me wild.

I whimpered and writhed against him but his hips kept me pinned to the mattress so I couldn't get any real relief. He opened his mouth over me and repeatedly dragged the flat of his tongue over my nipple as he sucked.

"Oh my God." Those three syllables came out as breathless pants.

Trey pulled back, the motion ripping the shirt off my wrists, freeing them. He reached behind me and unhooked my bra then tossed it aside. Scooting back, he unbuttoned my shorts and dragged them and my panties down my legs.

I watched his eyes focus on my pussy before skimming up my body to meet my gaze. The right corner of his mouth kicked up as he settled back between my thighs. Not breaking eye contact, he dragged his tongue along my slit, flicking it against my clit before he opened his mouth over me and sucked.

He placed his hand on my stomach to hold me in place when I tried to buck my hips off the bed. I dropped my hands to the mattress and gripped the sheet tight with my fists.

I thought he'd feasted on my breasts, but that was nothing compared to what he's doing down south. I shamelessly spread my legs wider and let my knees fall to the side giving him better access. Which he took full advantage of.

He slipped one finger, then two inside me and pumped in and out, in and out, in and out. I tightened my grip on the sheets when he curled his fingers and stroked me inside while his tongue worked its magic on my clit.

"Mmm Trey. That feels so good," I said, drawing out each word.

With his dark golden eyes watching me over the expanse of my body, he quickened his pace, obviously on a mission to make me lose my mind. Which was going to happen any minute.

The pressure of his fingers increased as he alternately licked and sucked my clit.

I released my hold on the sheet and dug my fingers into his hair.

"Right there," I panted. "Oh God, Trey. Right *there.*"

That last word was said on a long, low moan as my entire body tingled and my inner muscles spasmed against his fingers. His movements became slower and more soothing until the very last wave crashed through me then receded.

I let go of his hair as he pulled back and slowly slid his fingers out. He squeezed my hip, trailing wetness along my skin. It amazes me how wet I get for him.

He kissed my belly and as if he read my thoughts said, "I love how wet you get for me. It's so fucking hot."

My face heated at his words but before I could dwell on them, he pulled away and unbuttoned his jeans, then pushed them down his legs. His boxer briefs quickly followed and I licked my lips as his erection bobbed against his stomach.

I've never been a huge fan of giving blow jobs, but right now, there's nothing I want to do more than wrap my mouth around his cock. As he turned to retrieve the box of condoms from the nightstand, I shifted to my knees and crawled to the edge of the bed. He looked down at me as I reached out and wrapped my hand around his erection.

Granted, I'm a small person with proportionate hands, but he is large. This *job* is going to be a challenge, but I'll give it my best shot.

Trey's nostrils flared as he watched me move my hand up and down his length. I heard his breathing increase as I squeezed tighter and stroked faster. Leaning forward, I shifted my hand down his shaft and wrapped my mouth around his plump head. He sucked in a sharp breath as I moved down until my lips touched my fist then pulled back and repeated the motion over and over.

Trey's fingers tightened in my hair and I continued my ministrations, my mouth and hand working together to hopefully give him as much pleasure as he'd just given me. Squeezing the base of his penis, I pulled my mouth back but before I released him, I alternately swirled my tongue around the tip and sucked.

"Fuck! Nori...fuck..."

Trey dug his fingers into my scalp, but I'm not sure if it was to pull me closer or away. So I kept going. I countered the motion of his pulsing hips and took him as far against my throat as I could before pulling back then doing it again.

His grip on my hair tightened and he pulled me back. I let go of his dick with an audible pop and loosened my fingers one by one.

"You're killing me, you know that?"

His pained smile gave me a sense of achievement. It's

kind of nice driving a man like Trey Youngman to the brink.

I rested back on my elbows with my knees bent. Trey's eyes never left my body as he opened the foil packet then rolled the condom down his very considerable length. He rested his right knee on the bed then shifted forward and down onto me. I wrapped my legs around his waist and he slipped right inside. Our simultaneous groans echoed through the room.

"This isn't gonna take long," he muttered, more to himself than me.

He pulled out then thrust back in, slow and steady. My inner muscles welcomed him then clenched as he retreated, as if they were trying to keep him in place. When I squeezed my legs tighter around him, it shifted my hips and he hit me at a whole new angle.

"Oh God Trey, right there." I said those last two words in a whispered pant as he pumped in and out, faster and faster. "Right there, right there…" I continued to chant as he moved in and out, taking me higher and higher.

I dug my fingers into his shoulders and held on. The tingles started in my clit and then the pleasure burst through the rest of my body as my orgasm ripped through me. He thrust once, twice, three times more, then said my name on a low moan and collapsed on top of me.

TREY

NORI'S sleepy gaze met mine as we rested on our sides facing each other.

"You have the most beautiful eyes. When we first met, I

thought they were contacts, but then noticed how they change." She wrinkled her nose. "What was that for?"

"I almost got contacts to change the color of my eyes."

"Why?"

"When I first went to live with my dad and started at the new school, the kids kind of made fun of them. They said I looked like a cartoon character."

"Well, I like them. They're beautiful." I kissed her forehead. "So don't wrinkle your nose like that again."

"You know, your eyes are pretty spectacular too."

"Why?"

"They're not quite brown and not quite gold. The first time I saw you, they reminded me

of bourbon and I mentally started mixing colors to figure out how to replicate them." She smiled.

"And they're amazing on their own, but in contrast with your dark hair, they look even more spectacular."

I raised my brows and chuckled.

"I think I want another shot at describing your eyes. What you said just blew my compliment out of the water."

"What you said was perfect," she said and snuggled into the pillow.

It's obvious she's tired, but selfish bastard that I am, I don't want this time with her to end. I gestured for her to roll over then pulled her back against my chest.

"Tell me something about yourself."

"What do you want to know?" she asked around a yawn.

"How did you learn to draw? Did you go to school for it?"

Her hair brushed against my chin, getting caught on the stubble as she shook her head.

"My mom was a great artist and I don't remember a

time when I didn't draw. Once she died, it became my refuge, what I'd do to escape my less-than-happy reality."

I kissed the back of her head.

"I'm sorry about your mom and that you had such a tough time after you moved in with your dad."

She snuggled closer against me and I wrapped my arm tighter around her waist.

"I did take art classes in junior high and high school, but never got to follow through on my plans to study it in college."

"Why not?"

"My father felt art school was a waste of money. Why go to school for something you already know how to do?" She shrugged. "We negotiated and I agreed to go to college and major in something practical and minor in art. I went for the first half of the fall semester and when I went home for Thanksgiving break, he freaked out at how I looked. I'd gotten my first tattoo, pierced my ears a few more times, and shaved one side of my head."

Her muscles tensed and I ran my hand up and down her side in long soothing strokes to help her relax again.

"It's funny because I lived with the man for five years before going to college and probably could have walked around in a burlap sack and he wouldn't have noticed. Then when I was a legal adult and not living under his roof anymore, he decides to play daddy." She let out a sarcastic chuckle. "Do I need to tell you I basically told him to go to hell?"

"I'm not surprised."

"I told him I was an adult and could decide for myself how to look and dress. He said that as long as he was paying the bills, he still had a say. So I quit school and moved to Manhattan with Crispin. His family had trouble accepting his lifestyle so after high school he moved to the city with his grandmother who had no issues with it. Thankfully she welcomed me too."

"So you were eighteen and living in the city. What did you do?"

"At first, I did the art in the park thing, drawing caricatures and quick sketches of tourists. But that was no fun in the cold or rain and I wanted more of a steady paycheck, so I got a job at the coffeehouse on the ground floor of our apartment building. Nanny...that's what we called Crispin's grandmother...knew the owner and put in a good word for me. Which I needed because I didn't have any relevant experience."

"And that's how you got your first mural job, right?" She looked back at me, surprised. "Hey, I listen and remember things."

Turning around, she settled back against the pillow.

"What about you? I know you went to college. What was your major?"

"I went to a junior college and have an associate degree in communications."

"Why do you say it like that?"

"Like what?"

"You emphasized the words junior and associate. Like your degree isn't something to be proud of? Like it's not a real education?"

"Just to clarify what I have."

She glanced over her shoulder at me again and raised her brow. I chuckled and shook my head. When I agreed to tell her what she wanted to know, she turned around again.

"I told you about my dyslexia."

"Mmm hmm."

"My grades were never great and my SATs were even worse, so my choices for higher education were pretty much non-existent. My high school coach recommended that I go to a junior college. They're usually easier to get into and a lot of them have stellar baseball programs. I could develop as a player and either go into the draft after graduation or move to a four-year school, as long as I kept my grades at a certain level."

Besides Leo, I've never told anyone this. But if I want this thing between Nori and me to be real, I know I need to share, just like I expect her to.

"When I told my father my plan, he was less than happy. In fact, he was mortified that I wanted to go to a subpar institution. He'd planned on bribing my way into a school he considered appropriate so he didn't embarrass himself when he told his friends and business acquaintances where I was off to. He would have rathered I skipped school all together instead of going to a junior college and just enter the draft, but that would have been a disaster because I really wasn't ready."

"So how'd you end up going?"

"I got a full scholarship. That really pissed him off. He's so used to controlling people with money and didn't know how to react. So he just lashed out more and made nastier comments."

Nori laced her fingers through mine and squeezed.

"I'm glad you stood your ground and went where you wanted to go. And you met Leo there so it was definitely meant to be."

"Yeah, he and his whole family have been pretty great to me."

"And what about your family?"

"What about them?"

"Do you see them at all now?"

"I haven't seen or spoken to them since last year."

"Are you angry with them?"

She barely got the words out before she yawned again.

"That is a story for another day. We both need to get some rest."

I kissed the top of her head and pulled her closer against my chest.

"Be prepared to wake up early. I'm not done driving you wild yet."

Chapter Twenty-Five

NORI

I WOKE to the feel of Trey's warm breath on my skin as he trailed soft kisses along my back and shoulders. His hand moved back and forth along my thigh and hip in long, slow strokes adding to the delicious sensation. I moaned deep in my throat, torn between wanting to sleep some more and rolling over to rub against the erection poking against my ass.

Wriggling back against him, I let out a sound that could only be described as a purr. I opened my eyes and looked around the dark room and have no idea what time it is. It had looked exactly the same when Trey woke me in what I believe was the middle of the night with his wandering hands and we ended up making slow, sweet love.

"Good morning."

His scratchy morning voice vibrated against my ear sounding even sexier than usual.

"Is it morning?"

I felt him nod as he nibbled the side of my neck.

"It's just before ten."

"Ten?" I was about to get up but he licked at a particularly sensitive spot so I stayed put. "It's been years since I slept this late."

"Really?"

"Mmm Hmm. When I worked at the coffee shop in New York, I had to be there every morning at four to open for five and I got used to getting up early. Now my idea of sleeping in is eight."

"Then you must have been really tired."

He sounded proud of himself. And what can I say? He should be.

"I honestly don't know how you're so…" I pushed my ass against his hard cock. "Awake."

It's amazing how just his low sexy chuckle made my core clench and throb. As if he sensed that fact, Trey slipped his hand between my thighs and let his middle finger glide along the tiny bundle of nerves. I let out a low groan and shifted my leg back and over his hip to give him better access.

He stroked, flicked, and pinched my clit, until I just kept chanting his name followed by the word please. I'm not sure if I was begging him to stop, keep going, or increase the pressure. Thankfully, he knew exactly what I needed.

Tightening his arm around me, Trey slipped two fingers inside and stroked while his thumb alternately pressed against and circled my clit. It didn't take long before I felt the familiar tingles start deep inside then radiate through every erogenous zone in my body.

My pussy clenched with aftershocks as Trey removed his fingers. Cool air swept along my sweaty skin as he moved away from me. I was about to pull the covers over my shoulders when he was back in place.

He placed his hand on my knee and pulled it back higher on his leg. I felt the tip of his cock and shifted my hips to line him up against me. I'm so wet that when he pushed forward, he slipped right in, filling me completely in one long stroke.

"Mmm, you feel so good."

His warm breath whirled against my ear and my nipples tightened in response.

Trey pumped in and out, slow at first, before picking up the pace. I tightened my leg against his hip, pulling him closer. He slid his hand along my stomach and squeezed my breast before flicking his thumb against my nipple in time with his thrusts.

"Oh God Trey. That feels…Uh…"

I lost the ability to speak as he moved faster still and pinched my nipple between his thumb and forefinger and pulled, sending a zing right down to my core. My orgasm slammed through me and I clenched around him, squeezing tight while he plunged into me over and over before finding his own release.

He wrapped his arm around my waist and rested his head against my shoulder. As I caught my breath, I smiled in the dark room. I could get used to waking up like this every day.

It's funny, I was with Baxter for two years and never felt this comfortable with him. Being with Trey is just easy. And the more time I spend with him, the more I like him. Maybe even more than like him.

"You okay?" he asked before I could obsess about that last thought too much.

I looked over my shoulder at him and smiled.

"Do you even need to ask me that?"

"I just want to make sure I didn't hurt you." He hesitated for a second before adding, "Please don't get mad when I say this, but you're so tiny. Sometimes I worry that I'm being too rough."

"You're not."

"You'll let me know if I ever am, right?"

"I will."

"Good." He kissed me again. "So now that that's settled, I was thinking we could maybe grab some lunch before I drop you off and head to the stadium."

"That sounds good."

He rolled onto his back and I turned over and watched him reach out and grab a handful of tissues from the nightstand. After removing the condom, he sat on the edge of the bed and shifted to look down at me.

The corners of his mouth curled up and he tucked my hair behind my ear then stroked his thumb down my jaw.

"You look beautiful."

Since I never took my makeup off last night, I imagine I look like a raccoon with bed head, but he looked so sincere, I didn't mention it. Instead I just smiled and said, "Thank you."

"You can shower first while I shave." He leaned down and kissed my forehead before standing and smiling down at me. "I had quite a workout in the past twelve hours and I'm starving."

He winked then turned and walked toward the bathroom.

My stomach tightened and I'd like to chalk it up to being hungry too, but I know it has nothing to do with food and everything to do with the sexy, naked man walking across the room.

TREY

NORI SUGGESTED a local place with a deck overlooking the water. It's a hot day, but the ocean breeze makes it comfortable to sit outside, especially with the table umbrella keeping us shaded from the noon sun.

After we ordered, I figured it was time for another getting-to-know-you session. It's true, I know more about her than any other woman I've spent time with, but I want to know everything.

"So you mentioned the coffee shop this morning. I know you worked there and had your mural business in Manhattan. What made you move down here and start over?"

Nori looked at her glass, seeming fascinated with her index finger as she dragged it through the condensation. I didn't think she was going to answer and was surprised when she met my gaze and started to speak.

"Crispin moved down here about five years ago after Nanny died. It started out as an extended vacation then he decided he liked it and wanted to stay. I'm sure the fact that he met a guy and things between them got hot and heavy pretty fast had something to do with that. Also, he wanted to open a spa and the inheritance his grandmother left him offered more options here than in New York. He bought his house and started the business and still had some left over. Obviously that wouldn't happen in Manhattan."

I nodded when she paused, encouraging her to continue. After a quick drink of water, she did.

"He kept bugging me to move down here with him, but he was practically living with the aforementioned guy and

I'd moved in with my then boyfriend after Crispin moved here."

I clenched my jaw at the thought of her with another man then talked myself down from being so ridiculous. We're both in our thirties and obviously have history with other people. Only all my history is shallow. Hers is deep enough that she actually cohabitated with the guy.

"His relationship ended just before mine, about two years ago. The guy wasn't out of the closet and it ended up taking a toll on them." She smiled. "Crispin has been out since junior year in high school so it was difficult for him to get shoved back in, even for short periods of time."

"And what happened with you and your guy?"

I mentally patted myself on the back for asking that in a neutral tone, considering the turmoil churning through me.

"We got engaged, but then I found out he wasn't the guy I thought he was so I called things off. I came down here to commiserate with Crispin and decided to stay."

I wanted to keep the conversation focused on her first sentence.

"What did he do?"

The waitress brought our burger platters and refilled our water glasses then left us alone again. Nori popped a fry into her mouth then chewed and swallowed before answering.

"He was cheating on me, regularly, with multiple women." She shrugged. "The only reason he was with me was for business, specifically my father's business."

I widened my eyes. Her father's company is impressive...definitely not on the same level as Youngman Electronics...but Clay Somers does pretty well for himself. Regardless, it was definitely a dick move on that guy's part.

"I'll admit I thought it was strange when Baxter started

coming into the coffee shop and repeatedly asking me out, but I never imagined the whole thing was orchestrated."

"What do you mean?"

"His dad's company wanted to merge with part of my dad's. Apparently my father thought it would be even better if our families were fully connected and suggested Baxter pursue me. It was his screwed up way to get me back into the family fold." She shook her head. "It was so strange, like something from a soap opera."

I wish I could say I've never heard of something like that happening, but my father has used me as a pawn for his business more than once. Especially after I started playing professional ball.

"At first I turned him down, but eventually he charmed me enough that I agreed to a first date. Since he had inside information about me from my father, Baxter knew all the right things to say and do to pull me in."

Nori took a bite of her burger and looked out at the ocean as she chewed. I wasn't expecting this conversation to get so heavy and was about to tell her we could switch to a lighter topic when she looked at me and started speaking again.

"That's one of the reasons I was so hesitant to go out with you."

"What do you mean?"

"You reminded me of Baxter. Not your looks, but your whole air and appearance was similar."

"Was?"

She ate a fry and nodded as she chewed.

"When I got into that car, everything about you from your perfectly-styled hair to your polished shoes screamed entitled, cocky rich boy. You reminded me of Baxter and every other guy who attended my prep school. And you kept staring at me." I felt my eyes widen at that and she chuckled. "You were trying to hide it, but I felt you watching and figured you were judging me. Once he had me hooked, Baxter found a lot of stuff to be judgy about and that was before the pink hair dye."

"Before I respond to what you said, I have one question."

"What's that?"

"What made you decide to give me a chance?"

She nibbled at her bottom lip and smiled. The combination of the two made her look absolutely adorable.

"My shirt."

"Your *shirt?*"

"The one with *I Arted* on it. Baxter would have been mortified by it, but you not only weren't appalled, you asked where I got it to buy one as a gift."

"Angie loves it by the way."

"What's not to love?" She flashed a sexy smirk. "Now I'm curious to hear what you were really thinking during that car ride."

"To be honest, I was thinking a myriad of things. First, I was trying to figure out how that sexy voice was coming out of someone so small. Then I couldn't stop my mouth from watering because you smelled like cinnamon buns. Which I now know is from your lotion," I added with a smile. "I'll admit that your hair was a bit of a shock at first, but that faded when I noticed your eyes and I tried to figure out if the color was real or from contacts."

"Wow, you sure had a lot going on."

"I really did want to rest during the ride so I closed my eyes, but that didn't stop your scent or the charged air in the car from surrounding me. So I opened my eyes just a fraction and observed you." I chuckled and added, "Obviously not as surreptitiously as I thought."

"And?"

"And mostly I was trying to talk myself out of being attracted to you." Her brows drew together when I said that and I rushed to explain. "You know that I'm working on myself."

She nodded. "When I started down that road, I decided it would be best to do it on my own."

"So what made you change your mind?"

"I couldn't stop thinking about you and it just felt…" I shrugged. "Different."

Reaching over, I took her hand in mine and stroked my thumb along her knuckles. As much as I don't want her to know what a jerk I was, it's important that she does. She needs to know how special this is for me.

"I know it was only a few days, but that's more thought than I ever gave a woman before. So I asked my therapist if he thought it would be okay to pursue this."

"I'm assuming he gave you the green light."

"He said that the fact I was questioning it meant that it was okay."

She squeezed my hand. "Thank you for telling me that."

"Thank you for sharing with me." I pulled her hand to my mouth and brushed my lips across her knuckles before releasing it and leaning back in my seat. "And just so you know, while the pink hair shocked me at first, I kind of like it now. It seems to suit you. And I really do like your shirts. The only thing I like better on you is a Waves shirt with my number on it."

The smile that spread across her face gave me the same rush of feelings that had flooded through me last night when we were making love. I'm in uncharted territory here but it's definitely something I want to explore.

Chapter Twenty-Six

NORI

I FLIPPED the chicken in the grill pan then finished ripping romaine lettuce into a large bowl. Trey left this morning for a ten-day road trip and Crispin has a date after work, so it's just Eloise and me tonight.

For the past few weeks I've been either working or spending time with Trey and she's been hanging out with her friends, so we haven't seen a lot of each other. I'm hoping a girls' night will give us a chance to talk so I can get a clue of what her plans are. She can't stay here forever. Her quirkiness is losing its charm and Crispin is losing his patience. I probably would be too, but I've been in my Trey-induced happiness bubble so it would take a lot to bother me these days.

Just the thought of Trey puts a goofy smile on my face. Something definitely changed between us the other night. When he woke me to make love, it was different, more connected and emotional, and those feelings have remained front and center.

Eloise walked through the door before I could think about that too much. Her arms were loaded with shopping bags and I'm sure there are even more out in the car. Sure enough, she dropped the bags just inside the door, went back outside, and came in with another armful. Instead of taking them to her room, she left everything in a pile right there in the foyer and closed the door behind her.

"What are you making?"

"Grilled chicken Caesar salad."

"It smells good." She walked over to the wine rack and looked over the selection before choosing a Riesling. "Are you drinking wine?"

"Sure."

I turned off the stove, then removed the chicken from the pan and put it on the cutting board.

Eloise pulled two glasses out of the cupboard and set them on the counter. While she uncorked the bottle, I pulled a pan of cheddar biscuits from the oven and brushed them with the garlic butter I had melting on the stove. Once that was done, I removed a knife from the block and sliced the chicken then placed it in the bowl on top of the lettuce. Normally I'd top it with dressing and shaved parmesan cheese and toss, but Eloise limits her intake of pretty much everything, so I figured I'd leave the salad naked and we can each add what we want.

"I thought we'd eat in the living room and we can watch a movie. Maybe *Legally Blonde*?"

"That sounds good. I *love* that movie."

She grabbed the wine bottle and carried it and both glasses into the next room, set them on the coffee table, and sat on the couch. I brought the bowl with the salad and tongs in and set them next to the wine then went back to the kitchen for plates, utensils, and the biscuits.

I settled on the other end of the couch and grabbed the remote off the end table. After starting the movie, I grabbed my glass of wine and took a sip as Eloise picked through the salad, eventually adding some lettuce and chicken to her plate. Then she proceeded to cut them into tiny pieces.

Once she was done, I filled my own plate with salad, topped it with dressing and cheese, then added two biscuits before crossing my legs and relaxing against the back of the couch. I'd finished my salad and biscuits as Warner Huntington III was dumping Elle Woods at dinner and went back for seconds.

Eloise shifted her eyes in my direction and kept watching me as I settled back onto the couch.

"If I ate like you, I'd weigh five hundred pounds."

"I doubt that," I said, then took a bite of my biscuit.

"Seriously, you're so lucky. You eat whatever you want and stay so tiny."

"It's not like you're big."

"Yeah, but I watch every single thing I eat."

"I think that's more by choice than necessity."

"What does that mean?"

"You've been watching what you eat as long as I can remember just like all your friends. I think it's more a habit than anything, or maybe a contest. Like, 'Look how little I can eat and still survive.'"

"I just want to look my best."

"You see yourself in the mirror. You're gorgeous, tall and thin with curves in all the right places and legs up to your neck."

She placed a piece of chicken in her mouth and

chewed for what seemed like forever before she looked at me and tilted her head as she spoke.

"You know, sometimes I wish I was more like you."

"Why?"

"You were eighteen when you told daddy to take his money and shove it. I'm twenty-four and just can't do it. Not yet anyway. Maybe not ever."

Since she brought it up, I ran with it.

"What are your plans? You've been here for a while now and don't seem to be making any."

"I'm thinking about just going back to New York, maybe talking to Garrett again if daddy insists." She shrugged. "I don't think I'm cut out to be on my own."

Eloise placed her fork on the plate and leaned forward to set it on the coffee table. It doesn't look like she ate much, but I'm not going to call her on it.

"You're going to end up marrying a guy you don't want to be with just to make dad happy?"

She rolled her eyes as she shook her head.

"Nori, you just don't get it. I'm not cut out to struggle to support myself, and I don't have a Crispin or a sugar daddy to bail me out."

"What's that supposed to mean?"

"After you left dad, you lived with Crispin. Then you moved in with Baxter. When that ended, you came down here and are living with Crispin again. And now you're with Trey."

I stared at her with my mouth open then blinked.

"Crispin is my best friend. I never planned on living with him but it just worked out for both of us that I did and do. I moved in with Baxter because we planned on getting married and Trey and I are just dating. Please don't refer to them as sugar daddies. I don't like what it implies.

If that was all I wanted from a man, I'd be married to Baxter and still living in Manhattan."

She just shrugged at my words. I thought about saying more but didn't want to sound too defensive.

"Garrett isn't the worst guy in the world. I mean, he's kind of boring, but he has a *lot* of money and worships me. So I could do worse, I guess." She flashed a saucy smirk. "Or maybe Trey has a friend you can hook me up with. A baseball player might be a nice change from all the white-collar guys, especially since they're on the road a lot. It'd give me a lot of me time."

It's too bad my father didn't point Baxter in Eloise's direction instead of mine. She probably wouldn't have had a problem with their little scheme or the fact that he had women all over the city. Considering what she just said, she'd probably be happy she wouldn't have to deal with him full-time.

"But don't you want more than that?"

"I want to live comfortably and if I have a hot guy keeping me in the style I'm used to, that'd be even better." She arched her right brow. "Speaking of hot guys, why have you been hiding yours from me? I only met him one time and that was by mistake. If you didn't have to change that night, you would have opened the door. And yet, Crispin has been in his company multiple times."

"That's because Crispin happened to be here when Trey dropped my laptop off. And he's the one who arranged for us to go to the first game with Leo. You know he's a huge baseball fan."

"I could go to a game."

"*You* want to go to a game?"

"I would if we were going out after like you guys seem to do all the time."

I blew out a breath. There's no way I'd bring Eloise to

a game, she'd drive me crazy. But maybe I could have Trey over here when he gets back. He grew up in a world of women who act just like my sister or even worse so I'm sure he'll be able to handle her.

TREY

NORI and I had just hung up when I heard a knock on my door. I looked out the peephole and was surprised to see Leo standing there. Opening the door, I leaned my arm against it.

"Everything okay?"

"You tell me."

He walked past me and plopped down onto the couch.

"What are you talking about?"

I closed the door and sat in the desk chair across from him.

"You can't be upset about your pitching tonight," Leo said.

"Again I ask, what are you talking about?"

"You barely spoke at dinner and when you're quiet, it usually means you're stewing over something. And all I'm saying is that it can't be your pitching. You were on fire tonight and basically shut their offense down. My hand is still vibrating from your fastballs."

"No, I felt good tonight. Totally focused."

"So why were you so quiet? Something happen with Nori?"

I shook my head.

"No, we're great. In fact, I just got done talking with her." I know he won't stop acting like a mother hen if I don't tell him what he wants to know, so I spilled. "I'm just thinking about New York."

We have three more games here in Boston then head to New York for three. I'll be starting the second day we're there.

"I'm gonna put that first comment on hold for a minute and concentrate on the second. You'll be fine. You've been hitting all your spots and your velocity is steady. It's just another city, just another team."

I snort-laughed at that.

"It's where I crashed and burned last year."

"There aren't many guys who play this game that don't have issues at one time or another. You had some problems, dealt with them, and now you're back. Don't let what happened last year fuck with your head. You know what Yogi said, 'Baseball is ninety percent mental. The other half is physical.' Keep your head straight."

What he's saying makes perfect sense but that doesn't mean the insecurities aren't still there. But instead of dissecting that, I decided to change the subject.

"Weren't you going to meet someone after dinner?" He nodded. "So you left us at the restaurant, hooked up with this woman, and instead of focusing on her, you were thinking about why I was quiet?"

"Not exactly, but yeah."

I looked at the clock.

"Why are you back so early?"

"I don't remember her voice being so annoying." I raised my brow. "It's really high-pitched. I thought my eardrum was going to burst. And she kept doing this fake, staccato laugh. Between that and the voice, I couldn't stand it. So I bought her a couple drinks, put her in a cab, and came back here."

"Bummer."

"It is what it is." He shrugged. "So back to you and Nori."

"She's good. Things are good."

"This is a record for you, isn't it?"

"Pretty much. And you know, I'm kind of liking it."

"I knew she was going to be different the first time you mentioned her."

"You did not."

"Fuck if I didn't and you know it," he said, looking pleased with himself.

"If I'm being honest, I knew she was different too. I just didn't want to admit it."

"Well at least you took your head out of your ass before she got away."

"Every once in a while I get things right."

"But seriously, Nori is great. You're very lucky."

"Yeah, I think I am."

I felt the sappy smile spread across my face and there wasn't a thing I could do to stop it.

Leo's eyes widened.

"Holy shit!"

"What?"

He glanced left then right before looking me right in the eye.

"Are you in love with her?"

For whatever reason, he whispered the question.

"You don't have to whisper. No one else is here."

"Just answer the question."

"I haven't labeled my feelings for Nori as anything other than *different*. But rest assured, once I define it as something more than that, I'll be sure to let you know."

He threw back his head and laughed, then stood.

"I appreciate that. And you might as well copy Crispin

on the message, too. I'm sure he'd like to be kept in the loop."

"You're an ass."

"Yeah, but you'd be lost without me."

I stood and walked behind him and held the door open as he walked out then turned around.

"Don't let New York or your father get into your head. Just keep doing what you're doing and you'll be fine."

I nodded then slapped him on the shoulder.

"See you tomorrow."

Leo waved as he walked down the hallway and I closed the door and flipped the deadbolt.

I got into bed, grabbed the remote off the bedside table, and flipped on the TV. After scrolling through the guide, I switched the channel to watch *Schitt'$ Creek* and rested back against the pillows.

Normally the antics of the Rose family pull me out of whatever mood I'm in, but I just can't get into the show right now. I know what Leo said is true, but the mind is a funny thing and not letting New York or my father get into my head is easier said than done. But I'm gonna do my damnedest to keep moving forward instead of getting sucked back into the vortex I was in my entire life. Now that I know what real happiness is, I don't ever want to lose the feeling.

Chapter Twenty-Seven

CRISPIN STOOD and grabbed another slice then settled back onto the couch. He took a bite then shrugged.

"This pizza is actually palatable."

"Since that's your third slice, I guess so."

"I just don't understand why the pizza is so bad down here. It's not rocket science people." He took a bite and chewed. "Isn't there a transplant from New York who could open a shop and make something like they have in the city?"

"I have no idea. I'm just glad you found out about this place. It's definitely better than most we've tried."

The commercial ended and we turned our attention back to the game. The Waves are winning but it's only the third inning and the score is 6-4. Trey isn't pitching as well as the other times I've seen him, but he's hanging in.

"He's not smooth tonight," Crispin said. "He's aiming the ball instead of just pitching."

I have no idea what that means, but instead of asking, I focused on the game. The batter fouled four pitches into the stands, but finally popped one up that stayed in the field. Jimmy Chavez caught it just to the right of third base for the first out.

"So who do you think that woman is?" he asked.

As they've been doing in between New York hitters all game, the cameras switched to Trey's family, sitting in a private box. His parents and brother are there along with two men and a woman. She's stunning with long blonde hair and perfect features. Part of me wishes Eloise was home so I could ask if she knows who she is.

"I have no idea."

"His mother looks constipated."

I almost choked on my water when he said that.

"Don't say stuff like that when I'm drinking."

"But it's true."

I can't disagree with that so I just shrugged.

The camera switched back to a close-up of Trey standing on the mound. I've only seen his jaw clenched like that at the beginning of our shared ride from Fayetteville. That can't be good.

The next batter hit the ball in between first and second base for a single.

Once again, the Youngmans appeared on the screen and the announcers talked about Trey's issues in New York and why he got sent down to Triple-A last year.

"Trey looks just like his father, so at least you know he'll age well," Crispin said. "But his brother is definitely Trey Light."

"What are you talking about?"

"They resemble each other but that guy just doesn't have the *je ne sais quoi* that Trey does."

I can't dispute Trey's magnetism so I just nodded.

"Supposedly Leo's family is there. I wonder why they haven't shown them."

"Simple," Crispin said as he took a bite of his crust. "They don't own Youngman Electronics."

I turned my attention back to the game as the next guy stepped up to the plate.

Trey threw two balls in a row and Leo called time out and jogged out to the mound.

"Why do they do that?" I asked.

"What?"

"Put their gloves in front of their mouths like that."

"So no one can read their lips."

"It seems pretty unlikely that would actually happen."

"You never know and it's better to be safe than sorry."

Leo ran back behind the plate and the batter got back into the box.

The next pitch was called a strike.

"That looked better. His motion seemed more natural instead of forced," Crispin said. "Come on, let's get a double play here."

I swear the words just left his mouth when that's exactly what happened. The ball was hit to Jack Reagan at shortstop and he grabbed it then stepped on second base before throwing it to Dale Montgomery at first.

The camera followed Trey as he slowly walked toward the dugout.

"Those last two pitches were the best he's thrown all night. Maybe he's past his New York jitters."

"Do you think that's what the problem was?"

"I wouldn't be surprised. New York is a tough place to pitch and I'm sure Trey's history there doesn't make it any easier."

Crispin shifted to face me.

"I still can't believe you're dating him."

"I can't either. It all happened so fast, it's surreal."

"But you guys are great together. So adorable."

I don't know about *adorable*, but somehow we work.

Thankfully the next couple innings went smoothly for Trey. Whatever had been wrong the first three innings, he seemed to have corrected. He hasn't given up more runs and the Waves managed to increase their lead to 8-4 going into the bottom of the sixth inning. I'm guessing this will be Trey's last on the mound. Even in the games where he's done really well, I've never seen him pitch into the seventh.

Crispin stood, grabbed both of our glasses off the coffee table, and walked into the kitchen. The game had just come back on when he returned and handed me my refilled glass.

"Thanks."

"You're very welcome, *Mademoiselle*."

The first batter popped the first pitch up behind the plate and the camera followed Leo as he caught it.

"One pitch, one out. That's what we like," Crispin said.

Since dating Trey, I've learned a lot of things about baseball and I now know that they usually don't let pitchers throw more than one hundred pitches in a game. According to the little box on the screen, Trey is at ninety-three right now, so he doesn't have a lot of wiggle room here.

The next guy stepped into the box and Trey went into his windup and threw the ball right into Leo's glove for a called strike one. The batter swung at the next pitch and when he made contact, the bat shattered and the barrel went sailing toward Trey while the ball trickled toward third base.

Jimmy Chavez ran in and grabbed the ball with his bare hand and threw it to first base. It landed in Dale

Montgomery's glove a split second before the batter's foot hit the base. And thankfully Trey managed to jump out of the way of the flying bat.

Since the play was so close, New York challenged and we had to wait for it to be reviewed. During that time, they kept showing replays of the runner stepping on the bag and the ball going into the glove over and over again from all different angles, and the announcers debated whether or not the call was correct. The general consensus was that it was and a few minutes later, that was the official ruling as well.

I tucked my legs underneath me and crossed my fingers as the next batter stepped into the box. The first two pitches were called strikes.

"Oh he's in the zone now," Crispin said.

When the next two pitches were balls, I told him he jinxed it.

"Trey must really be rubbing off on you. You're so superstitious just like a baseball player." He glanced at my fingers and looked back at me with a raised brow.

Instead of responding, I shifted against the back of the couch, bent my knees in front of me, and wrapped my arms around them, my fingers still crossed. I watched the batter swing and the ball sail right under the bat to land in Leo's glove.

I relaxed my fingers, closed my eyes, and let out a relieved breath.

"Oh my God, look at that smile. It's scary."

At first I thought Crispin was talking about me, then realized he was looking at the TV. I followed his gaze and have to agree, Trey's mother did indeed look creepy as she smiled at the woman sitting next to her. Her grin made two things obvious. First, she's had work done and second, she doesn't smile often.

Which makes me wonder who the mystery woman is that she should elicit the rare facial contortion.

TREY

I PUT my head down and let the hot water pound some of the tension from my shoulders. That was a tough game. Thankfully our offense was on fire and we managed to take the lead despite my initial issues. I honestly didn't think I was going to make it past the first inning but somehow managed to keep my shit together and get through the sixth.

Thank God for that. This is my first game back here since getting sent down and then traded, and the reporters were all over me after the game. At least the last few innings I pitched were decent and I ended up with the win. Otherwise talking to them would have been torture.

Turning off the water, I slicked my hair back, wrapped a towel around my waist, then headed to my locker. Leo was getting dressed to my right and even though he wasn't looking at me, I know he's dying to say something. I dried off and slipped into my boxer briefs before facing him.

"Please say whatever you have to say now. I don't want this game to be the entire topic of conversation tonight."

Leo's whole family was at the game and we're meeting them for dinner. We'd probably already be on our way if I didn't get held up with interviews. But that's all part of the game.

"You had some trouble and worked out of it then eventually found your rhythm. All in all it was a good game especially considering where we are and who was here."

I wasn't thrilled to see my family up in that box, but did my best to ignore them. I assume the people with them were business associates. When I played for New York, the stadium was one of my father's favorite places to conduct business, especially when I was on the mound. It was actually the only time he pretended to be proud.

"You know, you sound just like Benji."

"I'll take that as a compliment."

"You should." I shrugged into a shirt and buttoned it. "He's a great coach."

Benji Alvarez is one of the main reasons I both made it through college and was skilled enough after two years of his coaching to enter the draft. He and Leo have very similar personalities and handle high-maintenance pitchers like me well.

I sat to put on my socks then pulled on my jeans and stood to drag them up my legs. I buttoned and zipped, leaving my shirt untucked then slipped my feet into a pair of brown loafers. We're going to a family-style Italian restaurant and it's pretty casual. Since Angie gave me a wardrobe makeover when she was visiting, I've gravitated to a more relaxed look. It seems to better suit my new, non-prickish personality. Plus, Nori seems to prefer it.

"Ready?" I asked Leo.

He nodded and we headed out the door. I cursed under my breath when I spotted my father in the hallway talking to one of the security guards. They all know him since I played here, which is probably why they let him into a restricted area.

"There he is," he said to the guard then walked toward me, his fake smile in place. "I tried calling but you must have your phone turned off."

I didn't comment because I can't guarantee whatever I

said wouldn't come out sarcastic. He didn't even blink at my lack of response.

"I wanted to tell you where we're meeting for dinner since I couldn't get through to you."

Satisfied he'd handed my father over to my custody, the guard excused himself. There were other people in the hallway, including a handful of reporters, so I nodded my head toward the exit and walked in that direction. I pushed the door open and took in a deep breath of warm city air as I walked outside. Leo was directly behind me, followed by my father. Every fiber of my being wanted to keep walking but I can't be sure of how my father will react to that, and there are people milling around out here. I really don't want any bad press. He's just not worth it. So instead, I stopped on the sidewalk and turned to face him.

"I have other plans for dinner."

His eyes shifted to Leo. "I'd like to have a word alone with my son."

Leo looked at me and I nodded. No reason to drag him into the middle of this awkward exchange. I watched him walk away and once he was out of earshot, turned my attention back to my father.

"That was an interesting game to watch," he said. "You've definitely had better outings, but at least you're here and not down in Triple-A."

I clenched my jaw to keep from commenting, or "engaging" as Dr. Fisher would say.

"My business associate's daughter is a big fan so I want you to come out to dinner with us. She's looking forward to meeting you."

"Like I said, I have plans so I can't."

He shifted his eyes in the direction Leo walked, then looked back at me.

"I'm sure you made plans with the Marakis family, but

I'm not taking no for an answer. If you answered even one of my calls over the past few weeks, you would have been aware of what was happening here."

"It's funny how you only called me *after* I got called up to the Waves. I didn't hear from you at all during the off-season or when I was in Triple-A."

"I figured you needed time to yourself after everything that happened."

I wanted to say that Leo's family had reached out to make sure I was okay, like most *normal* families would have. But again, not engaging, and I already said more than I should have.

"Well, I think I need more time."

That said, I walked away and surprisingly, he let me.

Chapter Twenty-Eight

NORI

MY PHONE WOKE me from a sound sleep. I rolled over and grabbed it off the bedside table and smiled when I saw Trey's picture.

"Hey," I said around a yawn as his actual face filled the screen.

"I'm sorry, did I wake you?"

"Yeah, but that's okay. I need to get up anyway." I yawned again. "I worked on some designs after the game last night and stayed up way too late."

"Sorry I bailed on our call last night. Leo and I went to dinner with his family after the game and we ended up closing the place down."

"Sounds like fun."

"It was," he said, but his face said the opposite.

"You don't look like you had fun."

"No, seeing Leo's family was great. It always is." He flashed a sad smile. "Seeing mine not so much."

"They kept putting your family on camera. I wondered if you ended up seeing them after the game."

"Just my father." He looked down and rubbed the back of his neck before looking at me again. "He ambushed me outside the locker room."

"They just let anyone down there?"

"Not usually, but since I played there, they know him." He shrugged. "He just assumed I'd go to dinner with my family and his business associates."

"We already established that you went out to eat with Leo's family, so how did he take it?"

"He wasn't happy, but he'll get over it." Shaking his head, he added, "Or not. I really don't care at this point."

Again, his face said something different, but I didn't call him on it. I know what it's like to feel conflicted about family.

"How do you feel after playing there and winning? Better?"

"If I gave a better performance, I'm sure I'd feel great."

"You had a couple rocky innings but pushed through, then really came alive."

"Listen to you sounding like a real fan."

"Seems I'm turning into one." I stared into his eyes through the screen. "But seriously, you did really well. You should be proud. I am."

"Thank you," he said around a sweet smile. "But enough about me, what's going on with you?"

"I just booked another local job."

"That's great."

"It's for a sports-themed nursery so it's a pretty easy design. I have it scheduled for next week. It'll only take a day and a half, two at most, so I squeezed them in."

"Pretty soon you'll be so busy, I'll have to make an appointment to see you."

"I'll give you first priority, I promise."

"I appreciate that. It's too hard not seeing you in person."

"I hear you," I said. "I'm just happy we have Face-Time. It's not the same as being in the same room, but it's definitely better than nothing."

"Agreed."

"So when do you leave for Baltimore?"

"Right after the game tonight."

"And you're not pitching there at all, right?"

He nodded. "I'm up the first game when we're back home."

"I'll be sure I'm available to go."

"I have the day before that off so maybe we'll be able to do something together."

"Sounds good."

Trey's eyes softened as they stared at me through the screen.

"I really miss you, and this is a whole new feeling for me so I'm still trying to figure out how to deal with it." He shook his head. "I've got a whole lot of new feelings going on where you're concerned. I'm in totally uncharted territory here."

My heart pounded at both his words and the vulnerable look in his eyes. But if he's opening up like this, I can at least meet him halfway.

"You don't have to worry, you're not there alone."

TREY

. . .

AFTER PRACTICALLY DECLARING my love to Nori over FaceTime, I hung up and sat back on the couch, putting my feet up on the coffee table. At least she seems to be on the same page as me. If she wasn't I'd probably be freaking out right now.

Things have been getting more serious and emotional between us for a couple weeks, but this road trip has really put it into perspective. I'm pretty sure I'm in love with Nori. I've never been in love before, never even pretended to be, but even I know the first time I say those three little words, we should be in the same room.

I don't have to be at the field until three and don't have plans to do anything until I have to leave. I was looking forward to just hanging out here until then, but now I feel antsy. I looked around my apartment. This place used to be my refuge, and now I feel like I don't belong here at all. I'm surrounded by all my things...as minimal as they are...yet I feel more at home in my hotel room in Myrtle Beach. Which is pretty sad since this is where I lived for a decade.

Speaking of home, I've been meaning to contact the realtor to have her start looking for a place for me in Myrtle Beach, but just haven't done it for whatever reason. No time like the present.

I swiped my phone open and scrolled through the contacts until I found the realtor my teammate recommended. I dialed and expected to leave a message, so I was surprised when she answered on the third ring.

"Joyce Rogers."

"Hi my name is Trey Youngman. My teammate, Sam Cherry, gave me your name. I'm new to the Waves and want to start looking for a house in the Myrtle Beach area. Hotel living is wearing on me," I added with a chuckle.

"That's totally understandable, Mr. Youngman. Do you know what you're looking for?"

"Please call me Trey, and I have a rough idea."

"Give me a minute to open my computer so I can take some notes. In the meantime, do you have a particular location in mind?"

I gave her Leo's address.

"I like that area or even closer to the beach or right on it if there's something available with the space I want."

"Okay, I'm ready to take notes. Now, let's start with the basics, do you have a preference for style?"

As she rattled off different types of architecture, I looked around my cold apartment.

"Any style except for modern. Ranch, two-story, and Cape Cod are all fine. I'd like three or four bedrooms and the more baths, the better. A pool would be great but if not, space for one is a must. And at least a two-car garage and a decent-sized yard."

"Do you want turnkey or is something that needs a little work okay?"

"I don't want to do tons of rehab but some work is okay." I smiled as I thought about watching that home show with Nori and the ridiculous things the people said. "I'm sure a lot of your clients say this and then drive you crazy, but honestly, I'm pretty open to anything."

She asked me a few more questions, including my budget and that was it. It was so easy, it made me wish I'd contacted her weeks ago.

"I'll pull some listings and email them to you. Look them over and if you like any, we'll set up a showing. If not, let me know what you don't like and that will help us narrow your wish list down."

"Sounds like a plan."

I rattled off my email address.

"Is this the best number to reach you at?"

"Yes, and you can text too if that's easier."

"All right," she said. "Thank you so much, Trey. I'll get some listings to you later today. I look forward to working with you."

"Thanks Joyce. I appreciate it."

I'd just hung up the phone when my doorbell rang. I walked over to the door and cringed when I spotted my father through the peephole. Taking in a deep breath through my nose, I slowly let it out though my mouth and opened the door.

His cold brown eyes skimmed me from head to toe.

"You look like a bum," he said and stepped past me into the apartment.

A sarcastic response was on the tip of my tongue, but I kept my mouth shut.

Don't engage. Don't engage. Don't engage.

Dr. Fisher's voice echoed in my head as I closed the door and walked into the living room behind him.

"What you did last night was unacceptable."

"I told you I had plans."

"Those people aren't your family. Your real family went to dinner with potential business associates after the game. They're big baseball fans and were looking forward to meeting you." He stopped speaking and just stared at me then narrowed his eyes. "Well? Don't you have anything to say?"

"I didn't hear a question and no, I don't have anything to say."

"Those people I was with own Nelson Tech and we're discussing a collaboration. We've been in negotiations for almost a year now. Like I said, Jim and Joe are big baseball fans, and Jim's daughter Clarissa is a fan of you specifically. Is it too much for you to play nice to help out your family?"

I dragged my fingers through my hair and rubbed the back of my neck. During my sessions with Dr. Fisher, he always asks if I want to totally cut my family out of my life. I've never been able to give a definitive *yes* to that question. It just seems so final.

What I want is to have a normal relationship with them. I just don't know if that's possible and I want to have myself figured out before I do anything too drastic that pushes them out of my life forever.

He must have seen me weakening and kept arguing his case.

"Since the game isn't until later and you're not pitching, I assume you don't have to be at the stadium until at least three. Max and I are meeting the Nelsons for lunch at one o'clock and I'd appreciate it if you'd make an appearance."

I glanced at my phone. It's ten-thirty now.

My father just wants to strut me in front of his friends like some prize pony and I should tell him to go to hell. But I know that if I do that, we'll be done for good and I'm not ready to shut that door yet, as crazy as that is.

"I'll be there."

Chapter Twenty-Nine

I PULLED up to the side door of Trey's hotel and had barely stopped the car when he climbed into the passenger seat. Without saying a word, he rested his elbow on the console, slid his fingers through my hair, and put his mouth on mine. I had enough sense to shift the car into park before wrapping my arms around his neck and eagerly kissing him back.

His soft lips feel absolutely perfect and when he urged my mouth open and applied a soft suction, I moaned deep in my chest. He leaned in closer and my aching nipples brushed against his hard chest as his tongue tangled with mine.

I dug my fingers into his shoulders and held on tight. The man makes my head spin in the best way possible. As he slowed the tempo of the kiss, I stroked my hands up and down his back, loving the feel of his muscles bunching and flexing against my palms. It's only been ten days since I touched him, but it seems like forever.

He slowly pulled back then kissed the tip of my nose before resting his forehead against mine.

"Hi," he said with a sweet smile.

"Hi."

"I missed you."

I nodded. "It was a long ten days, that's for sure."

Giving me a quick kiss, he shifted back into his seat and pulled on his seatbelt.

"But since we're sitting in a parking lot and I don't want to make you late, I'm going to keep my hands to myself." He looked at me with a sexy smirk and winked. "Until later."

"Are you sure you want to do this?" I asked.

"Absolutely. I want to spend time with you and this is what you're doing today." He held his hands up. "So that's where I want to be."

"Okay, let's go then."

I shifted into drive and turned around then headed out of the lot and onto the main road. When I booked this job, I had my days mixed up and didn't realize Trey was off today. I figured we'd just see each other later, but he surprised the hell out of me and asked if he could come.

"This is the sports mural, right?"

"Yep," I said. "And they already painted the walls pale blue so I can just sketch the design and start painting that today."

"Do you normally have to paint the room?"

"Sometimes. It depends. For something like the fairy garden I do because I use a custom blend of colors for the background. I ended up painting a blue accent wall for the Penn State room to make the rest of the design pop and also so I could paint a couple white jerseys and helmets." I shrugged. "But pale blue will be perfect to highlight everything I'm doing in this room so I don't think I'll need to change it anywhere."

"I promise I won't drive you crazy with questions when you're working. I'll just sit there and watch, kind of like you do when I'm working."

"Watching me paint will be less exciting, I'm sure."

"I don't know. I'm amazed at what you do. You're so talented."

"Thank you. I mean, I can't make a baseball defy gravity but I can draw one, so that's something," I said and turned into the development where the Ballards live. Six houses in, I pulled into their driveway, shifted into park, and turned off the car.

I popped the trunk then stepped out. Trey met me around the back

"Nice shirt," he said, his eyes glued to my chest.

Today's T-shirt says *Painters Gonna Paint* with a palette and paintbrushes in the middle.

Now that business is steady, I want to get some shirts printed with my logo so I can wear them like a uniform. But for now, my artsy shirts work.

He shifted his gaze to mine and said, "Just tell me what you need me to do."

I pointed to the ladders, tarps, and paint in the trunk.

"That all has to go inside."

Even though my ladders are relatively compact, I have the back seat down to accommodate their length. The trunk of the Accord isn't wide enough so I have to put them in vertically.

I saw the front door open and a very pregnant Gina Ballard stepped onto the porch.

"Why don't you go talk to your client and I'll carry this over?"

"All of it?"

If I don't have help, it usually takes me multiple trips to get everything inside.

He gave me a quick kiss then pulled back and smiled.

"I got it."

"At least let me carry the paint."

I admired Trey's ass in his basketball shorts as he leaned forward and reached into the trunk to get the box of paint. Since I'm only painting the design and not the walls, there are only a few quarts instead of gallons, so I can definitely manage, but he refused to let me.

Grabbing my computer bag out of the trunk, I slung it over my shoulder and headed up the sidewalk. Gina smiled as I approached.

"I'm so excited you're here. Thank you so much for fitting us in."

"You're welcome. I'm excited to be here. The design is so cute and I can't wait to get started."

I heard the trunk slam and looked over my shoulder and watched Trey walk toward me carrying both my multi-position and step ladders with the tarps and paint resting on top.

Gina opened the door and ushered us inside. I've already been here and know where to go but stood in the foyer until she walked in front of us to lead the way. Once we got to the nursery, Trey set the ladders down in the corner then walked over and took my laptop case from me and set it down too.

"Gina, I have a helper today. This is—"

Her eyes had shifted to Trey when I spoke that first sentence then widened as she finished the second one for me.

"Trey Youngman?" She blinked then glanced at me. "Oh my God, that's Trey Youngman."

I nodded.

"Yes, Trey Youngman."

"Nice to meet you, Gina."

He reached out to shake her hand and I thought she might faint, or go into labor. Neither would be ideal.

"My husband isn't going to believe this." Gina continued to shake Trey's hand and he slowly extracted it from her grip as she stared at him. "*I* don't believe this. Why are you in my house helping paint a mural?"

"Nori and I are dating and since I have a day off I figured I'd help out."

Her mouth dropped open and she looked over at me.

"You're dating Trey Youngman?" she asked in a reverent tone.

I bit my lip and nodded, fighting the urge to laugh but mustn't have done a very good job because Gina let out a nervous chuckle.

"I'm sorry I'm acting like such a fool, but it's not every day a professional baseball player walks into our house. It's a bit of a shock."

"You're acting just fine," Trey said and looked around. "But we should probably let Nori get started."

"Oh sure. I'll be in the living room if you need anything."

"Thanks Gina."

With one last glance at Trey, she left us alone in the room.

Once I was sure she was out of earshot, I said, "You know her husband will be here sooner rather than later."

"No doubt." He looked around. "We better get started so you can put a dent in things before he does. What needs to be done first?"

"We need to put the tarps down to cover the carpet."

He walked over and grabbed a tarp and together we

spread it over half the room, then put the other one over the rest. Then he set up the multi-position ladder near the far wall and attached the tray to one of the top rungs.

I opened my bag and took my pencils and paintbrushes out and set them on the floor, then grabbed my sketches. Since the drawings are relatively simple, I can work off them and probably won't need my computer.

"This is the plan." I held the sketches up one at a time for Trey to see, then rested each against the wall the design will be drawn on.

"So you have to draw all that on the walls then paint?" I looked up at him and nodded. "And it'll all be done by tomorrow?"

"Should be."

"I can't wait to see this."

TREY

NORI and I carried on a normal conversation during the ride back to the hotel, but the entire time, the air in the car crackled with sexual tension. By the time she parked in a spot just outside the side entrance, I was mentally counting the seconds until I had her alone in my room and naked. Since she jumped out of the car as fast as I did, I assume she feels the same way.

I kept my hands to myself in the elevator because once I touch her, I don't plan on stopping until she's either panting for breath or screaming my name, preferably both. The doors opened and we walked down to my room. I opened the door and stepped back. She brushed against me as she walked past then tossed her tote bag on the couch and turned to face me.

Her gaze never left mine as I stalked toward her. Slowly lowering my head, I placed a gentle kiss on one corner of her mouth, then the other. I pulled back and let my eyes take a lazy tour of her beautiful, flushed face and down over her curves. Reaching out, I circled my thumbs around her nipples, which are doing their best to poke through her bra and T-shirt. She dropped her head back and let out a shuddering breath.

Leaning down, I traced my open mouth up along her neck then licked my way back down as I continued to stroke her nipples.

"Trey."

"Mmm?"

"I really should take a shower before…" She trailed off as I nibbled and sucked at the base of her throat.

"Before?"

She nodded. "I have paint on me and I'm all sweaty."

I backed away and held out my hand.

"Come on, let's go get cleaned up."

I led her to the bathroom and reached into the shower to turn on the water. In the few seconds that had taken me, apparently Nori had stripped off her T-shirt and capris, because she stood in front of me in a matching pale blue cotton bra and panty set.

As I walked back toward her, I pulled my shirt off and threw it to the floor then kicked off my shoes. Nori slapped my hands out of the way and slid hers into the waistband of my shorts and dragged them and my underwear down in one swipe. They pooled at my feet and she reached out and wrapped her fingers around me and squeezed, then slowly stroked.

Watching her hand pump me made it feel that much

better and I closed my eyes hoping it would dull the sensation enough so I don't embarrass myself. That didn't work either so I focused on reciting the alphabet backwards to distract myself.

She tightened her grip on my shaft and pumped faster, circling her thumb around the head with each pass, nearly pushing me over the edge. When I couldn't take anymore, I covered her fingers with mine and slowly peeled them off of me. I kissed them all in turn before releasing her hand and reaching around to unhook her bra.

After dragging it down her arms, I tossed it to the floor then skimmed my hands over her breasts and down her stomach to slip my fingers into the waistband of her panties. I dropped to my knees in front of her and peeled them down her legs then leaned forward and placed an open-mouthed kiss over the juncture of her thighs. She squeezed her legs together.

"Trey," she panted. "Shower."

Thankfully this suite has a huge shower instead of a tub.

I stood and took her hand then walked backwards pulling her along with me until we stepped under the hot spray of the shower. She watched me with dazed eyes as I ran my fingers through her hair, slicking it back off her face. Leaning down, I opened my mouth over hers then slipped my tongue inside and feasted as the water cascaded down our bodies.

She rubbed her stomach against my raging erection and I dragged my mouth from hers. I kissed my way down her neck and chest then sucked on each nipple before skimming my mouth down her body until I was once again on my knees.

Forcing her legs apart, I slipped my tongue along her slick seam then gripped her ass and tilted her hips forward to give me better access. She dug her fingers into my scalp as I alternately licked, nibbled, and sucked her clit.

Holding Nori tight, I crawled forward, until her back was against the wall. I slid my hands down the back of her thighs and pulled her knees up to rest against my shoulders, opening her to me even further.

Holding her against the wall with one hand, I moved the other between us and slipped two fingers inside her and pumped in and out as I continued to lick, lap, and swirl my tongue around that tiny bundle of nerves. She let out a low groan then started chanting my name with breathless pants as I felt her pussy clamp down on my fingers. I stayed with her until the very last pulse subsided.

Kissing her inner thigh, I pulled back and slowly slid her legs off my shoulders and stood, holding her waist until she was steady on her feet. As much as I'd love to bury myself in her right now, I stupidly didn't bring a condom in with me, so that will have to wait.

I smiled down at her then reached for my shampoo and squirted a healthy amount into my palm.

"Turn around," I said.

She did as I asked and I rubbed my hands over her hair to work up a healthy lather, then massaged my fingers into her scalp. I've never washed anyone's hair but my own, but I have to admit, I'm enjoying myself despite my aching cock.

"Mmm, that feels so nice," she purred.

After washing her hair and giving her a thorough scalp massage, I tilted her head back and moved her into the spray. Keeping my hand on her forehead to keep the shampoo out of her eyes, I rinsed all the suds out of her hair until it was squeaky clean.

Reaching for the soap, I lathered it between my palms then ran my hands over Nori's body, making sure to remove any specks of paint. While she was rinsing off, I quickly washed myself then put the soap back and poured shampoo into my palm and gave my hair the same swift treatment.

Nori backed out of the spray and watched as I rinsed off. I reached over to turn off the water but she put her hand on my wrist and pulled my hand off the handle. Her lips lifted in a coy smile and she pushed me against the wall then kissed her way down my chest and stomach before sinking to her knees in front of me, just as I'd done to her.

My cock brushed against her chin as she nipped at my navel then licked her way down. With her eyes on mine, she wrapped her hand around the base of my shaft then opened her mouth and slowly, tortuously slipped her lips along my length until they met her fist.

I rested my head against the wall and watched her through slitted eyes.

She pulled her head back and I thought she was going to release me, but instead she swirled her tongue around just the tip and sucked then reversed direction until she met her fist again. Repeating that same motion over and over, her head bobbed up and down as she pulled me deeper into her mouth each time.

Releasing her grip on my shaft, she reached down and cradled my balls as my cock pressed against the back of her throat.

"Yes," I hissed through clenched teeth.

I fisted my fingers into her hair, fighting the urge to thrust my hips forward and fuck her mouth. Closing my eyes, I took in a deep breath of steamy air and fought to hold my release back, but she's not making it easy.

Opening my eyes again, I met her dark violet gaze as she picked up her rhythm, dragging me closer toward the edge. What she's doing feels too fucking good and I know I can't hold on much longer. Tightening my grip on her hair, I tried to pull her back, but she resisted and sucked me even further into her mouth.

"Nori, that feels so...*fuck*..." My balls tingled as her soft fingers stroked and tugged against them. "Nori, I can't...I'm gonna come...stop if you don't want..."

Her nostrils flared then she pulled back and dragged her teeth lightly across the tip of my cock. My balls tightened as she wrapped her lips wrapped around the head then slid down my shaft, her tongue swirling around me as she sucked, pushing me over the edge.

She slowly pulled back and released me then placed a gentle kiss against the tip. Moving her hands to my waist, she stood and I pulled her against my chest, her head resting over my racing heart.

Once I got my breathing under control, I kissed the top of her head then stepped back under the spray to rinse off again before turning off the water. Taking her hand in mine, I led her out of the shower and pulled a towel from the rack and quickly dried her off before dragging it over my hair and body. I tossed it on the floor then bent down and picked her up and carried her to bed. Nori rested her head against my shoulder and I slowly ran my fingers through her hair.

"Did I mention that I missed you?" I asked.

"Once or twice." I felt her smile against my chest. "Trey Youngman," she added, mimicking Gina Ballard's tone.

I tickled her waist and she squirmed away from me as she laughed. Kissing the top of her head, I pulled her close again.

"I'm sorry I wasn't with you the whole time. I was supposed to be helping you not having a meet and greet."

"You were a huge help. It takes me at least three trips to get all my stuff in the house."

"I can't believe you usually carry all that in yourself."

"If the clients are home, sometimes they help. And some have their own ladders and tarps. Otherwise it's just me." She shrugged. "At least it's good exercise."

"Just the drawing is good exercise. I got tired just watching you going up and down the ladder and I was only there to see part of what you did."

"I told you Ryan was going to be home in record time."

"Where the hell does he work? I swear, he showed up in less than a half hour."

"It's cute how people lose their minds when they meet you."

"You didn't."

"That's because I didn't know who you were." She shifted back and rested her chin on her hand as she looked at me and smiled. "But if I did, I'm sure I would have."

I kissed her forehead.

"I figured we would have had time to talk today, but since I spent most of my day with Ryan and Gina, I never got to tell you that I spoke to a realtor yesterday. So the search for a house is officially on."

"That's great. I know you're tired of living here."

"She emailed me a bunch of listings and I went through them last night. There were a couple that had potential so we're getting together later this week to check them out. Would you be interested in coming along?"

"Are you sure?"

I nodded. "Positive."

She nibbled at her bottom lip and smiled.

"I'd like that. Thank you for asking."

I leaned forward and kissed her, the new, but now-familiar emotions swirling through me. Sometime during my road trip up north, I'd defined what I'm feeling but sharing that

with her from another state didn't seem like a good idea. But right now, just might be perfect timing. Even if it's not, I can't hold it back any longer.

"Nori, I love you." Her eyes widened and held a slight sheen as they stared into mine. "I love you and I want you to spend a lot of time wherever I'm living, so it's important you like whatever house I buy."

She opened her mouth to speak but nothing came out. My heart pounded as I waited for her to respond. I've never said those three words to a woman before, never wanted to share my life with someone, so I didn't realize how vulnerable it leaves you feeling.

Before I could panic too much, she sniffed and wiped a tear that had escaped from her cheek then her mouth curled into a sweet smile.

"I love you too."

Chapter Thirty

NORI

I FINISHED ICING my cupcakes then carefully placed a strawberry on top of each. Crispin, Eloise, and I are going to Leo's for a barbecue. Since Trey and I exchanged the L-word a couple weeks ago, I can't keep her away any longer with the excuse that we're not serious.

After being in the Midwest for eight days, the Waves are back home for the next seven. Today was a day game so Trey and I get to see each other tonight and he doesn't have to be at the stadium until three o'clock tomorrow.

Eloise walked into the living room then sat at the breakfast bar and watched me work.

"What kind of cupcakes are they?"

"White cake with strawberry filling and whipped cream icing."

She wrinkled her nose. "I don't like strawberries."

"Trey's picking up brownies so there will be something chocolate there, too."

Not that she'll eat anyway, but I didn't say that. She's been in a really strange mood the past couple weeks, kind of moody and sarcastic and I don't want to get into anything with her before we go.

"What time is Crispin coming home?"

I glanced at the clock.

"He should be here any minute."

He's driving us over then he'll bring Eloise home and I'll go with Trey.

"So who's going to be at this party?"

"It's more of a get-together than a party. Besides you, Crispin, and me, it'll just be Trey, Leo, and Leo's brother Nicky."

"Don't they hang out with the rest of the team?"

"I'm sure they do, but not tonight."

Crispin walked in the front door before she could comment. His eyes shifted between Eloise, who's decked out like she's going to a swanky party in the Hamptons, and me, in white shorts, a black tank top, and flip-flops. We definitely don't look like we're going to the same place.

"Let me get changed and we can head out."

He's been limiting his interactions with Eloise and isn't thrilled that she's coming tonight. But I think that by keeping Trey away from her, it's making her want to meet him more. Once she realizes our get-togethers aren't like the gatherings she's used to attending, she won't want to come again and will stop bugging me about it.

I placed the cupcakes into the carrier and put the lid in place just as Crispin came out of his room dressed in a pair of board shorts and a polo shirt.

"Can I put these in your tote?" he asked, holding up a pair of shorts.

"Sure."

He walked over to the couch and put them in my bag,

then grabbed it and we all walked out to the car. I let Eloise ride shotgun so I don't have to listen to her complain about getting carsick in the backseat.

Leo's house is only a short distance away and we pulled into his driveway in no time. I saw the frown on Eloise's face as we got out of the car.

"What's wrong?" I asked.

"*This* is where Leo Marakis lives?"

"Yeah, why?"

"It's just not what you'd expect from a professional athlete."

"Eloise, don't be a snob."

"I'm just stating the facts."

Crispin stood at the front of the car watching us. I handed him the cupcakes.

"Can you bring these in? We'll be there in a minute."

He took them from me and I watched him walk around the side of the house toward the gate that leads into the backyard.

"Eloise, please don't say something like that in there."

"I'm not an idiot." She crossed her arms over her chest. "But Nori, the man makes eleven million dollars a year. If he wants to attract the right kind of woman, he should have a house to match his income. "

"How do you know how much he makes?" I asked, trying to keep my voice down.

"It's public record. Of course, that's only his salary, it doesn't include any endorsements he has, so he probably makes significantly more, but I didn't dig into that." I just stared at her with my mouth hanging open. "Haven't you looked up how much Trey makes?"

"No. Why would I?"

She rolled her eyes before looking back at me.

"He's wasted on you," she said, shaking her head.

"You'd be happy with someone who makes minimum wage yet somehow you're dating a guy who makes twenty-two million dollars a year." She flashed a sarcastic smile. "Again, that's before endorsements."

Holy shit.

I had no idea Trey makes that much. Not that it matters, but *holy shit.*

"Just please don't mention salary or Leo's house or anything else that might be considered offensive. Okay?"

She moved her right arm and drew a cross over her heart with her index finger.

"Promise."

After looking into the passenger-side window and checking her hair, she did a perfect runway walk across the sidewalk and around the side of the house.

I took in a deep breath and let it out slowly praying for patience. Because based on Eloise's mood, I know I'm going to need it.

TREY

HOW THE HELL can Nori and Eloise be related in any way? They're so fundamentally different, it doesn't seem possible they share even a fraction of the same genetics.

I may be clueless about some things, but I *know* when a woman is hitting on me and that's exactly what Eloise has been doing since she got here. Between the "accidental" touches and her batted eyelashes, it's pretty obvious.

Not that I think I'm special. She's been hitting on Leo too.

Of course, he's not dating her sister.

"That Eloise is something, huh?"

Leo's brother Nicky sat across from me at the table and I was happy to see he didn't mean that in a complimentary way. Eloise isn't really interacting with Nicky. Then again, she wouldn't look past the fact that he lives in Jersey and works at his parents' store.

"Yeah, she's something all right." I finished my water in one long gulp and crushed the bottle in my hand. "She said Nori's been keeping her away from us. Now we know why."

"It's a good thing Angie wasn't able to come. There'd be a cat fight for sure. Women like Eloise drive her crazy."

"Yeah, with good reason, and I'm pretty sure Angie would win."

The sad thing is that Eloise is the exact type of woman I spent time with up until last year. I would never have given Nori a second glance, chemistry or no chemistry. And that would have been sad because she's the perfect combination of sweet and sexy and I'm really happy with her.

Then again, last year I wouldn't have deserved her. I'm not sure I do now, but I'm at least working on it.

As if he read my thoughts, Nicky said, "I really like Nori. Seems like she's good for you."

I looked at him and smiled. "Yeah, I think so too."

"Angie is ready to add another honorary member to the family."

"I'm not sure Nori and I are there quite yet, but we are enjoying spending time together."

Before he could comment, Nori, Eloise, Crispin, and Leo returned from the basement. He's remodeling and wanted to show Crispin the space and get Nori's opinion on colors and of course, Eloise tagged along. Thank God for small favors though. It would have been awkward as hell if she'd stayed here with Nicky and me.

"Come on Nori, let's go for a swim," Eloise said as she whipped off her cover-up, once again revealing her minuscule bikini.

Nori took off the Waves T-shirt she was using as a cover-up and jumped right in from the side, going under water, and slicking her hair off her face as she popped back to the surface. Eloise slowly walked down the steps and leaned against the railing as she reached the bottom.

"So when's Sam Cherry supposed to be coming back?" Nicky asked.

"He should have been back by now but he's still having trouble with his leg during his simulated games."

"You've been doing great. Do you think they'll keep you in the rotation when he does come back?"

"I'm not sure what their plans are at this point. Honestly I'm not sure they do." I shrugged. "I'm just taking it one start at a time."

"I guess that's all you can do."

Leo walked over with the container of cupcakes Nori brought and placed them in the middle of the table. It's a hot night, so he had them in the refrigerator since they have whipped cream icing.

Nicky and I each grabbed one.

I peeled back the liner and ate half in one bite.

"Mmm, so good," I said around the mouthful.

Crispin sat at the table with his back to the pool but looked over his shoulder at Nori and Eloise before facing forward again and taking a cupcake. I'd finished mine and reached for another.

"These cupcakes are amazing," I yelled to Nori.

She smiled over at me.

"Thanks."

I finished the second cupcake in record time too then stood.

"Anyone want a drink while I'm going inside?"

Crispin and Leo asked for water and Nicky wanted a beer.

I made a face. "With cupcakes? That's gross."

"Hey, on vacation beer goes with everything."

Can't argue with that logic.

I walked into the kitchen, opened the refrigerator, and grabbed the last beer and a half dozen bottles of water. Setting them on the table, I walked over to the pantry to get more beer. After putting two six packs at the back of the bottom shelf, I crushed the cardboard holders and walked out to the garage to throw them in the recycling bin.

Eloise was standing near the island in that itsy-bitsy bikini as I walked back into the kitchen and I mentally groaned. There's not a snowball's chance in hell that I'm interested in this woman but I don't want there to be any misunderstandings.

I walked into the kitchen from the opposite side, putting the island between us.

"I just came in for a drink," she said, shifting to the side of the island.

"I'm bringing a bunch out."

As I reached out to gather up all the bottles, she wrapped her fingers around my wrist. When I froze, she walked her index and middle fingers up my arm to my chest and brushed them against my shirt.

"You had some cupcake crumbs," she said around a calculated smile as she batted her eyelashes.

"Oh." I looked down at her hand still resting on my pec and took a step back. "Thanks."

She took a step forward and just in case there was any

question of her intention, placed both her hands on my chest and slowly moved them up as if to wrap them around my neck.

I jumped back out of her reach then circled around the island and wrapped my arms around the bottles and pulled them against my chest.

"Eloise, I'm not sure what's happening here," I said even though I'm pretty sure I do. I clutched my plastic bottle barrier and added, "But I'm with Nori."

"Uh huh," she said, then tapped the tip of my nose with her index finger and offered a saucy smile as she walked away.

I turned to go back outside and spotted Nori in the doorway looking furious. It's pretty obvious she saw at least part of that exchange. I'm just not sure if she's pissed at Eloise or me.

Chapter Thirty-One

NORI

TREY PULLED INTO THE DRIVEWAY, put the car in park, and shifted toward me.

"Are you sure we're okay?" he asked.

"I'm positive." I cupped his jaw then leaned forward and kissed him. "I have no idea what Eloise's little display was about last night, but I'm sorry you got caught up in it. Like I said, she's been acting weird for a couple weeks but she's not telling me why."

After Eloise left the kitchen, Trey and I talked for a few minutes before we went back outside. I apologized for her behavior, even though I'm sure he's experienced worse. We left shortly after that and discussed it a little bit on the car ride, but once we got to the hotel, I didn't want to talk about it anymore. Alone time with Trey is precious and I didn't want to waste another minute trying to figure out my sister.

"Did I mention that I love you?"

My heart goes pitter-patter every time he says that, which he's been doing more and more often.

"You may have mentioned it once or twice."

"Is that all? I must be slacking," he said around a sweet smile. "I better show you."

That vow made, he nibbled at my bottom lip before placing his mouth over mine. And right there in the driveway, in broad daylight, he made love to my mouth with slow, sweet strokes of his tongue.

Pulling back, he ended the kiss and rested his forehead against mine.

"I'll see you at the game."

I nodded. "See you later."

That said, I opened the door and got out of the car. I felt Trey watching me as I walked up the sidewalk and I turned and blew him a kiss before going inside.

Eloise was sitting cross-legged on the couch, scrolling through her iPad. She shifted her eyes in my direction before looking back down.

"Hey."

I thought I'd let go of some of my anger overnight, but seeing Eloise's unapologetic face and her casual tone has brought it all back. After dropping my tote bag on the floor, I walked into the living room and stood behind the chair.

"What the fuck was that last night?"

She looked up, eyes wide. I rarely say that word so I used it specifically, knowing it would get her attention.

"What?"

"The bikini, the way you kept touching both Trey and Leo, the batted eyelashes, and whatever it was that I witnessed in the kitchen." My voice was taking on a shrill tone and I paused for a minute. Once I was sure I could speak normally, I continued. "You bugged me for weeks to meet Trey. Is that what you had planned all along? To what? Try to lure him away from me?"

"Nori, you're overreacting to nothing. Leo is cute and I thought maybe we'd hit it off but it's pretty obvious he's about as interesting as his house. As for Trey, I was testing him. You know, to see if he's worthy of you."

Normally I'd totally believe what she's saying but there's something in her tone I don't like and her look is too calculating. Crispin has always accused me of having a soft spot where Eloise is concerned and that's probably true. Part of me remembers the sweet girl she was when I moved in with my father and wants a relationship with her. But she's not that girl anymore, she's a woman who by her own admission will do whatever she has to in order to live her imagined version of her best life.

Last night, she said Trey is wasted on me. Does she believe she's more worthy of him? Is that the reason for her little performance last night?

Eloise placed her iPad on the coffee table and stood.

"I know you're angry with me, but trust me, I had my reasons. And maybe part of me did think Trey and I would be a better fit, but I decided it's not worth the effort. Or the cost. " Her gaze met mine as she said that last sentence and for once, I feel like her walls are down. "Daddy and I worked things out so I'm going back to New York tomorrow."

"I think that's a good idea."

"You think you're the only woman he's seeing but I seriously doubt that. He is a professional athlete after all." She rattled off a number. "That's the code for my iPad. There are some pictures you should see."

I watched her disappear down the hall then walked over to the coffee table and stared down at the iPad. Sitting on the couch, I swiped the screen then keyed in the code she'd given me.

My stomach tightened as a picture of Trey and the woman from the game in New York filled the screen. They were sitting next to each other at what looked like a restaurant and she was smiling up at him. I swiped and in the next picture her arm was resting on the back of his chair and his head was tilted toward her.

Eloise must have taken screenshots of a gossip blog because when I swiped again, I saw two pictures...one of the woman with Trey where they were smiling at each other and another of her with Trey's mother at what looked like a boutique. The headline read, *Could we be looking at another Youngman/Nelson merger?*

My head started to pound as I kept swiping and found more of the same. At least now I know who the mystery woman is. Her name is Clarissa Nelson and apparently her father and Trey's are working on some kind of business deal. I just don't know what she is to Trey.

If these pictures and headlines are to be believed, they're dating. I'm just not sure how or when that would happen. Since we started dating, Trey's only been in New York once, and he and I have spent most of his free time together when he's here. Unless she visits him on the road, it just doesn't seem probable. Of course, I lived with Baxter and didn't know he was cheating on me so anything is possible.

I pulled my phone from my pocket and forced myself to go through all the pictures again, this time taking a picture of each so I have my own copies then stood and walked to my bedroom. My mind is going in so many directions and the more I try to think, the more my head hurts. I need to take a painkiller and lie down in a dark room before it turns into a full-blown migraine.

TREY

AFTER GETTING through all my post-game interviews, I showered, got dressed, then high-tailed it out of the stadium to go check on Nori. She and Crispin were supposed to come to the game, but she'd texted saying she wasn't feeling well.

Somehow I managed to pitch well despite the fact that I'm worried about her. I honestly have no idea how the guys with wives and children handle this every season. Dan said you kind of get used to it, but I can't imagine how.

I pulled into the driveway and practically ran up the sidewalk and rang the doorbell. As soon as Crispin opened the door, I knew something was wrong.

"Is Nori okay?"

My voice held a hysterical tone, but I don't care. This is the first relationship I've ever had and it stands to reason there's a learning curve with this stuff.

"For the most part. She has a headache that's bordering on a migraine."

"Is she in her room?" I asked and took a step in that direction.

"She is, but I think we should talk first."

I don't think I've ever seen Crispin look so serious and it's kind of freaking me out.

He settled onto the couch and I followed and sat on the edge of the chair across from him.

"I'm just gonna rip the band-aid off here and blurt out what I know. Eloise shared some pictures and blog posts of you with a woman."

"What?" I jumped out of the chair and paced in the

space between it and the coffee table. "That's not possible. I mean, it's possible, but they must be old. From before Nori and I got together."

"As amazing as that would be, I don't think it's the case."

I stopped pacing.

"Why?"

"Because the woman in the pictures was in the box with your family at the game you pitched in New York."

"*Fuck.*"

I sat down in the chair again, feeling *my* head start to pound. My blood pressure is probably through the roof right now. This is what I get for doing something for my father. I should have known.

"She's more confused than upset at this point, but the pictures did trigger her a bit. You know her ex cheated on her?" I nodded. "So you can understand how upsetting this would be."

"I swear, it's not what it looks like."

As soon as the words left my mouth, I cringed, realizing how pathetic they sound.

"Normally I'd cringe at what you just said too, but something tells me you might be the first man who's ever said them and is telling the truth."

I started to explain, but he held his hand up, stopping me.

"Why don't you go tell Nori?"

"You think that'd be okay?"

"I do."

"Thanks Crispin."

I stood and made my way to Nori's room and knocked on the door.

"It's open."

I opened the door and entered the pitch black room. I

used the light from the hallway to figure a clear path to her then closed it behind me. Walking over to the bed, I sat on the edge, trying to think of what to say.

"Just please tell me it's not true."

"It's not." Needing to touch her, I rested my hand on her hip. "Yes, that woman was at the game I pitched in New York, but I never met her until the next day. I told you that after the game my father wanted me to go to dinner, but I refused because I had plans with Leo's family." She nodded. "The next day he showed up at my apartment and laid on a guilt trip because I didn't go out with them. He said he's in negotiations with those guys and they're baseball fans. Clarissa is supposedly a fan of mine and he promised they could meet me. So he set up a lunch and wanted me to stop by.

"My relationship with my family is fucked up. The only time my father really wants me around is when someone else is impressed by what I do. I know this. All my life, I'd held hope things would be normal between us and I knew that if I refused to at least make an appearance at lunch, we'd be done for good, and I wasn't ready for that. So I went and had lunch with them. But I swear, that was all I did. It was no different than any other meet and greet."

I waited for her to say something, but she remained quiet. My eyes had adjusted enough to the dark room that I could at least see the outline of her shape under the covers. As always, I'm surprised at how tiny she is. She has such a big personality, sometimes I forget.

"I really do have a headache. That's why I didn't come to the game."

"How are you feeling now?"

"Better," she said. "My head is still throbbing, but not like it was earlier."

"Is there anything I can do? Anything you need?"

"Hold me."

"Are you sure?"

"Positive."

I stood and took off my shoes then reached down, tugged the covers back, and slipped into bed behind her. Nori shifted back into me as I spooned her from behind and I kissed the back of her head.

"Nori, I'd never do anything to hurt you. I love you too much."

"Mmm, I love you, too," she said in a sleepy tone.

Her breathing turned slow and even and I closed my eyes but I couldn't fall asleep.

My father has enough contacts in the media that I know those pictures wouldn't have shown up anywhere unless he wanted them to. And even if I wasn't involved with Nori, it would be unacceptable.

Thankfully I have an appointment with Dr. Fisher tomorrow afternoon because I have a lot to discuss with him. I spent my whole life doing stupid stuff in reaction to my father's actions, but I don't want to do that anymore. I want to deal with his latest antics rationally and let him know what he did is inappropriate and that I won't be his show pony anymore.

In two days, I've had two strikes in my relationship with Nori, and none of them were even my fault. She's been understanding so far, but I don't want to find out how she'll react to a third strike.

<h1 style="text-align:center">Chapter Thirty-Two</h1>

NORI

"MMM. MMM. MMM." Crispin finished chewing, then swallowed, and took a big drink of his margarita. "If the whole art thing doesn't work out, you could seriously cook for a living."

"Why thank you, sir."

I finished my taco and watched as Rusty Russell struck out another batter for the third out of the inning. Since Trey isn't pitching, I've only been half-paying attention to the game but it seems like the Waves are doing well.

Trey pitched the last game in Houston yesterday. Now the Waves are in Tampa for three nights and he won't be starting again until their second game after they get home.

"Are you ready for another one?" Crispin asked, holding up his empty glass.

Mine is still half-full but I might as well have him top me off. When I held up my glass to him, he waved me off then went into the kitchen, grabbed the blender jar out of the freezer then came back and emptied its contents into our glasses.

I picked up my margarita and licked at the salty rim before taking a drink.

"Does Trey drink?" he asked as he set the empty jar down on the coffee table then settled onto the other end of the couch. "I've only ever seen him drink water, both in restaurants and at Leo's."

"I don't know. But now that you mention it, I've never seen him drink." I shrugged. "Although *I* don't usually drink when we go out so that could be why."

"Maybe it's all part of his transformation."

"He never mentioned that he has a drinking problem, if that's what you're insinuating."

My phone buzzed and I glanced at it and rolled my eyes.

"Eloise again?"

"Yeah."

"What's she saying now?"

I picked up my phone and read her entire text message. Clutching the cell to my chest, looked up at the ceiling and rolled my eyes, fighting the urge to scream.

"*Why* can't she just leave it alone?"

"What did she do?"

"She ran into Clarissa Nelson at a party and made it a point to talk to her about Trey."

"Oh. Em. Gee. What happened?"

"Clarissa said she never met Trey before that day they had lunch, but she's a big fan of his." I reread the last part of the text to make sure I was relaying facts. Or at least Eloise's version of the facts. "Apparently both of their fathers are in favor of them getting together and Trey's father is working on it." I looked up at him. "Whatever that means."

"Did Eloise happen to mention that you and Trey are together?"

"She doesn't, but probably not. You know Eloise."

"That I do," he said before taking a dramatic sip of his margarita. "But let's not talk about her. Let's discuss the fact that you and Trey were looking at houses before he left."

"Don't make it sound like *we're* looking at houses. *He's* looking at houses and asked me to go along with him."

Crispin raised his right brow and put his glass to his lips.

"And why exactly do you think he asked you to go with him?"

"For a second opinion?"

"Okay. Sure."

"Please wipe that look off your face."

He pointed to his face.

"This look?" He squinted his eyes and pursed his lips even more, exaggerating his look of sarcastic disbelief.

"Yes, your David Rose look."

"Well, I wouldn't have to resort to such measures if you didn't say such ridiculous things," he said. "Nori, the man is crazy about you. It's obvious to anyone who sees you together. Just enjoy it."

I finished my margarita in one long gulp and leaned forward to put the empty glass on the coffee table. As I settled back against the arm of the couch, I grabbed the pillow next to me and hugged it to my stomach.

"I do, but sometimes it freaks me out."

"He's not Baxter."

"It's still scary opening yourself up to someone."

"Oh, I know." He leaned forward and squeezed my hand. "But trust me when I say that you never looked as relaxed with Baxter as you do with Trey. Not to mention happy. And Nori, you deserve to be happy."

TREY

"PLEASE TELL me I'm not being like those people on *House Hunters*," I said as I pulled out of the driveway behind Joyce Rogers to follow her to the next house we're going to see.

"I don't think so," Nori said around a chuckle. "I never once heard you mention that you didn't like the paint color or carpets in any of the houses we've looked at."

"No, I guess I didn't, but I mentioned a whole lot of other stuff that I didn't like."

That was the twelfth house I looked at since I started working with Joyce and none of them felt right. Nori has been with me for most of those, although there were a couple I saw on my own two days ago because our schedules didn't mesh.

"Lot size, location, or having to do full kitchen and bathroom renovations are legitimate reasons for passing on houses."

"I honestly thought this would be easier," I said. "The apartment I bought in New York was the second one I looked at."

"You'll know when it's right."

I glanced over at her and smiled before shifting my eyes back to the road. That was definitely the case with her, even if I didn't initially want to admit it to myself.

We drove a couple more blocks before I pulled into the

driveway of the next house. I shifted the car into park and looked out the windshield at the sprawling ranch house.

"Two car garage. That's a good start," I said. "And I like the way it's set at an angle to the house." Looking at her, I smirked. "And I like the color."

"Grey with white trim is classic."

Joyce had gotten out of her car and was standing at the edge of the sidewalk. We got out and joined her then followed her into the house.

"This one just went on the market," she said as she led us through the foyer and into the open-concept living room, dining room, kitchen. "As you can see, this one has a lot of windows and while it is a large space, the vaulted ceilings make it seem that much larger."

I looked around and nodded as I walked through to the kitchen. Nori's eyes widened when she spotted the top-of-the-line appliances.

"The countertops are quartz, the cabinets and drawers are all soft-close, and the faucets in both the main and prep sink are touchless." Joyce said. "That's a stainless steel Viking six-burner gas stove with a double oven. As you can see, there's also a full-size wall oven."

I'm not much of a cook beyond breakfast foods, but Nori looks like she's fallen in love with this room. If nothing else, I can appreciate its aesthetic.

"This house has four bedrooms?" I asked.

"Yes, four bedrooms and an office."

She led us down the hall to the master suite, which also has the large windows and vaulted ceilings. There are his and hers walk-in closets as well as a large bathroom with a multi-jet shower, a large soaking tub, and a double vanity.

Across the hall is another large bedroom with an ensuite bathroom and down the hall are two bedrooms with a Jack and Jill bathroom in between. The office is a good size and it has built-in bookshelves all along one wall. We checked out the laundry area and half bath off the kitchen then walked through to the spacious two-car garage.

"Why don't we head outside and then we can go into the basement?" Joyce suggested.

"Lead the way," I said.

The wall of windows in the dining room opens up to a large deck which looks out over the back yard.

"Oh I love this," Nori said as we walked down the stairs to the patio area which boasts an outdoor kitchen. "And the pool is amazing."

"The freeform pool has a beach entry, a sitting ledge all around, and a spa with a waterfall spillover. There are also LED lights in both the pool and spa," Joyce said. She walked over to the wall of windows off the patio and slid one open. "And of course, this is the finished basement complete with a wet bar, so it's a great space for entertaining."

Instead of a TV, there's a projector and surround-sound speakers mounted to the ceiling.

"Lots of blank walls in here," I said to Nori. "You better start designing."

Her eyes widened. "Is this the one?"

"I'll give you some privacy to talk," Joyce said and walked back outside.

"I really like it. What do you think?"

"What do I think?" She looked around the basement then out toward the pool, before meeting my gaze. "It's amazing."

"There's just one thing."

"What's that?"

"My cooking will never do that kitchen justice. Do you

promise to come over and make use of it as often as possible?"

A smile spread across her face as she nodded.

"I promise."

"Come on then, let's go tell Joyce to draw up the paperwork."

I leaned down and kissed her then wrapped my arm around her waist. As I led her out to the patio, I felt like I was walking on air even as my heart raced in my chest.

Because if I wasn't absolutely positive before, I am now...this house isn't the only thing that I know is perfect for me.

Chapter Thirty-Three

I PULLED the prime rib out of the oven and set it on the counter to rest, resisting the urge to lift the foil and take a peek. Changing the oven temperature, I slid the pan of green beans, coated with olive oil and parmesan cheese, onto the middle rack. I checked on the boiling potatoes and decided to give them another couple minutes.

Trey should be here any minute. We're celebrating the official closing of his house. If it was up to him, that would have happened the day we looked at it, but the owners had asked for thirty days to vacate so he had to wait.

I ran to the bathroom to check my hair and makeup. My cheeks are flushed from the heat in the kitchen but other than that, everything looks okay. The doorbell rang just as I finished adding a fresh coat of lipstick.

After taking one last look in the mirror, I went to open the door. Trey smiled as his eyes skimmed me from head to toe before meeting my gaze.

"You look beautiful," he said.

"Thank you." I took in his khakis and untucked, white button-down shirt. "So do you."

I stepped aside so he could enter and closed the door behind him.

He held up a bottle. "Since it's a celebration, I brought some champagne."

"Bollinger Rose. Pretty fancy."

"It smells amazing in here," he said as he set the bottle on the counter.

"It's just about ready. I was waiting on the potatoes, which should be done now."

"Can I do anything to help?"

"Why don't you grab a couple glasses from over there?" I pointed to the cupboard on the other side of the kitchen. "And open the champagne. It'll only take me a couple minutes to finish everything here."

I turned and grabbed the pot of potatoes from the stove and drained them in the sink. After adding butter, milk, and some cloves of roasted garlic, I opened the drawer and extracted the hand masher and got to work.

A pop sounded from the dining room as I scooped the mashed potatoes into a serving bowl. After adding a spoon, I set it to the side. I pulled the foil off the prime rib and smiled at how perfect it looks. I cut it into even slices, placed them on the platter, and spooned some of the juice on top then put the rest into a gravy boat.

I glanced at Trey standing near the breakfast bar and held out the platter.

"Would you put this on the table?"

He held out his hands and smiled.

"With pleasure."

"You can sit then. I'll be right in with the rest."

I turned off the oven, pulled out the green beans, and

placed them on a plate then carried them and the mashed potatoes into the dining room and set them down on the table.

Trey shifted his gaze from the food to me as I sat adjacent to him.

"Nori, this looks amazing. Like something you'd get at a five-star restaurant."

"Hopefully it tastes good, too."

"I have no doubt it will. Thank you for taking the time to cook this dinner to celebrate my closing. It means a lot to me." He picked up a champagne flute and handed it to me before picking up his own and holding it up. "To the new house and to us."

He clinked his glass against mine and we stared into each other's eyes as we took a sip. After all, how could I not drink to that?

"Mmm, this is yummy," I said and took another sip.

"I've never seen you drink so I wasn't sure whether or not to bring it but then figured it's a celebration so what the hell?"

"I've never seen you drink, either."

"After last year, I took a little break," he said. "I'm not an alcoholic or anything...at least I don't think I am and neither does my therapist...but the partying did get out of hand for a while. So I stopped. What about you?"

"The first couple times we went out, I didn't want to do or say anything stupid so I stayed away from alcohol just in case." I shrugged. "Honestly, I don't drink that often when I'm out. I'll have wine at home if Crispin opens a bottle and I always make margaritas when I cook tacos but my tolerance isn't that high and the older I get, the longer it takes me to recover so I just usually abstain. But that's enough on that topic." I gestured toward the food. "Help yourself."

Trey and I both filled our plates and dug in.

"Nori, this is amazing," he said after he took a few bites of everything.

I basked in his praise, but the meal is pretty good, if I do say so myself.

We talked about my business and how unbelievable it is that the regular season is almost over. This is the first time we've had dinner at home, just the two of us, and it feels very domestic. But it also feels very right.

After we finished eating, Trey helped me carry everything back into the kitchen. I put the dishes in the dishwasher while he covered the leftovers. He opened the refrigerator and looked over his shoulder at me.

"Are those lemon tarts?" I nodded. "Did you make those, too?"

"I did. I wanted to make something light for dessert since the meal was so heavy."

"That meal was amazing," he said as he placed the leftovers in the refrigerator.

Trey reached my side as I closed the dishwasher then dried my hands. Placing his hands on my waist, he pulled me against his chest and kissed the top of my head.

"You're amazing." He shifted back to look me in the eyes. "And I look forward to sharing many meals with you in our new home."

My head is a little buzzy from the champagne, but I swear he just said "our" instead of "my" but before I could dwell on that too much, he lowered his head and kissed me until the only thing I could think about was the feel of his mouth on mine.

Chapter Thirty-Four

NORI

I LOOKED around at all the boxes. What could he possibly have in them?

Angie had supervised the movers when they packed up his New York apartment. Instead of selling it, he decided to rent it out fully furnished, so he was only having his personal things shipped here. All the household items were staying there.

The Waves have an afternoon game, but since he's not pitching, I volunteered to be here to meet the movers. It also gives me time to unpack all the kitchen items that got delivered yesterday. He let me pick everything out and I had so much fun. I've never outfitted a full kitchen before. As Eloise pointed out while she was here, I went from my mom's house to my dad's then to Baxter's and now Crispin's. So I never had a place of my own to shop for.

Not that this is my place. I have to keep reminding myself of that.

Trey has had me with him through the whole process of furnishing this house so I feel invested. Plus he keeps alluding to the fact that he wants me here more often than not. He's even mentioned setting up a studio for me in one of the extra bedrooms.

After emptying the plates and silverware out of the dishwasher and putting them away, I filled the top rack with everyday glasses and the bottom rack with pans then placed some serving utensils in the silverware holder. I added a gel pack, closed the door, and turned it on.

I've made some decent progress here in just a few hours and it's really starting to come together. Well, the kitchen is anyway. The rest is a work in progress. We've picked most of the furniture out but other than his bedroom set and one couch in the living room, we're waiting for it to be delivered.

I broke down the boxes I'd emptied and placed them into the largest box and put it out in the garage. After grabbing a glass of water, I sat on the couch and took a long drink. This domestic stuff is hard work and I've worked up a sweat despite the air conditioning.

Just as I opened my email and started scrolling through, I heard the doorbell ring. I thought all the boxes had been delivered but it's possible I'm wrong.

I set my glass on the counter as I walked to the front door. Looking through the sidelight, I spotted Trey's father standing on the porch and opened the door. I debated whether or not I should admit that I know who he is and decided against it. It seems unlikely he knows who I am and I don't want to explain that, not without Trey present.

"Can I help you?"

His eyes took a quick tour of my pink hair, cutoff denim shorts, and *I Do It for the Monet* T-shirt and obviously found me lacking. I thought his expression was dismissive when I opened the door, but it was even more so now.

"I'm looking for Trey."

"He's still at the stadium."

He looked down at his watch that probably cost more than my car.

"He should be here by now."

I'm sure this man is charming when he wants to be but since he's obviously judged and found me lacking with one glance, his words sound short and scathing. But I've dealt with people like him before and know it's best to act unaffected. And, since he didn't ask me a question, I didn't offer a response.

His eyes narrowed.

"So where is he?"

"I'm not sure, Mr...."

"Youngman. I'm Trey's father."

"I'm not sure, Mr. Youngman but I can let him know you stopped by."

"Don't bother. I'll just come back."

He turned and walked back to his car, giving me one more dismissive glance before he closed the door and backed out of the driveway.

I pulled my phone out of my pocket to text Trey and give him a warning, but it rang before I could and Crispin's picture appeared on the screen.

"Hey, what's up?"

"I was in a car accident."

"Shit, are you okay?"

"For the most part. I'm banged up and have a broken wrist but my car is a mess. Can you come get me at the hospital?"

"I'll be right there."

TREY

AS I TURNED into the driveway, I was surprised when I didn't see Nori's car. I opened the garage door, pulled in, and closed it behind me, making a mental note to get her set up with the app so she can park inside too.

I walked past the empty boxes and through the laundry room into the kitchen. Wow, she really got a lot done today. Things are really starting to come together...in here anyway. I looked out at the boxes piled throughout the living and dining rooms and cringed. It's amazing how much stuff you accumulate through the years.

Most of the boxes are filled with clothes and I'll probably donate a good chunk of them to charity. I'll keep some suits and tuxedos for events, and my New York gear, but the "douche uniforms," as Angie dubbed them, can go. The rest probably hold awards and memorabilia, which I'll set up in the office.

As I settled onto the couch, I pulled my cell from my pocket to double-check if Nori texted and I just missed it. She didn't. So I sent her one asking where she's at.

Resting my head back, I looked around the room. I really do like this house and I imagine I'll like it even more once we get it furnished and organized.

We.

I've been using that word more and more in the past few weeks. I'm sure I would have bought this house on my own, but once I saw the look on Nori's face when she walked inside, there was no question. And while I haven't officially asked, I've been dropping hints that I want her to live here with me.

My phone rang and I rushed to answer when I saw Nori's image pop up.

"Hey. Everything okay?"

"Yeah, with me anyway."

"What's wrong?"

"Crispin was in a car accident and I just brought him home from the hospital."

"Fuck, is he okay?"

"He's banged up and has a broken wrist, but he'll be fine." She sighed. "But I'm gonna stay here to keep an eye on him."

"I'll grab takeout and come over."

"Are you sure?"

"Of course. Anything in particular you'd want?"

"Crispin loves the chicken marsala at Molinaro's."

"Then Molinaro's it is," I said. "What would you like?"

"Surprise me."

"Will do. I'll see you in a little bit. Love you."

"I love you, too."

I hung up and pulled up Molinaro's menu on my phone. After deciding on a good assortment, including cannoli for dessert, I placed the order online then went and packed a duffle so I can sleep there tonight and head straight to the stadium tomorrow afternoon.

It seemed to take forever to pick up the food then get to Crispin's house but in reality it was only a little over an hour. I leaned down and kissed Nori as soon as she opened the door.

"Keep it rated PG over there."

I ended the kiss and looked over at Crispin reclining on the couch, a bandage on his forehead and a splint on his wrist. Nori stepped back and I walked inside and set the bag on the kitchen counter.

"How you doing?" I asked him.

"Okay right now but I'm sure I'll feel like shit tomorrow."

"What happened?"

"A guy in a Jeep crossed the line and slammed right into me. I saw him coming but had nowhere to go. Thankfully there wasn't anyone behind me or I would have really been screwed."

Nori put Crispin's meal on a plate and held it up for him to see.

"Do you want to eat there or at the table?" she asked.

"I think I'll eat at the table. It'll probably be easier."

He put his legs on the ground then shifted forward and paused.

"Do you need help getting up?" I asked.

"I think I'm good." He grunted as he stood and made his way over to the table. "Thankfully it's my left wrist that's broken or I'd be helpless." Picking up his fork, he dug in. "I'm sorry to be so rude, but I'm starving. I was at the hospital for hours and they wouldn't let me eat. And since I was in a no-signal zone, I couldn't call Nori either until I was ready to come home. So I sat there like a prisoner waiting for them to set me free."

Nori placed the rest of the containers and some plates on the table then went back to the kitchen to get us drinks.

"Don't worry about us," I said. "Just enjoy."

"Thanks so much for picking this up. It's my favorite."

Nori and I filled our plates while Crispin continued to eat.

"The kitchen looks great," I said.

"Thanks. I'm happy with what I got done."

She added some calamari to her plate and popped one into her mouth then looked at me, her eyes wary.

"What?"

"Your father stopped by."

"My father?" She nodded. "What did he want?"

"To talk to you. When I told him you were still at the stadium, he said 'he should have been home by now.' Then he said he'd come back later."

"Well, I won't be there then either."

"Just so you know, I pretended I didn't know who he was when I saw him and he didn't ask who I was."

"That's not surprising."

He would have taken one look at Nori's pink hair and dismissed her. I cringed when I remembered I'd initially done the same thing. But even on my worst day, I wasn't as rude as Reg Youngman.

Needing to change the subject, I looked over at Crispin who'd finished his meal and was picking at some of the appetizers I brought.

"So your wrist is broken?"

He nodded. "I have to go to the orthopedist once the swelling goes down in a couple days to get a real cast."

As I half-listened to Nori and Crispin talking about what he needs to do in the morning to take care of the salon, I couldn't help but wonder what my father is doing in town. Whatever it is, I know it can't be good.

Chapter Thirty-Five

NORI

"ARE you sure you'll be okay here by yourself?"

"I'm fine. You've been stuck to my side for three days and I appreciate it, but I'll be okay."

As predicted, Crispin was pretty sore for a couple days so I stayed close to help him out. We just got home from the orthopedist so now he has a real cast instead of just the splint. He'll have that on for three weeks.

Thankfully he mostly manages the salon and only cuts the hair of certain clients, so he only had to shift around a few appointments. And as he pointed out the day of the accident, at least it's his left hand so he's definitely not as limited as he would have been if it was the right one. He's giving himself one more day off then he'll go back to work. We're picking up a rental car for him tomorrow so he won't be dependent on me for rides.

"Do you need anything before I go?"

"Nope, I'm good." He clicked on the TV. "I'm going to turn on something mind-numbing and take a nap. Tell Trey good luck tonight." Smiling, he added, "Good luck to you, too. Going to the game by yourself like a big girl."

I said goodbye to Crispin, walked out the front door, and got into my car.

Yes, I am going to the game by myself, but I think I'll be okay. Trey told Hannah Reagan I'm going stag and she offered to sit with me. She usually ends up sitting near Crispin and me when we go to the games anyway, but tonight she's meeting me near the turnstiles. I told Trey I'd be fine making my own way to my seat, but he said Hannah insisted.

As for Trey, he's slept here the last few nights since I didn't want to leave Crispin alone and he said he didn't want to sleep without me. I'll admit I melted a little bit when he said that.

While I took Crispin to the doctor, Trey went home to wait for his living and dining room furniture to be delivered, which should have happened a couple hours ago. He's pitching tonight and will be heading to the stadium in about an hour.

I'll see him for a few minutes after the game but then the team is leaving for Chicago and he'll be gone for a week. So when the frame shop called and said my housewarming present was ready, I picked it up and can't wait to give it to him. I'll make it to his house in plenty of time before he leaves, then I'll just hang out there and empty more boxes before I go to the game.

I pulled into the driveway and cringed when I saw the car Trey's father had been driving the other day parked there. Call me a coward, but I grabbed my bag out of the trunk then walked around the back of the house and went in through the basement. I'll just hide out down here until Reg Youngman leaves.

After setting my bag near the stairs, I walked around the basement and looked at the walls. Trey keeps saying he wants me to paint something on a couple of them but isn't giving me any indication of what.

Most of the basement murals I've done have been sports-themed, but he's not thrilled with that idea. He said it would be too cliché. There's a wall next to the bar that would look great with a pub scene or possibly a custom beer and liquor bottle design. Since there's a projector, I could do a movie or Old Hollywood theme and he could get some low-slung couches and set it up more like a theater room.

I heard raised voices from above and walked closer to the stairs and strained to listen. Their voices are similar and it's difficult to tell who's speaking or what exactly is being said. I should just mind my own business, but can't stop myself from creeping up the stairs and standing on the landing to listen.

TREY

"I REALLY DON'T WANT to discuss this right now."

"Then when? You keep ignoring my phone calls and the clock is ticking."

"Dad, I seriously doubt your business deal will be affected by what I do or don't do."

"You've been with women like Clarissa. Ones whose fathers have the means to give them everything they want.

She's never heard the word no." He glared at me. "And she wants *you*."

"Well she can't have me and *that* isn't up for negotiation."

Realizing his bullying tactics weren't working, my father tried charm.

"Trey, I know you've taken your own path, but you can't play baseball forever. I'd always imagined you'd take your rightful place at Youngman Electronics. It is the family business after all."

If he'd said that to me a few years ago, I would have done anything to make it happen. Then again, a few years ago, I would have gone out with anyone he put in front of me without question.

Dr. Fisher's voice is screaming in my head not to engage but I can't hold back.

"My entire life, you've told me that I'm a moron and you'd never allow me near your precious company. So now you're telling me if I fuck this girl, I'll be welcomed with open arms."

"Don't be crude, Trey," he said, nostrils flaring. "You could do worse than Clarissa, and as far as *what* you do with her, that would depend on what she wants."

I dragged my hand through my hair. This is un-fuck-ing-believable.

"No." I shook my head. "It's not happening."

"Is it because of the Somers girl?"

My stomach flipped at the mention of Nori. I swear, if he starts ripping her apart, I will lose my shit.

"Did you think Clarissa wouldn't mention to her father that she met her at a party? The girl couldn't have been more obvious, grilling poor Clarissa."

"What are you talking about?"

"Eloise Somers," he said. "I mean, she's your usual

type and if Clarissa didn't have her sights so set on you, I'd consider your association beneficial. Somers Property Group is a big fish in a little pond and I'm sure we could use them for something."

I opened my mouth to tell him I'm dating Nori, not Eloise, but decided not to share that. The less he knows about my life the better.

"Dad, I'm not sure why you're all of a sudden so interested in who I'm spending time with, but it's really none of your business."

"It's *all* my business and it's all about business. My father did what he had to in order to start the business. Then when I married your mother and we acquired her father's company, Youngman Electronics doubled in size. Now it's you and your brother's turn to step up to grow the legacy we've started. Max would be all over Clarissa Nelson in a second, but she wants you." He shrugged. "There's no accounting for taste, I suppose. But you have a pretty face and for whatever reason people are fascinated by the fact that you can throw a ball." He let out a sarcastic chuckle. "Despite the fact that you can't read a book."

He's just trying to push my buttons. I know he is, and I fought back the urge to lash out because that's exactly what he wants me to do. I'm a grown man and have to stop acting like an adolescent where he's concerned. I don't need him for anything and it's important that I remember that and let go of any hope that we'll ever be a regular family.

I clenched my jaw and glanced at the clock then looked back at him.

"This conversation is getting ridiculous and I need to get going."

"What's ridiculous is your attitude. I don't understand what the issue is. It's not like you haven't done this before.

You've always been willing to do your part keeping the ladies happy while I schmoozed their fathers. It's the only thing I've ever been able to count on you to not screw up. And it's not like Clarissa is hideous. Honestly, she and Eloise Somers are interchangeable, so what's the difference?"

"The difference is that I'm done." I slashed my hand through the air. "Done allowing you to make me feel like shit so I do stupid shit. And I'm done hoping we'll have any kind of normal relationship."

I walked toward the door, beyond ready to show him out.

"Trey, I don't know what's going on with you recently. All the trouble you got into last year, embarrassing yourself and this family getting sent down to Triple-A." His eyes skimmed me from head to toe before meeting my gaze again. "And with the way you're talking, looking, and dressing lately, you're more suited to that pink-haired girl who was here the other day than any woman I'd want you to spend time with. So I expect you to clean yourself up, play nice, and do what needs to be done."

Every word he's saying is fueling the rage within me. For all the years I wasted trying to gain his approval and for all the stupid things I did when I didn't get it.

I don't want to talk to him anymore. I just want him out of my house and out of my life.

As I opened the front door, I spotted Nori's car parked next to my father's then heard a sound from the side of the house. Before I fully processed that she's here, I saw her run across the driveway and jump into her car. I yelled her name, but have no idea whether or not she heard me. Instead of even looking in my direction, she backed down the driveway and her tires squealed as she turned onto the main road and sped away.

I leaned my arm against the door and rested my head against it. If she heard that whole conversation, she won't understand why I didn't tell my father that she *is* the one I'm dating. She also probably won't be too thrilled about the fact that I essentially used to act as my father's gigolo.

Strike three.

Chapter Thirty-Six

NORI

I WALKED along the water's edge hoping the feel of the sand under my feet and the sound of the ocean would calm me. If I go home, Crispin will immediately know something is wrong and I'm not ready to talk about it, not even with him.

The way Reg Youngman was talking to Trey was horrible, but what I'm having trouble with is the fact that he never admitted we're together. Not when his father thought he was dating Eloise, not when he said there's no reason he can't see Clarissa Nelson, and not when he said that Trey is more suited to "that pink-haired girl" than his high-class women.

Then of course there's the fact that Trey was no different than Baxter in that he spent time with women through the years just so his father could make business deals. It seems like Trey is different now, but that still stings.

If he at least told his father about us, I probably

wouldn't have been so triggered by the second thing. But I feel like he didn't say anything because he's embarrassed. I've been with a guy who claimed to be accepting and then tried to change everything about me and refuse to do it again.

I found a secluded spot in the sand and sat just watching the ocean. The rhythm of the waves really is soothing and eventually the knot in my stomach loosened a little bit.

Glancing up at the sky, I noticed the sun had shifted quite a bit since I've been sitting here. Trey kept calling me so I left my cell in the car. I don't want to speak to him until I have a chance to sort out my thoughts.

Standing, I wiped sand off my shorts then made my way back toward the walkway leading to the parking lot. I washed off my calves and feet then slipped my sandals on and got into the car.

I looked at my phone and saw ten missed calls, one voicemail, and a text…all from Trey.

Nori, we need to talk. I need to explain anything you might have heard.

He also left a message that said pretty much the same thing. The anguish in his voice tore me apart but I'm not ready to talk to him. Besides, he's pitching tonight so he'll be at the stadium already doing his pre-game workout.

I thought about skipping the game, but I don't want to bail on Hannah at the last minute. Not that she won't be there anyway, but it'd still be rude. Plus if I go home, I'll just watch on TV and stew in my misery. And I know Trey will be upset if I don't show and I'd feel horrible if that affected his game.

Pulling out of the lot, I drove the few miles to the stadium. Trey had gotten me a VIP parking badge so I drove to the garage right next to the stadium and showed it to the guard in the booth. He raised the gate and I pulled ahead and found a spot.

I checked my face in the rearview mirror and finger-combed my hair before getting out of the car. Hannah is meeting me near the turnstiles, so instead of going to the will call window like Crispin and I usually do, I walked until I spotted her.

She waved and gestured for me to walk right through the turnstile. I followed the people in front of me and once I got through, she gave me a hug then handed me my ticket.

"I'm sorry, I should have had you meet me over by the gate so you didn't have to wait in line."

"Oh, it's not a problem," I said. "I appreciate you meeting me, but I hate making you change your schedule."

We walked through the concourse, away from the heavy crowd at the entrance.

"It's not a problem. Gives me a reason to get away from my desk early." She patted her stomach. "I've been told to slow down, but it's not easy."

"You look great. How do you feel?"

"Surprisingly well. I mean, I feel like a cow, but since the morning sickness ended after the first trimester, I've been full of energy. I'm taking advantage of that because I can't imagine it's going to last as I get bigger." She chuckled. "And Jack will be home full-time for the last couple months and I know he's not going to let me do anything."

"That's sweet."

A look of pure love crossed her face as she smiled and nodded.

"Did you want anything to eat before we go to our seats?"

"No, I'm good for now."

My stomach is in such knots, I can't imagine putting anything in it.

I followed Hannah to our seats and scanned the field for Trey as I sat. He must still be in the bullpen because I don't see him.

"How's Crispin?"

"He's a little banged up and has a broken wrist, but it definitely could have been a lot worse."

"That's good to hear. It's so scary how something like that can happen so fast."

"Yeah, but he was lucky. He wasn't going very fast and there was no one behind him."

She shifted toward me and straightened her legs as much as the seats in front of her would allow.

"Sabrina loves the way her hair turned out. She said Franco is a miracle worker. Crispin's business should triple because she's telling everyone."

"Crispin would be thrilled if that happened. He's got big plans for Haven."

I heard Hannah respond but have no idea what she said because when I saw Trey walk out of the bullpen and cross the field, everything else faded away. He'd been looking down but as he stepped onto the infield, he looked up and spotted me. Even from a distance, I saw him inhale, then he smiled. He looked relieved and sad and happy all at the same time.

He paused and held my gaze before stepping down into the dugout. It's amazing how much was said with just a look.

I stared at the spot he'd been standing for several heart-beats after he disappeared from it. I'm still sorting out my feelings and my mind is whirling.

"Is everything okay?"

Blinking the tears from my eyes, I nodded then looked

at Hannah.

"Yeah, fine."

She looked toward the dugout then back at me. The corner of her mouth kicked up.

"It's probably none of my business, but based on the look I just saw on Trey's face, I'm

guessing he did something stupid." My eyes widened and she laughed. "Sorry to be so blunt. I'm going to blame it on the hormones."

"No, it's fine. I just…" I gestured, trying to figure out what to say.

"I'm sure you'll work it out. Jack and I had a couple bumps in the road but we obviously got past them." She laughed and placed her hands on either side of her belly as she said that last sentence. "Relationships with regular men are difficult enough and these guys are anything but regular. Add in the brutal schedule during the season and it takes a lot of work, especially at the beginning."

I nodded, acknowledging her words then looked down as the Waves took the field.

Trey glanced up and met my gaze as he stood on the mound, and I imagine his look of anguish is mirrored on my face. He looked away to catch the ball Leo tossed him and by the time he put his foot on the rubber and threw his first warmup pitch, his game face was firmly in place.

TREY

"SO WHAT ARE YOU GONNA DO?" Leo asked as he stretched his legs out in front of him.

"There's really nothing I can do until then. Right?"

"Are you asking me?"

"I guess I am." I blew out a breath. "You know that I don't know anything about relationships. I've just been limping along, praying I'm doing it right. Nori left that message letting me know she wasn't meeting me after the game and asked me to give her space. She said we'd talk when I get back. I feel like I should respect that, but then another part of me wonders if I should ignore what she said and call to let her know I'm committed to working through this."

"As you know, I'm no expert with women either, but I do have three sisters. From what I've observed with them, the answer depends on the woman in question. It seems to me that Nori is a lot like Angie and, that being said, I'd do what she asked and give her time. Otherwise she's either going to get pissed off or shut down. Neither one would be good for you."

I nodded and rested my head back as the lights dimmed in preparation for takeoff.

Closing my eyes, I tried to sleep but as with the car ride I shared with Nori, she invaded my thoughts too much for me to relax. I have no idea how long I struggled for before popping my eyes open.

Leo was reading a book on his phone but looked over at me when I shifted in my seat.

"You know you hit triple digits a few times."

"Yeah, one of the reporters mentioned it after the game," I said.

"How's your hand?"

"I'll live."

On a good day, my fastball is in the mid-nineties, but today I was throwing hard. All game. I also hit all my spots. If nothing else went right today, at least I pitched well.

"Warning, I'm gonna channel my inner Benji here," Leo said and I raised my brow.

"This whole thing with your father sucks, especially since Nori got stuck in the middle. But instead of getting all mentally fucked up and blowing your start, you channeled everything into throwing harder."

"Yeah, at least that's something. I'd hate to blow my relationship and my career on the same day."

"You and Nori have something special. I'm sure that by the time you get back, she'll be ready to pick up right where you left off."

"Hopefully."

"So did you finally tell your father you and Nori are dating?"

"I told him that and a lot more." I dragged my hand down my face then looked at Leo. "We're done."

"Are you sure about that?"

"I'm pretty positive. I mean, it wasn't going well when I refused to play gigolo anymore, but when I told him about Nori it really went downhill. He made some nasty comments about her and it took all my willpower to keep from punching him in the face." I chuckled. "I did however grab him by the arm and physically throw him out of my house."

"I wish I could have seen that."

"I'll never forget the look on his face."

I rested my head against the seat but before I closed my eyes, Leo spoke.

"I know we're not blood, but you know my entire family considers you one of us."

I looked at him and smiled.

"Yeah, I know and I credit that for the fact that I never turned into a total douchebag like my father." I chuckled. "Although it was touch and go there for a while."

"Can't argue with that."

Chapter Thirty-Seven

NORI

"ARE you sure you want to watch this?" Crispin asked as he turned on the Waves game.

"I'm sure." I shrugged. "It's not as if when Trey's out of sight, he's out of mind. I think about him all the time anyway, so I may as well watch the game. I'll just be wondering what's happening anyway."

After winning just one of three games in Chicago, the Waves traveled to Cincinnati and won last night. Trey is pitching tonight, then they have two more games there before he comes home. So essentially I have forty-eight hours to figure out what I'm going to say to him.

As if he read my mind, Crispin asked, "So I've been trying to play it cool and not bug you about this, but I can't hold back anymore. Trey will be home soon. What'd you decide?"

"I don't know. I'm still thinking."

He just stared at me, eyes wide, his face frozen into a mask of indifference which I know means he disapproves.

I sighed. "Just say it."

"Say what?"

"Whatever it is you're thinking. Your face is screaming disapproval."

"I really need to teach my face to use its indoor voice." He wrinkled his nose. "You know I love you, right?"

I nodded and braced myself. If he's starting with that, I'm probably not going to like whatever it is he's going to tell me.

"Other than yours truly—" he paused, and dramatically placed his hand on his chest. "You have had *the* worst men in your life. And trust me, I know all about sucky men. But I digress," he said then waved his hand in front of his face as if to clear his thoughts. "Your father was an ass and probably still is, considering you've been down here for two years and haven't heard from him. Then he got Baxter in your life and, let's face it, he was a fucking douchebag who didn't deserve to breathe the same air as you. But Trey, no matter what he was like before you met him, is a good guy and he worships you."

The topic of our conversation's face appeared on the TV screen. Apparently the Waves' offense did well while Crispin and I were talking and Trey is starting the game with a three-run lead. We watched as the first batter got into the box and Trey went right after him with a fastball on the inside corner.

Crispin whistled.

"Well, if nothing else, you two having issues has increased his velocity. He's been consistently throwing in the high nineties the past few games."

The next pitch was another fastball and the batter

swung late for strike two. Then he threw some sort of curving ball for strike three.

Once again, the camera switched to Trey, with his game face. He looks even more intense and focused than usual. The announcers even commented on it.

The second batter popped the first pitch up to Dale Montgomery at first base and he struck the third guy out.

When they cut to commercial break, I addressed what Crispin had said.

"These past couple months have been amazing and in my head, I know that everything you said is true. I also know Trey is different, both from Baxter and from how he used to be, but it still doesn't explain why he didn't tell his father about us, why he'd let him think it was Eloise he's dating." I looked at him with pleading eyes. "Do you have any idea how much it hurt to hear his father talk about me that way and hear silence on Trey's end?"

Crispin nodded then scooted over next to me and wiped a tear that had escaped off my cheek. He wrapped his arm around me and I rested my head on his shoulder.

"That's because you were triggered. You never really dealt with what Baxter and your father did to you. You just shut the door on them and moved down here. That hurt has been festering all this time and when you heard the conversation between Trey and his father, it all came back, making it seem worse than it was." He squeezed me closer and kissed the top of my head. "As far as why he didn't correct what his father said, that's something only he can answer."

I wrapped my arm around his waist and settled against him to watch the game and think about what he said. By the time Malik Walters got the last batter out, I'd mentally replayed what I'd heard at Trey's house at least a hundred times and have come to the conclusion that Crispin is right.

Now I just have to figure out what to do to make things right between Trey and me again.

TREY

I LOOKED at my cell as I walked to my car hoping to find some sort of communication from Nori.

"Nothing?" Leo asked from beside me.

"No."

"Are you gonna call her?"

"I don't know yet. It's late so I should wait until tomorrow, but I don't know if I can wait that long." I shrugged. "I'll decide when I get home."

He nodded and opened his car door.

"Good luck with whatever you decide," he said.

"Thanks, I'm probably gonna need it."

As he drove away, I tossed my suitcase into the trunk and slammed it shut then got behind the steering wheel. I rested my head against the seat and took a deep breath in through my nose. After letting it out slowly through my mouth, I started the car and pulled out of the parking lot.

That road trip was only seven days but it seemed like forever. It's amazing how I've been doing this for ten years and never minded being away, never talked to anyone regularly during the season, and never missed anyone while I was on the road. And now, after just a few months, I dread the weeks away, look forward to talking to Nori every night when I'm on the road, and miss her like hell when I'm gone.

I pulled into my empty driveway and opened the garage door and pulled inside. I'll admit that part of me had hoped to find Nori's car here, but logically had figured chances of that were slim.

After closing the garage door and grabbing my suitcase from the trunk, I made my way into the house. Since I'm in the laundry room, I emptied my dirty clothes into the hamper and shoved my now-empty suitcase onto the shelf over the door.

I'm suddenly exhausted and just want to sleep. I don't have to be at the stadium until four tomorrow. If I don't hear from Nori by noon, I'll bite the bullet and give her a call.

I stripped off my shirt as I walked into my room and tossed it on the floor. After kicking off my shoes, I sat on the edge of the bed and rubbed the back of my neck.

"Don't stop there. Things were just about to get really good."

At the sound of her voice, I jumped off the bed and flipped on the lamp next to me.

The sight of Nori tucked in my bed wearing one of my Waves T-shirts is the best thing I've ever seen. She looks sleepy and sexy and a little nervous.

"Hi," she said.

"Hi."

I sat back down on the bed as she shifted up to sit against the pillows.

"I hope it's okay that I'm here, but I really wanted to talk to you tonight and I wasn't sure what time you'd be home. I wanted to surprise you so I had Crispin drop me off." She nibbled on her bottom lip and shrugged. "This seemed like a good decision at the time."

"It's fine. Perfect actually." I moved closer and tucked her hair behind her ear and stroked her cheek. "I hope the fact that you're here means you forgive me for being such an ass."

Even though she's in my bed wearing my shirt, my stomach tightened when a sad smile crossed her face.

"Trey, I'm not sure there's anything to forgive. I mean, I thought there was, but Crispin made me realize that the conversation I overheard between you and your father triggered me more than anything."

"No, I should have just shut him up, told him about us, and kicked him out. Which is what I ended up doing after you left."

"Really?"

I nodded.

"When my father thought I was dating your sister, I didn't correct him because I didn't want him to know anything about my life now, never mind the best part of it." She smiled at that, so I continued. "Then when he said that thing about you, I was about to tell him the 'pink-haired girl' is the one I'm seeing when I heard the side door slam and saw you get in your car."

"I'm sorry, Trey."

"What are you sorry for? I'm the one who screwed up."

She shook her head.

"I let my past experiences cloud my judgement of what happened. I shouldn't have run out like that. Instead, I should have stayed and discussed it when your father left." She chuckled. "Although if I stayed, I would have heard you setting your father straight."

There's so much I want to say and ask, but right now, there's something I want to do more.

"Can I kiss you? I'm dying to kiss you."

Instead of answering, she lunged toward me, wrapped her arms around my neck, and pressed her mouth against mine. She took me by surprise and I fell back against the pillows with her on top of me. Not a bad position to be in.

I smiled against her lips then opened my mouth over hers, quickly escalating the kiss. As our tongues tangled, Nori shifted her leg over my waist and I groaned deep in my chest as my erection settled against the juncture of her thighs. Sliding my hands down, I gripped her ass and pulled her closer. She rocked against me faster and faster, then groaned and pulled her mouth off mine and sat back.

"Too many clothes," she said and shifted back enough to unbutton my jeans. After slowly lowering the zipper, she pulled my pants down my thighs then quickly removed her panties.

Resting her hands on my chest, she straddled me again then whipped her shirt off and threw it across the bed. As she rose up on her knees and settled over my aching cock, I dug my hands into her waist and stopped her from sinking down.

"Condom," I managed to rasp out.

Her deep violet eyes met mine.

"I'm on the pill and I know I'm clean. I was tested after —" she shook her head. "—when I moved down here and there hasn't been anyone since then."

I haven't had sex without a condom since I was a foolish teenager. One pregnancy scare in high school taught me a big lesson and I've used protection every time since. Every. Single. Time. Whether the woman said she was using birth control or not.

But this is different. Nori is different.

"I'm clean too. I have regular blood tests for the team."

I loosened my grip on her waist and we both groaned as she slowly slid down my entire length. We stared into each other's eyes as she first moved up and down on my dick, going faster and faster before she rested her hands against my chest and rode us to climax.

Chapter Thirty-Eight

NORI

TREY DRAGGED his fingers up and down my back as our heartbeats slowed and our breathing returned to normal. He kissed the top of my head and I snuggled against his chest.

"Can I ask you a question?"

"Sure."

"What were you doing here that day?"

"I came to give you your housewarming present." I rolled off him and settled onto my side to face him. "When I saw your father's car in the driveway, I decided to go in through the basement and wait until he left to make my presence known. When I heard shouting, I snuck up the stairs to eavesdrop." I felt my face heat. "I probably shouldn't have but I couldn't help myself."

He shook his head.

"You have every right to be here at any time and know

everything that goes on. He's the one who doesn't belong. But I'm pretty sure he won't be coming back."

"Are you okay about that?"

"I am. It was a long time coming." He kissed my cheek. "But let's go back to the most important thing you said."

"What was that?"

"Present?"

After kissing him, I shifted back onto my knees and reached for the T-shirt I'd borrowed from his drawer. It hangs down to my knees so I didn't bother searching for my underwear before crawling out of the bed.

"I'll be right back."

I jogged through the living room and down to the basement and grabbed the bag

that was exactly where I left it at the bottom of the stairs. Just as quickly, I made my way back to the bedroom where Trey was waiting, resting against his pillows. I handed him the bag and climbed back into bed next to him.

"Open it," I said.

He reached inside and pulled out the custom frame then flipped it over. He looked at the picture then shifted his gaze to me.

"Did you draw this?"

I nodded, feeling suddenly shy for some reason.

"Nori, it's…" he ran his index finger along the glass, tracing the lines of the picture below. "It's amazing. Perfect." Leaning toward me, he placed a sweet kiss on my lips. "Just like you."

⚾

TREY

. . .

I'M TORN between kissing her and looking at the gift she made me. Since she looks nervous about my reaction, I decided to pay attention to the picture I'm holding.

I grew up surrounded by priceless art, but none of it holds a candle to this. Nori created a perfect replica of this house and it's stunning. Not that I'm surprised. I've seen pictures of her murals and she has a way of drawing and shading that brings her images to life.

In the dark grey matting of the frame, *Youngman Est. 2021* is engraved in rich silver script. I looked around the edges of the picture searching for a signature and when I didn't find one, I frowned.

"What's wrong?" she asked.

"I don't see a signature."

"It's signed on the back."

I flipped the frame over and released the metal tabs holding the cardboard in place and removed it, revealing her signature as well as a note.

Trey

As soon as we pulled into the driveway of this house, I knew this place was as special as you. With every day that passes, it's feeling more and more like a home and I know you'll be truly happy here.

I love you.

Nori

The words blurred as I read them a second time and I blinked to clear the tears from my eyes before meeting her gaze.

"Thank you." I rested the frame against my stomach then reached over and slid my fingers through her hair to cup the back of her head. "I love it." I kissed her and pulled back. "And I love you."

I chuckled when I thought about the day I met her.

"What's so funny?"

"I'm just thinking about when we met."

"Yeah, who'd have thought we'd end up here from a shared car ride?"

"Not me, that's for sure."

"Why do you say it like that?" she asked with a snarky smirk.

"When Leo insisted I was interested in you, I told him that women with pink hair and tattoos who smell like dessert are nowhere on my list. But it turns out, you're the only woman on my list."

"Good save, Youngman." She leaned in for a quick kiss. "But I'm thinking about getting rid of the pink."

"What? Why?"

"I dyed it as an act of rebellion, to reclaim my life." She shrugged. "I don't need to rebel anymore and my life is pretty much perfect right now."

I looked at her hair then met her gaze again and smiled.

"Pink, blue, green, tie-dyed...it doesn't matter to me. I love *you*, Nori Somers."

"How about blonde?"

"If you insist on being so boring, I'll learn to live with it," I said around a dramatic sigh.

Tearing my gaze from her beaming smile, I replaced the back on the frame and picked it

up to look at it again. Tracing my finger over *Youngman Est. 2021*, I couldn't hide the smile that spread across *my* face.

I know she put it there to represent the year I bought this house, but if I have my way it will mean much more than that. With any luck, it will also be the year Nori and I become an official family.

But that question will have to wait for another day.

THE END

Are you ready for Leo's story?

323

Chapter 1

Leo

I shifted into a reverse warrior pose, fighting to keep my balance as every muscle in my body protested the movement. Blinking, I crinkled my nose in an attempt to divert the sweat that somehow still managed to trickle into my eyes even though I'm looking up at the ceiling.

The curses ricocheting through my brain mocked the incense-and-serenity vibe in the studio. But seriously, this is bullshit. I've been through every cardio, strength, and flexibility training Major League Baseball has to offer and haven't struggled or sweat this much. I've already done all these poses on the other side of my body and am definitely feeling it.

At least this hell is almost over.

"Exhale and come into an extended side angle pose by placing your right forearm on your right thigh. Then extend your left arm and hover it over your ear."

I followed Clay's directions, breathing through the *discomfort* as he had me flow through triangle and half-moon poses.

"Step back to downward dog and you can rest there for a few breaths, or if you'd prefer, move into child's pose."

Oh trust me, I'd *prefer*.

I lowered onto my knees and, reaching my arms forward, rested my forehead on the mat, thanking every supernatural power in the universe that this torture is almost over. I could have stayed like that forever, but once again, the taskmaster shouted out a command.

Okay, he told me what to do in a soft, calm voice, but either way, he was making me move.

"Shift to a seated position with your legs straight in front of you."

My knees cracked as I moved onto my ass and stretched my legs out. The back of my right calf settled into the wet spot my sweaty forehead had created and I shifted it slightly to the left.

"Inhale and straighten your spine then bring your arms straight out to the side and up over your head, reaching toward the ceiling. Draw your spine up and inhale, keeping your torso long. As you exhale, lean forward from your hip joints, not your waist."

My hamstrings, hips, and lower back protested as I did what he told me. I breathed deeply, compelling my muscles to give in to my will. But as I've learned in the past week of classes, it will take more than determination to make things happen.

"Don't grit your teeth. Keep your face and jaw relaxed and with each inhale, lengthen your spine and with each exhale, fold deeper. Imagine your belly coming to rest on your thighs, rather than your nose coming to your knees. Keeping your feet flexed, grab hold of either your toes or your ankles."

My toes? Yeah right.

I glared up at Clay, my jaw clenched. His raised brow and muted smirk would have made me laugh if I had the energy and enough breath. Despite my sneers and groans, it's the first time in a week that he's dropped his professional demeanor during our private sessions.

"Keep your neck a natural extension of your spine, don't look up or down."

I looked forward again and slicked my hair back off my face before grabbing my ankles.

"Keep breathing and if you're able, deepen the stretch with each exhale," Clay said.

Sweat dripped off my chin and immediately soaked into my shorts, forming a blotch that got larger with each subsequent drop. He had me hold that pose for what seemed like forever before saying the words I've been waiting for since this torture session started.

"Release your hold on your ankles and come back to a seated position. Now, with your core engaged, exhale and slowly lower your back to the mat. Rest your hands at your sides with your palms facing up and put your feet mat-length apart. Close your eyes and transition into Savasana, allowing your body to be just as it is and yourself to be whole and complete, simply lying there, breathing."

My body felt heavy as I eased onto the mat and my muscles relaxed. I closed my eyes and listened to the soothing background music and focused on regulating my breathing until it settled into a slow, comfortable rhythm.

In my opinion, this is the best kept secret of yoga. I think if everyone knew the torturous classes ended with this relaxing pose, they'd be packed. The first few times I did this, my mind wandered, thinking about all the things I had to do once I left the studio, not to mention how much pain I was in. But after just four classes, I'm learning to Savasana like a pro.

My mind and body totally relaxed and I enjoyed just lying on my mat breathing. Then a beat pounded into my consciousness. I opened my eyes and looked around, trying to figure out its source.

I spotted Clay through the glass door of his office. He'd started going in there after my first class when I said the thought of him watching me in Savasana was giving me the wiggins.

Sitting up, I twisted first to the right side then the left and shook out my legs. I grabbed my water bottle and finished its contents in one gulp. As I swallowed, I identified the song that had intruded on my Savasana. *Boom Boom Pow* by The Black Eyed Peas is an awesome song, but not something to listen to while in a state of total relaxation.

"You have five more minutes," Clay said from behind me.

"I was rudely interrupted by your music."

"I wasn't playing music." He frowned, then cocked his head to the side. The music changed to a slightly slower tempo as *Sorry* by Buckcherry started to play. "The floors must be finished downstairs."

"What does that mean?"

"The floor was being refinished in the pole dance studio downstairs, which is why there haven't been any classes there this week." He looked at his watch. "Although there aren't usually classes this late on a Sunday. Down there or up here. Which is probably why whoever is down there wasn't too concerned about blasting the music."

I got up and walked across the room to grab a spray bottle and rag off the shelf. Kneeling down, I sprayed down my mat and wiped it clean.

"I appreciate you meeting with me privately."

"No problem. I can't have you in my class distracting everyone with that pretty face," he said with a chuckle.

"Smart ass."

"But seriously, we'll do whatever works for you."

"You're the one with the busy schedule." I sat and slipped on my socks and sneakers, then rolled my mat and stood. After returning the spray bottle to its home, I tossed the rag into the hamper. "I'm free most anytime since it's the offseason. So if you need me to come during the day, I can."

I reached down and grabbed my water bottle and mat.

"Mornings or early afternoons might actually be better during the week. I'll text you tomorrow and let you know about Tuesday."

"Sounds good."

"It's getting easier, right?"

"No comment."

"Well, I see improvement in the few sessions we've had. Your balance is better and you don't seem to be protecting your lower back as much, so it must be loosening up."

"I do feel more loose, but this is harder than I thought it'd be. When the Waves' trainer recommended yoga, I had no idea it'd be so tough."

Clay patted me on the back and opened the door.

"You'll get there."

"I'll take your word for it."

That said, I stepped into the hallway and walked toward the stairs. I was rounding the landing when the unmistakable thump of *Fat Bottomed Girls* pounded out of the open door on the first floor. I jogged down the rest of the way and walked over to peek inside.

Holy shit!

I never believed in falling in love at first sight, but good Lord, I fell into something the moment I spotted her. With her long limbs, porcelain skin, and platform boots, she looked like some kind of goddess as she climbed the pole. When she reached the top, she released her left hand and extended her arm out to the side and held on by her right hand and her ankles as she spun around and around. With her body away from the pole, she gripped it with her right hand near her thigh then wrapped her right leg around the pole and continued to spin with her right arm extended.

My sister Angie used to have a musical jewelry box with a ballerina inside that would spin around when the top was opened. That's exactly what the woman on the pole looked like.

I watched in awe as she straightened her legs and rolled around the pole then tipped back and hooked her left leg, seeming to hang on by the back of her knee. She arched and grabbed the heel of her right boot as she kept spinning around and around. I was getting dizzy just watching.

She let go of her boot and kicked her left leg back toward her head. And I don't know how it happened, but next thing I knew, she was hanging upside down in a full split.

Hooking her left leg around the pole again, she wrapped one arm behind her and grabbed on. Twisting her body, she straightened her legs until she hung upside down with her back against the pole. She looked like a sexy bat.

Freddie Mercury continued to sing about how fat-bottomed girls make the world go round and I have to agree. Not that the enchantress in front of me has a fat anything, but her bottom is perfectly rounded, especially in comparison to her slim figure and tiny frame.

Releasing her hands, she let her arms hang toward the ground while just her knees held her to the pole. She slid down slowly until her fingertips brushed the floor as she continued to spin. Around and around she went until she finally placed her hands flat on the floor slowing the momentum. Once the spinning stopped, she let her legs fall back until her feet landed against the hardwood floor with a bang.

She stood, whipping her hair over her shoulders and gripped the pole again. Before executing another mind-boggling trick, her eyes widened when she spotted me.

Her sky-high heels added a sexy sway to her hips as she walked in my direction. My mind raced as I tried to think of something to say that would accurately convey how much her performance blew me away. But I didn't have to worry about it because she didn't give me a chance to speak.

"Show's over," she said, and slammed the door in my face.

Anjannette

I placed my hand over my chest, as if that would still my pounding heart. When I looked up and saw that man watching me, it took all my willpower to hide my initial panic. Thankfully, I noticed the yoga mat under his arm and realized he must have been upstairs with Clay before I totally freaked out.

Resting my back against the wall, I slid down to the floor. After unzipping both of my boots, I slipped them off and rubbed my feet. For eight-inch heels, they're pretty comfortable, but still squeeze my toes a little.

I heard a knock on the door and stood. Turning the knob, I opened it a crack and breathed a sigh of relief when Clay Moody stood on the other side of the threshold instead of the Greek god that had been there a few minutes ago. Whether he's Greek or not, that's what I'm calling him since he looks just like John Stamos.

"Hey Clay."

After opening the door, I walked over to my iPad and lowered the music.

"What do you think of the floors?" he asked as he stepped inside.

"They're beautiful. I'm really happy with them."

Picking up my tank top, I shrugged into it before turning around.

"How was your vacation?"

"Relaxing," I said. "It's the first one I've taken in a long time and I made the most of it."

"Do anything special?"

"Nothing fancy. A few friends and I rented a lake house in the Poconos. We hiked,

kayaked, and drank way too much."

"Sounds like a good time."

"Yeah, it was." I nodded. "I'm surprised to see you here."

"That's actually why I stopped in. I'm doing private sessions with a friend of mine so I'll be here at different times for the next few months."

"I saw your car in the lot, but didn't realize you were with someone. I hope my music didn't totally kill your session."

"No, he was halfway through Savasana when it started."

"Oh good. Besides the fact I had the music cranked up louder than usual, I left the door open because there are still some fumes in here." He blinked then shifted his eyes toward the door I'd had to open for him. "Your friend stopped by and I slammed it in his face," I explained with a shrug. "Sorry about that."

"No worries. It'll keep him humble," Clay said with a chuckle. "Anyway, I just wanted to stop in to welcome you back and let you know that you may be seeing me here at weird times."

"I'll be sure to keep the music at a decent decibel and the door closed."

He nodded and walked toward the door. "Have a good night."

"You too."

A minute later Keera arrived.

"Guess who I just saw downstairs."

"Clay?"

"No, not Clay." She waved her hand in a dismissive gesture. "When I pulled into the parking lot, I saw Leo

Marakis getting into his car, but he pulled out before I could talk to him."

She said the name as though I should not only know who that is, but I should also be impressed. I just looked at her and blinked.

"Leo Marakis," she said again, raising her voice slightly on the last word making the name sound like a question.

I lifted my brow and shook my head.

"Leo Marakis."

She drew out the five syllables, as if saying the words more slowly would magically give me the knowledge she seems to think I should possess.

"You can say the name as slow or loud as you want, but I have no idea who that is."

Keera rolled her eyes.

"Have you been living under a rock? He's the catcher for the Carolina Waves and one of the hottest guys in professional baseball."

"You know I don't follow baseball or any other testosterone-filled sports."

"They're worth watching for the eye candy alone." Keera's train of thought switched tracks and she seemed to have an epiphany. "Wait a minute." Her eyes widened and she grabbed my hand and squeezed. "He was carrying a yoga mat. Was he in this building?"

Her question was asked with a quiet reverence that made me laugh. She removed her hand from mine and crossed her arms over her chest.

"Look, just because you're a total misandrist doesn't mean the rest of us don't enjoy the company of a hot guy."

This is not the first time Keera has said that exact thing to me. And I'll admit that the first time I heard the word, I had to look up the exact definition of *misandrist*. It's not exactly in my everyday vocabulary.

"I don't despise men," I said. "I just don't have the patience to deal with egotistical pretty boys."

"You don't have the patience to deal with men, period." Keera rolled her eyes at my shrug. "You've got to get back out there sometime. You broke up with Travis the Weasel three years ago. Don't you miss sex?"

I'll admit that at first I did, but for the past couple years, not so much. In fact, all my toys have been collecting dust. Now I channel all my sexual energy into my business. The fact that Peaches & Pole is generating enough revenue to allow me to cut back on my web design business says a lot.

Instead of answering her question, I said, "I'll admit your Leo Marakis is easy on the eyes."

"You saw him?"

"I'm guessing the man you're talking about is the one Clay just told me he's doing private sessions with. Dark hair and eyes?" Keera nodded. "Looks like John Stamos?" Her eyes widened and she nodded again. "He was watching me freestyle."

"And what did you do?"

"I slammed the door in his face."

"Seriously?" I nodded. "*What* is wrong with you?"

"What would you do if you thought you were alone then looked up and found a guy watching you dance?"

"If he was a muffin like Leo Marakis, I know *exactly* what I'd do." She bobbed her eyebrows.

I grabbed my grip spray and coated the top of my feet, shins, and inner thighs. After placing the cap back on and returning it to the shelf, I turned to face Keera again.

"You and I both had shitty exes and are dealing with our breakups in our own way. Your dick band-aids seem to be working for you, but at this point in my life, casual sex would only make me feel worse."

"I'm not saying you have to go out and throw your cat at every guy you see, but don't you think it's time to put yourself out there again?" When I didn't answer, she continued. "By not dating, I feel like you're still letting Travis have power over you."

Instead of answering, I grabbed a spray bottle and rag and walked over to the pole I'd used. After spraying the rag, I tucked it in my bra and climbed to the top, cleaning the grip off as I slowly slid down. Just for good measure and to give me extra time to collect my thoughts, once I reached the ground, I gave the lower half an extra scrub.

"He doesn't still have power over me. This doesn't have anything to do with Travis. Not specifically anyway."

Other than my therapist, I haven't talked to anyone about this. But maybe it's time. If anyone would understand, it's Keera. She had a shitty ex too. I didn't know her when she was with him, but from what I understand, he was just as bad as Travis.

I walked over to the iPad and turned the music back on but lowered the volume. What I'm going to say is difficult enough to admit, I don't want my words echoing through a quiet room. Keera had settled on the floor and I sat across from her and rested my back against the wall.

"After I left Travis, my therapist made me realize that since I started dating in junior high, I hadn't been single for longer than a month. I've been stuck in a cycle of relationships, moving from one guy to the next, always focusing on fitting the mold of whoever I was with at the time. I've given up pieces of myself or ignored my own wants just to make whatever guy was in my life happy."

I shifted my gaze to the side and blinked away the tears that threatened to fall. Drawing my knees up, I wrapped my arms around them before looking at her again.

"Travis was a dick and borderline mentally abusive, but

the fact that it took me three years to realize that tells its own story. I made it easy for him to totally bend me to his will. I lost myself in that relationship because I didn't really know who I was."

Looking around the studio, I smiled. Pole is the one thing I wouldn't give up for Travis. At first he thought my dancing was cool but quickly started to resent the time I spent at the studio. After a while, I compromised and only attended classes I taught and trained on my home pole the rest of the time. That appeased him at first, but after a few months, he pushed for me to totally stop again. Thankfully I had one brain cell working and didn't give in to his demand.

"After I finally broke up with him, my therapist suggested that I take a six-month dating hiatus. The fact that I had such a hard time being single at first made me realize how much I needed a break from men and I decided to extend it to a year. And now, I'm happy with myself and my life, my friendships. I know who I am and what I want." I shrugged. "Part of me is afraid that I'll backslide and lose that if I get involved with someone new."

"Not if you're with a good guy," Keera said.

"The fact that I'm a bad picker is a whole other therapy session and the reason I've been taking an extended break from anyone with a penis." I released my knees and shifted to my feet. "But we're here to figure out the end of our routine and practice, not lament on my sexless existence."

Keera stood and walked over to give me a big hug. With her arms still around me, she pulled back to look me in the eye.

She released me and stepped back.

"Why didn't you tell me this before? I would have shut up."

"I didn't tell anyone. It's not exactly something you want to shout from the rooftops."

She nodded and seemed resigned to let the subject drop.

"Now that I've brought down the entire vibe, I need some feel-good music."

I scrolled to an upbeat playlist but just before I hit play, Keera spoke again.

"But you have to admit that Leo Marakis is seriously hot."

Full disclosure, my hoo-ha had perked up for the first time in more than a year at the sight of Leo Marakis. But I'm keeping that to myself. I've shared enough already today.

www.ingramcontent.com/pod-product-compliance
Lightning Source LLC
Chambersburg PA
CBHW061113310726
48974CB00002B/515